For Shawn & Jill, who never failed to ask me "Hey, Goose, how's the writing going?" over the last twenty-plus years. And for Mom & Dad, my first readers and biggest fans. I would not have gotten here without you.

PROLOGUE
Saturday, October 14, 1989

His own eyes, blue, red-rimmed, haggard, stared back at him. He grimaced, shifted the backpack's weight on his shoulders, turned away from the mirror, and left his house for the last time.

His walk to campus was slower than he'd expected; he hadn't realized his load would be so heavy. He finally reached the top of Bascom Hill and leaned against the statue of Abraham Lincoln for a brief rest. His heart slammed against his ribcage, either from adrenaline or physical exertion. Maybe both. Amplified voices, cheers, and applause drifted up the hill from the festivities below him. He shuddered, then stood and adjusted the heavy red backpack against his spine again. Anxiety gripped his chest; he didn't have much time.

The clock was ticking.

He loped down the south side of Bascom Hill, eyes on his prized red Converse sneakers, ignoring anyone who passed him. The old limestone buildings that lined three sides of the quadrangle were silent. No classes on Saturday. At the bottom of the hill, he stopped for a moment and adjusted his backpack again. *Fuck, this thing is heavy.* More thunderous applause, louder now, floated toward him from the other side of busy Park Street.

He took the footbridge over Park Street and followed the sidewalk toward the crowd that packed Library Mall. He saw Lauren Dailey on the stage, gesturing wildly and whipping up the crowd. He saw Ben Packard at the top of an abstractly-shaped concrete tower, a favorite spot of hoarse-voiced evangelists, holding a squirming black puppy to his chest. He did not see Sara.

He glanced at his wristwatch and his heart lurched: nine fifty-seven. *It's time.* He took a deep breath and moved toward the tower. Sweat dripped down his back. The item in the backpack shifted and jabbed into his ribs. He grunted, but didn't stop walking. Keeping his eyes focused straight ahead, he pushed through the crowd.

"Hey!'

"Watch it!"

"Dude, what the —"

He stopped just behind the stage, to the side of the tower, where he was most exposed. Out of the corner of his eye he saw Scott Schlosser's massive back. He grinned, appreciating the magnitude of what he was about to do. A certain peace covered him like a warm blanket. *I win.*

His watch ticked over to ten o'clock. Grinning maniacally, he held his arms out wide at his sides, took a heaving breath and screamed his last word.

"MOTHERFUCKERS!"

He allowed himself the pleasure of watching Scott Schlosser start to turn before the timer in his backpack flipped from :01 to :00, beeped once — and sent them all straight to Hell.

2019

CHAPTER ONE
Monday, October 14, 2019
Morning

Sara

The dream always played like an old-school filmstrip with the scratchy voiceover like she'd watched in elementary school.

"Mommy? Shouldn't you wear these ones to work?" Her own small, innocent seven-year-old voice asked; the image showed her little arms straining to hold up a pair of steel-toed work boots.

Clackity-clack. Scene change.

"He just…he looks so sad." This voice was foreign. "Now I kind of wish I'd said yes when he asked me to be his Bio Lab partner. I really am some kind of jerk." The voice was clearly speaking to someone, whose face never quite came into focus.

Clackity-clack. Scene change.

"No matter what, I always have you." Bat's furry black face with huge inquisitive green eyes popped in. This was a phrase she uttered to her feline companion when the constant assholerie of humanity was more than she could deal with. Those were the days she locked herself in the house with a pint of Chunky Monkey and *Dateline* on TV. There were many of those days.

Clackity-clack. Back to Scene 1.

Beep. Beep. Beep. The alarm's steady rhythm wrested Sara from her strange nickelodeon dream. She rolled onto her back and sighed, eyes still closed; the dream left a slimy coating of dread on her consciousness that she knew would take hours to fully shake. *What is that, six nights in a row I've had that dream?* She picked up her cellphone and snoozed it into silence.

Sudden weight appeared next to her on the bed, and little paws, like little dumbbells, slowly and deliberately walked the

9

entire length of her body. Bat started up his motor and tickled Sara's face with his whiskers. *Breakfast!* Sara groaned and sat up, her blonde hair falling in a tangled web over her face. "I'm up," she muttered thickly.

Bat jumped down from the bed with a trill and made a beeline for the kitchen. Sara slipped her feet into her battered slippers and stumbled after him. She filled his food and water bowls and watched him enthusiastically chomp his dry kibble. "Damn cat," she said, then turned for the bathroom.

She brushed her teeth, then leaned over the sink to get a better look at her face in the bathroom mirror. Her startlingly bright hazel eyes gazed back at her. *Golden eyes,* her mother had called them once in a rare moment of sobriety. Except it seemed the dark circles under her eyes had grown from carry-on to checked bag size over the past week. *Not getting enough sleep.* Sara sighed through her nose. *If this is what my thirty-five looks like, I can't wait to see what forty will do to me,* she thought, the familiar vertical crease appearing between her eyebrows.

She pulled her hair back in a haphazard ponytail and wrapped her oversized terrycloth robe around herself. She'd accidentally bought it in the wrong size, but decided to hang on to it; the thought of her average body cocooned in this massive robe started her days with a wry little smile. Most days it was the only smile to cross her face.

She padded back toward the kitchen. Boxes with labels such as MOVIES and KITCHEN SHIT scrawled across the sides in black permanent marker sat piled atop one another in every room; she'd moved into the house almost a week ago, but hadn't finished unpacking. Some of these boxes would probably never get unpacked, relegated instead to an attic or basement storage space to await her next move.

She hadn't unpacked most of her life yet, but the coffeemaker was sure as hell the first thing to get plugged in. As it spit out her morning joe, she looked out the kitchen window at the decrepit house next door. According to Beckie Wyatt, Sara's real estate agent, it had sat abandoned for as long as anyone could remember.

"Are you sure you want to live next to the neighborhood eyesore?" *Beckie asked. They had walked the entire interior of the house, and now they were now standing in the front yard. Beckie regarded the house next door with a look of vague distaste on her pretty face, as if she'd accidentally taken a swig of spoiled milk. The wide aluminum siding might have been white at one time, but was now a dirty non-color. The front gate hung by half a hinge, swinging halfheartedly in the breeze. The mailbox at the end of the crumbling walk canted alarmingly out toward the street.*

Sara nodded. "How can a house sit empty for so long?"

Beckie shrugged. "It can sit empty forever, as long as the property taxes are paid and the grass doesn't get too long. I looked this property up; according to the county, it's owned by an R. Porter, and taxes are current. So somebody's paying them. Although, I imagine if the structure gets any more rundown, the city's going to start taking notice."

"I'm surprised they haven't already," Sara said.

Bat appeared at Sara's feet and twined himself around her ankles, purring. Sara blinked, coming back to the present, then picked him up and buried her nose in his silky black fur. The cat bashed his forehead into Sara's cheek affectionately. Thinking of her strange dream, she softly said, "No matter what, I always have you," then set Bat down on the tile floor and watched him trot back to his food bowl, tail straight up in the air like a flagpole.

The coffeemaker abruptly stopped burping. She poured some of the steaming black coffee into her chipped coffee mug and carried it into her bare living room. She set her coffee on the scarred side table next to her comfortable old easy chair in 1993 plaid – the only two pieces of furniture in the room – then headed for the front door. The light thump of her slippered footsteps echoed against the empty walls and wood floors.

She stepped out to the cool October morning. Her recurring dream, with its seemingly random points in time and unfamiliar voices, still picked at the edges of her mind as she looked around for her morning newspaper. *I wonder what it means,* she thought. *I don't --*

Sara's train of thought was stopped dead by the faint sound of a large crowd cheering and applauding. *What the hell?* She looked up and down the street, which was crowded with cars parked bumper-to-bumper along both curbs; she was, quite possibly, the only person on this stretch of Mound Street who was awake at this hour.

She listened; there it was again. The unmistakable sound of a large group of people cheering and clapping. It reminded her of the crowd noise at a Badger football game. She wondered if something was going on at Camp Randall Stadium, the home of Wisconsin Badgers football and only about six blocks away, then remembered the early hour and dismissed the idea.

The sound seemed to swirl around Sara's head. She moved to the sidewalk and stepped a few paces to the east; the sound grew fainter. She centered herself in front of her house again and walked a few paces to the west; the sound grew louder. Frowning, she zeroed in on the abandoned house next door. Shingles with curled edges peeled up from the roof. The porch floor was rotting and had holes in some spots. Pieces of old siding hung askew. There was no movement, no sign of life; the whole place had that air of long-term neglect.

And then, silence. Sara cast a final suspicious glance at the house, then spied her Wisconsin State Journal lying on the boulevard grass between the sidewalk and the street. She picked it up and shook it with one hand to unfold it. The front page bugled: MADISON REMEMBERS. The creases on Sara's brow deepened as she read the subhead: "Thirty Years Later: The Library Mall Bombing." Eyes on the paper scanning headlines and photos, still carrying her mug, she went back inside. She settled into her well-worn armchair to drink her coffee and read about a thirty-year-old tragedy.

Madison Remembers
Thirty Years Later: The Library Mall Bombing

Jeffrey Kjersten, Wisconsin State Journal

It's been three decades, and many questions remain unanswered. Why would someone carry a powerful bomb onto packed Library Mall and detonate it, killing 82 and injuring scores of others? What prompted such a deadly outburst? And who was the famous but still unnamed Library Mall Bomber?

It was Saturday, October 14, 1989. The day was sunny and unseasonably warm, a perfect day for a fundraising event. UW sorority Kappa Delta and fraternity Sigma Alpha Tau held their annual "Paws for a Cause" Humane Society fundraiser. An estimated one thousand people packed the mall to see the festivities and possibly adopt a pet.

"Nothing seemed out of the ordinary," says Kelly Caldwell, then a UW sophomore and now a financial planner in Milwaukee. "Everyone was having a great time."

Caldwell was sitting with her friends on the edge of the Hagenah fountain, a hundred feet from the stage, when the bomb went off at exactly 10:00 a.m. "The explosion was unbelievable. It knocked me and my friends backwards into the fountain; the cover broke under our weight."

The explosion was indeed powerful; powerful enough to leave a hole three feet deep in the sidewalk where the bomber stood. Library Mall's concrete platform and elevated stage were destroyed. Buildings all around the site, including UW's Memorial Library, the Wisconsin Historical Society, the University Club, and the St. Paul's University Catholic Center sustained heavy damage. Windows were blown out of the Memorial Union, the Red Gym, the Mosse Humanities Building, and the University Bookstore. People enjoying the morning lakeside on Memorial Union Terrace reported being showered by debris. Some victims' belongings were fished out of Lake Mendota a week later.

65 people were dead at the scene. 17 more would die later of their injuries. 112 were injured, many critically. The Library Mall bombing, the worst catastrophe in terms of human casualties in Wisconsin's history, has become an event that the city of Madison cannot forget.

"We still don't know who the bomber was," says Chief Mike Daniels of the Madison Police Department, who was a patrol officer on the State Street beat that day. "The carnage was unbelievable, the death toll unthinkable. It's hard to come to terms with an event like that when nobody can answer 'who' or 'why.' It's Madison's most famous cold case."

Very little is known about the bomber. "There wasn't much left of the bomber after the explosion. Pieces, basically," Daniels says. "There weren't even enough teeth left to compare against dental records. We did find one red Converse Chuck Taylor shoe at the bottom of the crater, but there's really no telling if that belonged to the bomber or a victim."

When asked about the bomb itself, Chief Daniels said, "All we know is that it was a large pipe bomb with a timed trigger, constructed with readily available materials. It was packed with shrapnel, which caused most of the catastrophic injuries."

A task force consisting of representatives from agencies such as the MPD, UW Police, Dane County Sheriff's Office, Wisconsin Division of Criminal Investigation, the Federal Bureau of Investigation, and the Bureau of Alcohol, Tobacco and Firearms worked around the clock for weeks, working to identify the bomber. They reviewed missing persons records, investigated known violent criminals across southeastern Wisconsin and northern Illinois, and followed up on over three thousand leads. One of those leads came from the Hammersley Quarry in Fitchburg, which had been burglarized just days before the bombing. Investigators were never able to determine whether the materials stolen from the quarry were used in the bombing.

The identity of the Library Mall Bomber remains a mystery to this day.

And what of the victims? What was left of Library Mall became a large memorial. Julius Keller, of Wauwatosa, lost his brother Michael in the bombing. He visited the site several days later. "There were flowers piled

14

three feet high all around the place, outside the crime scene tape. Candles everywhere. Messages written on the sidewalk in chalk. I'd never seen anything like it."

UW's Greek system bore the worst of the casualties. 36 of the dead belonged to the Kappa Delta sorority – its entire membership. The Sigma Alpha Tau fraternity lost 42 men, leaving just three surviving members. Kappa Delta and Sigma Alpha Tau both closed their UW chapters after the bombing. Officials from either organization could not be reached for this story.

Walk Library Mall now, thirty years later, and you'll still see scars. When the mall was reconstructed in the spring of 1990, hundreds of names and messages were scratched into the new concrete. A proposal to replace the vandalized concrete was brought before the City Council in 1991, which unanimously voted to leave it as is. A plaque, donated by the Class of 1989 in memoriam to the fallen, was placed on the spot where the elevated stage had stood at the intersection of State Street and Library Mall.

Thirty years later, Madison still mourns, and hopes to someday find the answers to those two timeless questions: Who? Why? Even if we had those answers, one thing is certain: Madison will never forget.

Sara examined the black and white cover photo closely while her coffee went cold in her hand. In the background, slightly blurred, she could see a ragged crater in the sidewalk, either bloodstains or scorch marks (she couldn't tell which) on what was left of the platform, blackened trees stripped of their leaves and bark, a bank of animal cages toppled over with one door standing straight up, concrete chunks and glass shards strewn everywhere, and holes that had been windows in building façades. In the foreground, right in the center of the photo in clear focus, lay a single women's white hi-top athletic shoe, the kind with laces and two hook-and-loop strap closures over the tongue. She could see the name Reebok stitched into the side of the shoe, even on newsprint. It gave her chills.

Sara had lived in Madison for the better part of a decade, and hadn't heard about this particularly tragic chapter in the city's history before this morning. Her heart hurt for the victims. *So many people died, and so young. Boom. Gone. And the families see no justice because they couldn't figure out who the bomber was. Just awful.* Her hand trembled slightly with her next sip of coffee. *What I would give to turn back the clock, give those poor kids a chance.*

She sighed and drank the last of her coffee. Bat, who had curled up on Sara's lap while she read, lifted his head and blinked sleepily at Sara. "Sorry, Batman, I have to get up," Sara said, scratching the cat's head.

Her recurring dream had again faded from her consciousness. But it wasn't completely gone.

The Library Mall bombing was on Sara's mind all morning. Her corporate job kept her busy, but it wasn't particularly challenging; she should have been answering emails or preparing for an afternoon meeting. Instead, she hid in her bare cubicle and Googled the Library Mall Bombing to learn more about it. Surprisingly, there wasn't much on the internet. Because it happened in 1989, long before everything was easily available on the World Wide Web, finding original news coverage was frustratingly difficult. She propped her chin in her hand and sighed, debating whether paying to search newspaper archives would be worth it.

"Hey Sullivan," a deep voice brought her out of her concentrated reverie. She looked up to see Luke Marshall peeking over her bare cube wall, grinning. She genuinely liked Luke, with his wide, friendly smile and sparkling blue eyes. At first glance, he didn't look like a corporate ladder-climber, currently a Director of something or other; with his freckles, he looked like a kid fresh out of college. There was something about the way his sandy-colored hair stuck up in an Alfalfa spike at the back of his head that Sara found endearing. Much to Luke's consternation, it wouldn't lie down no matter which way he combed it.

"Hey Luke."

"Up for lunch today?"

"Yes," Sara said. *Pathetic. Loser.* The ghost voice whispered softly. Sara shook her head, and the whispers blew apart like smoke.

"Outstanding," Luke said. "Let's head over to Trang's. It's Crab Leg Monday, you know."

As she gathered her purse, Luke made an observation. "Your cube is so bare. You spend like a third of your life at work, don't you want it to feel a little more like home?"

Sara's cubicle felt exactly like home. Her colleagues had photos of family and pets on their desks and calendars hung on their walls, and some even had small plants or tchotchkes. Sara's workspace was devoid of all decoration save for her bus schedule pinned haphazardly above her phone and a stained coffee cup sitting next to her mouse. Unwilling to admit to Luke that she didn't have photos of actual people to set on her desk, she shrugged. "I dunno. I guess I could bring in a picture of my cat."

"You should. Spruce up your space a little, you know?"

They left the office and walked down Carroll Street toward their favorite Chinese buffet. As they walked, Sara turned her face to the sun and appreciated the eclectic feel of this neighborhood that was a part of what the locals called Capitol Square.

The Wisconsin Capitol and the streets that encircle it in two successive square-shaped rings are oriented to the points of the compass. Other streets run straight out from the square like spokes in a wheel, creating a star effect when downtown Madison is seen on a map or from the air. The most notable of these spokes is State Street, which runs due west, connecting Capitol Square directly to the University of Wisconsin campus.

The streets that form the squares ringing the capitol building are lined with buildings ranging in age from gleaming new apartment buildings featuring all of the amenities any self-respecting millennial could possibly want, to dusty old three-story brick structures with a restaurant or storefront on the main floor and apartments, sans amenities, on the upper floors. Sara rather enjoyed the dissonance these buildings created on Capitol Square and throughout downtown, inhabiting the same space but illustrating different times in Madison's long and proud history. This gave the city an eclectic feel – a progressive city working hard to preserve its past. *My favorite part*, she thought as she and Luke walked, *is that the best Chinese buffet in town is hiding in one of these old buildings.*

At Hamilton Street and West Main Street, one block south of Capitol Square, delicious odors of garlicky fried rice and tangy sweet and sour chicken beckoned Luke and Sara through a small door set in a dingy, windowless façade and into Trang's Chinese Buffet Emporium. A smiling Chinese woman with a rudimentary understanding of English seated them. The room, with its tube metal chairs upholstered in olive green vinyl, green patterned laminate tabletops, gold-flecked mirrors on the walls, and dusty fake greenery, hadn't seen an interior decorator in decades. Sara didn't care; she was here for the famous egg rolls. Roughly a dozen other people had come on their lunch breaks as well.

After filling her plate with cream cheese wontons, crispy fried egg rolls, and chicken fried rice, Sara sat and watched Luke walk unsteadily back from the buffet line holding a plate piled high with nothing but white and red snow crab legs. He plopped unceremoniously in his chair and set his plate on the table, nearly losing his cup full of drawn butter to the floor.

That's the kind of guy every girl says she wants, Sara thought bitterly, biting into a wonton and savoring the warm, melty cream cheese. *Handsome. Smart. Successful. Completely untouchable.*

Luke had asked her out several times over the last two years; she declined every invitation, unable to ignore the voice in her head that quietly asked *What makes you think I would ever want to be with a pathetic loser like you?* Yet he still seemed to want to hang around her. Sara didn't get it; she couldn't figure out what he wanted. She enjoyed his company, so she allowed it – with many conditions.

"They need bigger plates in this dump," Luke grumbled good-naturedly and smoothed his green linen napkin across his lap.

"Or maybe just take fewer crab legs and make more trips to the buffet line," Sara pointed out. She took a sip of the steaming hot tea placed in front of her by a small Chinese woman, then skillfully loaded fried rice into her mouth with her chopsticks.

"Nah, what's the fun in that?" Crab legs cracked and crumbled in front of Luke as he hunted for the tender white meat inside the shells. A thin stream of juice squirted from one crab leg directly onto Luke's pressed blue shirt. "Damn," he muttered. He dabbed the spot with his napkin.

Sara ate in silence for a few seconds, then asked, "Did you read the State Journal this morning?"

Luke shook his head. "I read the Capital Times after work, so I'm always a half day behind in the news. Or a half day ahead, depending on the news in question."

"The front page was covered with a story that I can't stop thinking about. Did you know that there was a bombing on Library Mall thirty years ago today?"

Luke dunked a hunk of crab meat in his drawn butter and popped it in his mouth. "I sure do. Thirty years already, huh?"

"Do you remember it?"

The Chinese woman returned with more hot tea for Sara and another Coke for Luke. He took a gulp of his soda and nodded. "Yeah, vaguely. I was nine years old when it happened. It was all anyone could talk about for weeks. Months, even. I remember my mom took me down there a week or so after the bombing, and the place was a mess. There were pieces of glass and chunks of concrete everywhere. There was a big hole in the ground. They had the whole mall cordoned off with yellow CAUTION tape. It was pretty gruesome."

"Doesn't it make you wonder what kind of bomb that guy must have been carrying? I mean, it was enough to leave a big hole in concrete. I couldn't even imagine." She sipped her tea, breathing in the soothing steam.

"They never did find out who that guy was, did they?"

"That's what the article said. Nothing left but unrecognizable pieces." Sara shuddered at the thought.

Luke shook his head and took another bite of crab leg. "I wonder what would possess someone to do something like that."

"I've been thinking about that too," Sara said. "I don't think anybody causes that kind of damage – or blows himself up like that – by accident. Especially in the middle of a college campus. 1989 was a time of relative peace, right?"

"So you're thinking it wouldn't have been a war protest, or anything political like that."

"Exactly." Sara shifted in her chair; it was missing something at the bottom of one leg, and wobbled with her movement. "It was a Humane Society fundraiser. I wonder if it was an animal rights group."

Luke sat back in his chair, his crab legs reduced to a mountain of cracked shells in front of him. "Does PETA have something against the Humane Society? I'd think they'd be cool with Humane Society's efforts to place pets into homes."

Sara picked up the fortune cookie sitting on the table in front of her. "Who knows. Those organizations look for all kinds of reasons to be pissed. Maybe they had a problem with spaying and neutering." She pulled the cellophane wrapper off the cookie and broke it open. "What else could there be?"

"Well, it was a Greek function, wasn't it?" Luke opened his own fortune cookie. "Weren't a sorority and a fraternity throwing the party?"

Sara considered this. "Somebody pledged and didn't get in, maybe?"

"Whatever it was, it must have been pretty major," Luke observed as he unfurled his fortune. "Never, ever do karaoke," he read. He looked up at Sara, one eyebrow raised. "What kind of fortune is that?"

"Mine says, 'You will pass a difficult test that will make you happier.'" She shook her head. *Yeah. Right.*

Luke popped a piece of fortune cookie in his mouth. "You could be on to something there. Suppose this person had been rejected all his life, and losing out in the fraternity was the last straw for him. Kinda like Parkland or Columbine or any of those other school shootings the last twenty-five years. Kids who've spent their whole lives at the mercy of bullies finally snap, whip out Daddy's AR-15, and blow away the sons of bitches who make their lives hell." He shrugged and took a gulp of his soda.

Goosebumps crawled up and down Sara's arms. She opened her mouth to say something, and discovered that her voice wouldn't work.

"Besides, isn't that what the Greek system's really all about?" Luke continued, oblivious to Sara's shocked silence as he placed items on the table — soy sauce bottle, ceramic container filled with daintily wrapped pairs of wooden chopsticks, Chinese New Year placemats — back in their proper places. "Social acceptance or rejection of people trying desperately to fit in, by people who decide whether or not they meet the standards?" He leaned back in his chair again and inspected his tie. "Which, by the way, are usually just two things: money and status. Can you tell I had better things to do in college than mess around with fraternities?" His eyes moved to Sara's face, and the ironic smile disappeared from his face. "Sullivan? Hey, are you okay?"

Sara blinked and breathed deeply. "Yeah…yeah, I'm okay. Sorry. You said something that struck home for me, is all." She picked up her teacup and sipped.

"What's that?"

"Well…if what you said about being bullied was somehow true about the bomber, let's just say I can relate to that." Her eyes fell to the table in front of her, and a miserable flush crawled up her neck. She wished she hadn't said that, but it was out there now.

"What do you mean by that?" A frown crinkled his forehead

The small smiling Chinese woman set the check on the table and left with a dainty bow. Sara grabbed it. "Never mind. I'll buy lunch today."

"Oh, no. You don't get to buy my disinterest here, Sullivan. What did you mean by that?"

She looked up from her wallet, directly into Luke's eyes. "Just drop it. Okay?"

He sat back and crossed his arms, his baby blues regarding Sara with intense interest. "Okay." She could almost see the thoughts running through his mind like a marquee: *What happened? Who? When? Why? Is that why you won't go out with me?*

The check paid and fortunes read, Sara and Luke walked back to the office, both preoccupied, neither saying much.

CHAPTER TWO
Monday, October 14, 2019
Evening

Sara

When Sara had finally had enough of the emotional and financial drain of her mother's raging alcoholism and decided it was time to leave Minneapolis, she threw a dart at a map and it bullseyed on Madison. So she packed what few belongings she had into her old Chevy Celebrity and moved east. She'd felt welcome in Madison; it was a progressive Midwestern college city that didn't much care what you did as long as you didn't make life harder for your neighbors. This kind of laid back lifestyle perfectly suited Sara, and allowed her to rebuild her life on her own terms.

Her first place in Madison was a room for rent in what passed for a high rise in this town, near the Capitol. Her roommate had been a nice enough person, but had a tendency to bring unsavory men home from the bars on the weekends. Sara awoke late one night to find one of them standing over her bed, watching her sleep with a creepy drunken look on his face. Sara, recalling in living color all the times her mother's "boyfriends" had tried to lay a hand on her as a kid, had screamed bloody murder, and he disappeared.

She was grateful for the flexibility that came with renting; it was so much easier to be able to pull up stakes and move on short notice when circumstances required it. By the following weekend Sara had moved out and into another room for rent an old Queen Anne-style house a few blocks from Lake Mendota. She soon tired of the anxiety-inducing chaos that came with having three roommates; she lasted less than six months with them.

Finally she'd found Janice.

Janice Harper was an elderly widow who needed a bit of help around her neat little rambler near the northern shore of Lake Monona — and she had a mother-in-law apartment in her basement for rent. Janice was the perfect roommate for Sara: quiet, unobtrusive, and she always had her teapot bubbling on the stove. Sara enjoyed Janice's company for over eight years — until the old woman's family moved her to a nursing home and put her house up for sale.

Sara had saved enough money for a down payment by that time, and after Janice's son Steven set her up with Beckie Wyatt, she finally found a place she could call her very own: a 1920s red brick Cape Cod in the Greenbush neighborhood on Madison's near south side. Built mostly by Italian immigrants, African Americans and Jews in the early 20th century, "the Bush" as locals called it was now inhabited mostly by transient UW students stuffed into once-grand old houses that had been converted to multi-unit moneymakers. Sara felt lucky to find her single-family home in the vibrant, jostling urban neighborhood.

Janice was on Sara's mind as the city bus moved fitfully through downtown traffic after work. She sat alone, her briefcase on the red plastic seat next to her to deter anyone thinking they might want to be her seatmate today. She thought of Janice's timeworn face, wispy white hair, and thick glasses that magnified her eyes like Mr. Magoo. *I should go see her*, Sara mused. *I could use a cup of her Earl Grey and some of her wisdom.* She stared at the back of the spiky blond head in front of her without really seeing it, making a mental note to call the nursing home and set up a visit with Janice when she got to the office the next morning. She closed her eyes as her thoughts turned to her lunchtime conversation with Luke, and it replayed like a movie behind her eyelids.

Suppose this person had been rejected all his life, and losing out in the fraternity was the last straw for him. Kinda like Parkland or Columbine or any of those other school shootings the last twenty-five years. Kids who've spent their whole lives at the mercy of bullies finally snap, whip out Daddy's AR-15, and kill the sons of bitches who make their lives hell. Luke's words sent almost-forgotten tingles of humiliation and shame down her spine. He'd said it so casually, unaware of the effect his words had on her, unable to see the rashes of gooseflesh on her arms. His words had dug into her brain and pulled up memories she'd tried so hard to banish. She sighed, leaning her head against the cool bus window.

All the cruel giggles and spiteful laughs when I tried to speak in class, she thought. She closed her eyes against the tears, but couldn't stop them from leaking down her cheeks. The memories flooded over her now, not to be stopped. She saw Mandy Huber's cheerleader face in her mind's eye, along with the equally contemptible faces of her friends Lisa Martin and Jessie Jarvis, and shivered.

How many times did they trip me up in the lunchroom, trying to get me to spill my lunch on the floor? She rubbed her elbows against the shivers. *How many times did they steal my clothes in the locker room after gym class, throwing them between each other, calling me "Salvation Army Sara" while I stood there naked and crying?* The humiliation of the memory sent more tears down Sara's face. She remembered Mandy Huber's candy-sweet smile; her signature Miss Mauve lipstick couldn't mask her hateful eyes, so full of contempt. Sara shuddered.

Another face popped up in her mind's eye, and she cringed. *Kirk Brockman.* North High's basketball god. His chiseled face had contorted in disbelief and disgust when she'd finally asked the question she'd been told he wanted to hear. *What makes you think I would be seen at Snowball with a pathetic loser like you? Wait, I know. How about instead, you just go kill yourself. Nobody would miss you.*

How they had all laughed.

"Hey, lady. You okay?"

Startled, Sara opened her eyes and sat up straight. A pair of concerned brown eyes watched her over the seat in front of her. Two silver hoops threaded through one dark eyebrow. Another hoop decorated the nostril of a thin straight nose. The young man's spiky hair, blond in the back, was dyed green at the tips in the front.

Sara tried to compose herself. "Um, yeah. I'm fine." Her tone was short. She couldn't meet those eyes again; the compassion in them would make her cry. She busied herself with trying to find a tissue in her purse.

The bedecked young man faced forward again without another word.

"Next stop, Randall Avenue." The tinny voice told Sara that her stop was coming up. She drew a shaky breath and rubbed her gritty eyes. *Get a hold of yourself, Sara. You've worked so goddamn hard to put that shit behind you. Just leave it be and move on.*

This was excellent advice, but much easier said than done. The bus came to a jerky stop at the corner of Regent Street and Randall Avenue. Purse and briefcase in hand, Sara disembarked and headed south across Regent, walking past the 7-Eleven and down Randall Street. She tried to stuff the old memories back into the triple-locked vault in her mind they'd escaped from, but they weren't done with her. Not yet. She watched the cracks pass beneath her kitten-heeled pumps as she trudged down the sidewalk, lost in memories that were now nearly two decades old.

The smug look on Mandy's face, and the realization that the whole thing had been a setup expressly designed to humiliate Sara, were each a separate punch to the gut. Sara took off running down the hallway, struggling to breathe, the troll-like laughter of Kirk and his basketball buddies trailing behind her like a piece of toilet paper stuck to her shoe. She stumbled into the girls' locker room—thankfully it was empty at this hour--and shut herself inside the handicap toilet stall. Hot, desperate tears flooded down her face. She felt so fucking stupid for believing Mandy — for allowing this to happen to her.

It was a bitter pill to swallow.

After Ms. Bachman, the phy ed teacher, found her hiding in the locker room just before fourth period and sent her on her way to her next class, Sara decided to go home instead; she couldn't bear the thought of facing anyone else's laughter or cruel comments. She signed herself out sick. This had become such a common occurrence that the secretary didn't bother asking questions anymore.

As she walked home, she wondered what sort of shape her mother would be in.

She didn't have to wonder long. Ignoring the catcalls and keeping her eyes down, Sara walked past the group of pot-smoking wannabe gangsters loitering on the front steps of their blighted apartment building. She didn't dare challenge them or even acknowledge them; the mere idea of finding herself on the wrong end of the barrel of a gun terrified her. So she scurried, trying to avoid trouble.

Sara hated this place.

She let herself into the dingy apartment; the sour odor of fresh vomit washed over her. She found Melinda in the dust-streaked living room, barely dressed in a tattered old pair of boxer shorts and a stained white tank top, passed out cold on the matted brown carpet. She still clutched a mostly empty bottle of Stoli in her hand. She hadn't even made it to the bar today. Looking at her mother was a bit like looking in a mirror for Sara; she had inherited Melinda's straight nose and blonde hair. But Melinda's narrow face was puffy and her eyes, a different shade of hazel than her daughter's, were sunken — just a couple of the many effects of her severe alcohol addiction.

By that time the smell of vomit didn't bother Sara anymore. She cleaned up the mess as best she could and cracked the one window that would still open. Then she returned to where her mother lay, crouched down next to her, and hooked one arm under her neck.

"I didn't have a good day today, Mom," she said, then grunted as she tried to guide Melinda's limp body up to sitting. "Mandy told me that Kirk

wanted me to ask him to the winter dance. I believed her, and I finally worked up the nerve to ask him in the hall between third and fourth period." Sara had maneuvered Melinda just enough to wrap an arm around her mother's back and hoist her up to standing.

"Uhhhhh…" Melinda moaned, her head lolling forward and her stringy hair falling in front of her face. She dropped the Stoli bottle. Sara could hear what was left of the vodka gurgling out onto the carpet. *Another mess to clean up,* she thought.

Sara wrapped Melinda's left arm around her own neck, holding tight to her hand to keep her from falling, and held on to Melinda's waist with her own right arm. She encouraged Melinda to walk. "Come on, Mom, take a step. Yeah, there you go." They slowly made their way to Melinda's bedroom. "Anyway, I asked Kirk to the dance, and he laughed at me in front of everybody. All his buddies did too." Her voice cracked on that last word, and tears prickled behind her eyes again at the memory. "He said I should just kill myself, and nobody would miss me."

Another step. Then another. "Why did I fall for that, Mom? I mean, Mandy has hated me since the ninth grade. But she seemed so…so sincere. And excited for me. I can't believe I believed her." A breath that sounded suspiciously like a sob escaped her. "I really am stupid."

Melinda moaned again, her chin still touching her chest. The muscles in Sara's arms and back sang from holding up her mother's dead weight

"Come on, another step. That's it. I don't know, I guess I really wanted to believe that a boy likes me. Especially the boy I've liked since tenth grade. I mean, how cool would it be to go to Snowball with the captain of the basketball team? Everyone would want to be my friend then, wouldn't they?"

More slow progress down the dark hall. "He…he was just so mean, Mom. Why did he have to be like that? I've never done anything to him. To any of them." Another small step. "And you should have seen the look on Mandy's face. I let her play me a like a cello and she couldn't have been more proud of herself." A tear snaked down her cheek.

They finally reached Melinda's bedroom; it was bare save for a threadbare fleece blanket on a stained queen-sized mattress, a pile of ruined *clothes in the corner, several Stoli bottles scattered across the floor, and broken mini blinds on the window. Sara carefully laid her mother on the mattress and covered her with the blanket. Then she sat on the floor next to Melinda, who had started snoring.*

"I wish you would wake up and talk to me," she said, starting to cry in earnest.

A sob escaped Sara, blowing the bad memories into smoke. Her heart literally hurt; Sara had grown up taking care of her mother, rather than the other way around like it was supposed to be. Being a girl with a mother who was absent in every way but physically had made life exponentially harder for Sara, especially during her teenage years. She should have been arguing with her mother about what she wore to school or whose car she rode in, not cleaning up vomit and making sure her mother ate something every day. She sighed and forced the tears back again.

She turned left onto Mound Street and admired the little wildflower garden in front of the Mound Street Yoga studio. Most blooms had succumbed to autumn frost, but a few hardy ones refused to give up their color and beauty just yet. They eased the pain in her chest, and she drew a deep cleansing breath. She walked halfway down the block to her house and climbed the front steps. She clucked at Bat's silhouette in the living room window as she pulled her mail from the box next to the door; she shuffled through the envelopes. *Bills, bills, junk, junk.*

She was interrupted by the mysterious cheering crowd sound she'd heard this morning. It was faint, as if the crowd was some great distance away or the sound was playing from an old radio with the volume turned way down. This time she knew it could not be coming from Camp Randall; she had gotten off the bus just outside the silent and empty stadium. She turned and faced the house next door. There was no movement over there, no light, and yet the strange sounds continued:

louder, softer, swirling around her head. She had the distinct feeling that she was being…beckoned.

Curious, Sara set her purse, her briefcase, and her mail on the stoop and walked over to the ramshackle house next door. The faint cheering and applause – even a whistle or two – still swirled about her head, and grew louder as she neared the ruined house. She stepped gingerly onto the porch steps, bracing herself in case a rotting riser should give way under her weight. Several pieces of siding had fallen off, revealing old tarpaper underneath. The trim around the windows and door might have been red, once upon a time.

She walked carefully across the sagging porch and tried to look through the pane of beveled glass set in the heavy wooden door. It was so dirty that she could only see muted brown shapes on the other side. The pungent wet smell of decades' worth of rotten tree leaves wafted through the holes in the porch floor.

I'll try the doorknob, Sara thought. The door swung open easily at her touch. Surprised, Sara snatched her hand back. The cheers stopped abruptly. She stepped back, her open hands hovering near her chest. *Shouldn't that be locked?* she wondered. Her curiosity got the best of her. Three tentative steps later, Sara was inside.

Standing just inside the front door, she looked uncertainly around. The evening light fell through opaque windows, leaving dim streaks on the dirty wood floors. Everything was covered in a blanket of thick gray dust. The air was cold and smelled of old cigarette smoke and mummified mice. *God, it looks like someone just up and walked away decades ago,* Sara thought, running her finger over the ancient Bakelite phone on the small wooden table next to her. Her fingertip left a clean black stripe and came away with a thick glob of dust stuck to it. She wiped her hand on her pants.

The living room was spacious, with dark-stained hardwood floors and trim. A flowered velour couch in various shades of 1970s brown and gold with wooden arms sat against one wall. An olive green easy chair and a heavy brass floor lamp with a yellowed macramé shade sat in a corner near the front door. All faced the big television set in a wooden case that sat dark and silent against the other wall. Above the TV hung a large portrait photo of an elderly woman in a gaudy frame with broken glass. Sara stepped closer to get a better look through the dust and spiderweb cracks that radiated out from a center point between the old woman's eyes where something must have hit the glass.

She could see that the woman's gunmetal gray hair was cut short; her perm appeared to be loosening to the point where some hairs were somewhat wavy, and entire chunks were almost completely straight. Rheumy gray eyes and crooked yellow teeth showed among the deep wrinkles and horizontal lines carved into her browned face by years of smoking.

The old woman appeared to be smiling, except...something was a bit off. It took Sara a few seconds to realize what it was: the eyes. The lady had on her best Mona Lisa smile, as if she were posing for the church directory – but her eyes were flat. Calculating. Unsettled, Sara stepped back again and continued her journey through the living room on tiptoe. She felt like the old lady's eyes followed her.

She tried not to disturb the almost morbid silence. Dust bunnies the size of her fist scattered at her feet with every step. She stopped next to a 1950s-style chrome dinette set that sat in the small dining room between the living room and the kitchen. Several college textbooks – Accounting, Biology, Statistics, and a jacketless volume titled *Selected Works of Shakespeare* – sat in a messy pile in the center of the table. Sheets of loose-leaf paper, some covered with faded scribbles and doodles, cascaded out of an old school green Trapper Keeper. A black pocket calculator sat nearby next to two #2 pencils.

Who uses a Trapper Keeper anymore? Can you even get them anywhere outside of Amazon these days? She moved past a set of built-in wooden shelves full of dusty ceramic knick-knacks and into the kitchen. *Whoa. Someone left a mess,* Sara thought as she stepped onto the cracked brown and yellow patterned linoleum. A pile of dishes sat in the sink, the foodstuffs stuck to them long since turned to dried brown goo. Dead flies lay on every surface. Copper gelatin molds and large utensils carved from wood hung on the walls. The refrigerator's deep gold door was devoid of magnets. *I'm not gonna open that.*

Sara headed toward the stairs on the back side of the kitchen and climbed them as quietly as she could. She shivered in the chilly air. *It's like someone's life was interrupted, and nobody's noticed for decades. How is that even possible?* She poked her head into the bigger of two bedrooms. The room was sparsely furnished, with a twin bed that looked like it had last been slept in decades ago, a chest of drawers, a small bedside table. *Doesn't really look like a grandma's room, does it?* she thought. She headed toward the other end of the short hallway to inspect the second bedroom. She glanced into the bathroom on her way by and saw her own reflection in the mirror over the porcelain pedestal sink. She changed course and went into the bathroom; she couldn't help but gaze at herself in the sparkling glass. *My God, it's so clean!*

The mirror's beveled edges were engraved with the letters in the Greek alphabet. Each engraved letter, about an inch and a half tall, sparkled with its own mellow light. Sara stood, mesmerized. Her eyes seemed to glow. And then they turned blue. Sara blinked. *What the hell?* Her eyes were still blue. *Wait…those aren't my eyes.* She stepped closer yet to the mirror, and the glass shimmered with her movement. Sara watched as the form and face of someone else slowly faded in over her reflection. A dark shadow at first, details and features slowly came into view as if a hidden sun rose over a mysterious horizon.

It was a young acne-scarred man, lanky, coarse blond hair cut in an 80s-style mullet, big bloodshot blue eyes, and ears that stuck out on either side of his head like teapot handles. His thin lips turned down at the corners, and Sara's heart tugged in her chest. If the pain in her heart had a face, this would be it. Then, completely out of the blue, she thought: *He looks so sad.* Her brow furrowed as she tried to place where she'd heard that phrase before. Then blinked to make sure she wasn't seeing things.

The young man was still there in the mirror, motionless, not seeing her – then turned to go. Startled, Sara uttered a small gasp and compulsively reached out to the ghostly figure in the mirror as he moved away from her. The glass rippled like waves on water at her touch. She snatched her hand back and inspected her fingertips, expecting pain and blood. There was nothing but a cool phantom wetness where her fingers had somehow penetrated the mirror's shiny surface. Eyes wide, heart skipping, she reached out again. Her fingertips disappeared in the metallic shimmer. Then her knuckles, her wrist, her elbow…still she felt no pain.

Hypnotized, aching, she leaned into the mirror's glass…

1989

CHAPTER THREE
Tuesday, September 5, 1989
Morning

Sara

"…just like a prayer…your voice can take me there…" Madonna's voice, normally smooth like a sip of thirty-year-old Scotch, sounded crackled and tinny. Sara groaned and rolled over, bringing her hand over to slam the alarm into silence. Instead she hit a cold uncompromising wall, sending bright pain through her fingers and up her arm.

"Ow!" Gritting her teeth, Sara sat up and held her injured hand against her chest. She kept her eyes closed against sunshiny brightness, refusing to let go of sleep just yet. *Come on, I couldn't close the curtains last night?*

The pain in her hand had dulled to a throb by the time Sara made her next realization. *Wait a minute. I don't use a radio alarm clock.* She mulled this over, eyes still closed, and then another thought: *And what the hell did my hand hit?*

Any hope of more sleep gone, Sara cracked her eyes open, squinting against the light. A new voice crackled on the radio, an ad for a local Oldsmobile dealership. She didn't recognize the name.

She also didn't recognize her surroundings, and her eyes snapped open wide. The pain in her hand forgotten, Sara gaped as she looked around. She was in what appeared to be a narrow college dorm room. A single door stood between a pair of closets at one end; at the other was a window, its brown curtains thrown open. A utilitarian dresser sat at the foot of her bed, a matching desk at the head.

Another bed, another dresser, another desk sat along the white painted cinderblock wall on the opposite side of the room. The other bed was empty, its geometric-patterned bedding crumpled at the foot. Posters covered the walls on that side of the room: Bon Jovi. New Kids on the Block. A young Bruce Willis – with hair – glowered out from a Die Hard movie poster. Everything looked hopelessly dated. *I guess whoever those belong to is a real '80s buff.*

The walls on her side were bare, save for one big black and white poster of Einstein on the wall above the bed. A tan-colored push-button phone sat on one side of the desk; on the other, a framed photo of an older couple standing cozily next to each other, Mount Rushmore in the background. There was no TV in the room. *What is this?*

The door flew open and a strikingly beautiful young woman with black hair and skin the color of cocoa strode in, clad in a red bathrobe and carrying a small plastic basket full of shower necessities: shampoo, conditioner, soap, a washcloth. Her hair fell in curly wet strings to her collar. She saw Sara and grinned, showing straight white teeth and rabbit-like crinkles around her nose. "Good morning, sunshine!" She didn't seem the least surprised to see Sara sitting there. In fact, she behaved as if Sara belonged there.

Sara opened her mouth but couldn't make anything come out of it. She could only sit, dumb, and watch as the roommate of whoever was really supposed to be here flitted cheerily around the room.

"Oh, I didn't turn my alarm off. I'm sorry, Sara, I didn't mean for that to wake you up." Sara blinked at her name. The roommate flipped the switch on the clock radio with red digital numbers, silencing Madonna, then went to her closet to stow her shower basket. That done, she turned and looked at Sara, forehead knitted. "Are you all right?"

Sara stared at the roommate, still unable to speak. All she could muster was a feeble "Uhhhh…"

The roommate sat next to Sara on the bed and looked at her intently, yet affectionately. "You don't look so hot, my love."

Sara had to make a quick decision: play along as best she could, or confess to this complete stranger that she had no idea what was going on.

"Oh. Uh, I'm okay. I'm fine," Sara stammered. Thinking quickly, she said, "I hit my hand on the wall just now, it kinda hurts." She held up the hand in question.

"Are you okay? Do you need me to grab you some ice?"

"I can get it," Sara said, standing abruptly. She needed to get out of this room and go home, and she recognized her opportunity. She looked down to find herself wearing an oversized red nightshirt that looked like a football jersey. Number 27. *Pants,* she thought. *I need pants.* She felt the roommate's eyes on her as she moved to the dresser and began opening drawers. Panic started rising in her chest. *Where are the goddamn pants?*

Then she spied a pair of stonewashed jeans lying on the closet floor like they'd been worn yesterday. She stuck one leg in, nearly fell over sideways when she forced the other leg in, and spent entirely too much time on the five-button fly. Her hands were not moving fast enough. *Who the hell wears button fly jeans anymore?* she thought, exasperated. Not caring a single iota that her nightshirt was half tucked and half hanging out, Sara headed toward the door. Something occurred to her, and she stopped. Sheepish, she turned to the roommate. "Um. Where is it?"

The roommate's perfectly shaped black eyebrows shot up. "The ice machine is in the commons room, next to the soda machine." Recognizing Sara's complete confusion, she pointed to the left. "That way."

Sara ducked out the door without another word. She found herself at the end of a long hallway, which was lined with five identical doors on each side, confirming her suspicion. *This is a dorm. I'm in a college dorm. Dear god, what did I do last night?* Most of the doors were closed, but some were open; voices echoed down the hall. Each door was decorated with occupants' first names and hometowns: MONICA OSHKOSH WI and JULIE EDEN PRAIRIE MN lived across the hall from the room she just left, which had LAUREN OZAUKEE WI and SARA WAUSAU WI pasted on the door. The cinderblock walls between the doors were painted with custom murals; she walked past an adorable portrait of Bert and Ernie from Sesame Street, painted by LUCINDA '88.

Breathing deeply to stave off what felt like an impending panic attack, Sara tried not to look into anyone's rooms, not even when someone called "Hey Sara!" as she padded by on her bare feet. The linoleum-tiled floor was cold. She passed a communal bathroom, and then the hallway finally gave way to a central commons room, currently unoccupied. She looked around and saw a Mr. Coffee (a handwritten sign on the wall above it reminded users: FINISH A POT, START A POT. Sara remembered how much coffee she'd consumed as a college student and thought this sound advice), a soda machine, an ice machine, a heavy tube TV with a convex glass screen mounted to the ceiling, a magazine rack, a couple study carrels, and several hospital-quality couches and chairs upholstered in a uniquely 1980s combination of mauve and gray. A small kitchen was tucked behind a split door in one corner. A bank of two elevators stood to her left, and she could see two other hallways, each jutting out at roughly a forty-five degree angle from this central room.

Remembering every hotel she'd ever stayed in, Sara walked to the elevator bank and examined the sign above the buttons. CHADBOURNE HALL 7 IN CASE OF FIRE USE STAIRS.

Okay, Sara thought. *I know where I am.* She was about a mile from her house, on the seventh floor of Chadbourne Residence Hall on the UW-Madison campus. She'd driven by the 13-story Y-shaped building hundreds of times over the years she'd lived in Madison. *But how the fuck did I end up here? In someone else's pajamas?* Her eyes teared up in frustration, blurring the floor sign; the stick figure walking calmly down the stick stairs in the fire safety illustration looked like he was swimming. She shuffled to a couch and sat, massaging her face with her fingers, trying to remember what she'd been doing the day before. She remembered having lunch at Trang's with Luke, and the flowers in front of the yoga studio on the way home from the bus stop. After that, it was like the film had run out; nothing but blank white.

Sara sat up straight and blew air out of her mouth. *I have to get out of here. Right now. I'm going to be so late for work.* She stood and moved back toward the elevators. Just as she was about to press the button, her eyes fell on a bright green poster hanging on the wall; in thick black letters it announced: GREAT WHITE – TESLA – DANE COUNTY COLISEUM – OCT. 1, 1989 – 7PM – FOR TICKETS CALL 267-3976.

Hold on, Sara thought, and reread the poster. Her eyes stopped on the date and her fingers fell away from the elevator button. *1989?*

"Sara?" The unexpected voice startled Sara; she whipped around to find the roommate – she remembered the sign on the door that said LAUREN – standing outside the door to the bathroom, dressed for the day in a plain white t-shirt tucked into high-waisted acid-washed jeans, watching her with some concern. "Are you all right?"

Sara didn't know how to answer that question, so instead she asked, "Can I ask you something?"

"Shoot," Lauren said.

"What's the date today?"

A bemused chuckle from Lauren. "Seriously?"

Panic bubbled in Sara's chest again. "Please? Can you just --"

Lauren must have seen something in Sara's eyes; she grew serious and said, "Okay. Today is September 5, 1989. Tuesday. It's the first day of class."

All of the air seemed to leave Sara's lungs. She felt a little sick.

Lauren took a step forward. "Are you sure you're all right?"

In the absence of any information that might help Sara understand what was happening to her, she decided that continuing to play along was probably the best thing she could do. She tried to compose herself, smoothing the front of her pajama shirt. "Um, yeah. Yeah, I'm fine. I guess I was just confused there for a second. I, uh, I found the ice machine."

Doubt moved across Lauren's face like a wave. "Okay, well, you should probably get dressed. We have Biology Lab in about twenty minutes."

"I'll be there in just a sec."

Lauren disappeared down the hall, leaving Sara to stare at the concert poster for a bit longer. *1989. What the hell is going on here?*

Charlie

First on the schedule: Biology Lab. It didn't make much sense to Charlie to start the semester with Biology Lab before Biology Lecture, but today was Tuesday. Lab day. He slowly climbed the stairs to the third floor of Noland Hall, a nondescript brown brick building on the south side of campus, listening to his footsteps drag up the empty echoing stairwell. He kept one hand on the cold metal railing, his eyes on the rubber-covered toes of his new red canvas basketball shoes. After spending his childhood with his feet in old, ill-fitting, holey shoes, Charlie always relished a new pair of footwear. These particular shoes were special because not only were they new, they were *cool*. They were *trendy*. They were so fancy that he could bring himself to wear them only on special occasions, like the first day of classes — reserving his tired white sneakers for ordinary days. He had high expectations for these shoes: he was pretty sure they would help him fit in.

He reached the third floor and followed the hallway, head down. He resisted the urge to reach out his right hand and drag it along the wall as he walked. People passed him on their way to class as if he were invisible. Charlie watched the floor, glancing up only occasionally to check room numbers. He arrived in front of Room 341 to find the door open, lights on inside, and other students milling around. His chest locked up with panic, but he forced himself to step forward.

He scurried to an empty table in the back of the room, not looking at anyone as he went. The pressure in his chest threatened to crush his heart. Sweat popped out on his forehead, despite the air conditioning. He dropped his backpack on the table and sat in the hard plastic chair closest to the wall, struggling to gain control of his panic attack. *You fucking loser,* he thought, and squeezed his eyes shut. He laid his head on his backpack and tried to breathe normally.

Panic gradually loosened its hold on his chest, and finally Charlie was able to lift his head, open his eyes, and look around the lab. Twelve two-person lab stations arranged themselves in two columns down the long room. Diagrams of cells and internal organs hung on the walls. A long green chalkboard spanned the front of the room. The morning sun shone through two narrow windows. Locked cabinets lined the back wall.

As he inspected the room, Charlie noticed a girl sitting at the table directly in front of his. Her blunt cut blonde hair fell straight down to her shoulders, the sides tucked behind her delicate ears, her bangs slightly feathered. Her hazel eyes darted around the room, trying to take everything in at once. They settled on him for an extra beat. His heart lurched. He lowered his head to his backpack to catch his breath.

He lifted his head again after a minute or two. *Maybe I should say hi.*

That girl? She doesn't know you exist. His grandmother Ruth's voice, roughened by decades of smoking full-flavored Pall Malls, chimed in. She was always there to help him feel even worse about himself in any situation.

Maybe not, Charlie thought. *But she looks…lost. Maybe even a little scared. Maybe if I ask her to sit with me…*

Don't know why you would bother, Ruth scoffed.

Trembling, Charlie gathered every ounce of courage he had and opened his mouth. It was so dry that his tongue stuck to the roof for a panicky second. "Um, excuse me," he said, rather timidly.

She turned; those remarkable golden hazel eyes fell on him again, taking his breath away. He struggled to form words. "I – I mean –" He cleared his throat. "I was wondering if you'd like to…to…"

She didn't say anything, but her amber eyes held his gaze steadily, almost expectantly. The rest of the words died on his lips and he gestured feebly at the empty chair next to him.

"Good morning, class." The booming voice was immediately followed by the professor, a big white-mustached man in a tweed coat. A pretty woman – he thought maybe she was mixed race – took the empty chair next to the girl at the table in front of him.

The prof pointed a latecomer, a dark, handsome young man, toward Charlie's table; he took the chair Charlie had just tried to offer to the girl with the golden eyes. "Hey bud, how's it going?" the young man asked, grinning.

Charlie ignored him. His stomach churned. The professor, named Hilliard, started class by handing out the mimeographed syllabus. Charlie took his and stared at the purple type without reading it. He heard the professor's booming voice without comprehending what he said. All he could see was the blonde girl with the amazing golden eyes sitting seven feet from him. He learned from roll call that her name was Sara Sullivan, her tablemate's name was Lauren Dailey, and his own new partner was Ben Packard.

Professor Hilliard finished reviewing the syllabus and announced, "Get to know the person you're sharing a table with, folks – they'll be your Biology 101 Lab partner every Tuesday for the rest of the semester."

Sara's hand shot in the air. "Excuse me, sir?"

"Yes. Ah," He consulted his class list. "Sara, is it?"

"Yes. I was wondering if I could switch partners. I love Lauren here, but she's my roommate."

Lauren leaned closer to Sara and whispered something in her ear. Sara shook her head. Then, to the professor: "I thought we could mix things up with the table behind us."

Hilliard looked confused but willing to play along. "By all means," he said, making a sweeping gesture with his right arm.

Sara turned to look at Charlie. For a moment he was sure those amber eyes could see directly into his soul. "Wanna be lab partners?"

Charlie turned to Ben expectantly, sure that she was actually talking to him. Ben was already looking at him with the same expectant look on his pretty boy face, and made a gesture with his hand that said, *Well? Aren't you going to answer her?* Confused, Charlie looked back at Sara, who nodded. A hot flush climbed up his face. "Oh. Uh…okay," he mumbled. His eyes fell to the table.

Sara gathered her belongings and stood up. Ben did the same and moved to sit next to Lauren. Sara sat down next to Charlie and introduced herself. "Hi. I'm Sara."

It was hard to meet her gaze; when he finally did, he managed to say, "I'm Charlie."

Hilliard started his lecture, and they all faced frontward. Charlie kept stealing little sidelong glances at Sara, unable to believe his good luck. *This kind of shit never happens to me. Why does she want to be lab partners with me, and not with pretty boy there?*

Charlie didn't know, but he was glad she did.

CHAPTER FOUR
Tuesday, September 5, 1989
Afternoon

Sara

Sara didn't quite know why she'd felt compelled to ask Charlie to be her Bio Lab partner either. He was skinny, and his limbs seemed a little too long for his body. He had clearly suffered from severe acne as a younger teenager; his face was a bit ruddy and pockmarked with acne scars. He wore his coarse blond hair in a style that Sara had known in middle school as "hockey hair": cropped close to his head, and a bit longer on top and at the nape of his neck. His oversized ears stuck out from the side of his head like sugar bowl handles. His thin lips seemed to be always moving, as if he were constantly on the lookout for an ambush. His big blue eyes seemed familiar somehow.

Sara had never seen this guy before today, but when she'd first caught sight of him, a movement in her chest signaled that she needed to pay attention. She couldn't imagine why that was; she was a stranger to this time and place. A random thought shot through her consciousness – *I really am some kind of jerk* – a split second before she unexpectedly raised her hand. It was almost as if she wasn't operating under her own power.

He'd seemed nervous after she'd moved to his table; he never spoke a word, and he would look at her only out of the corner of his eye. When Hilliard dismissed class, he shouldered his red backpack and scuttled out the door without a word. She watched him go, noticing his Atari logo t-shirt, jeans that hung from his skinny butt and legs, and shiny new red Cons, and thinking *He is like the epitome of a late-eighties geek*. She wondered if perhaps she'd made a mistake.

Sara had no idea where she was supposed to go after Bio Lab, so after Lauren headed for her College Composition class, she decided to go back to Chadbourne Hall. As she trudged across campus, she saw evidence everywhere that supported Lauren's crazy claim that this was 1989. Flat-brimmed plastic trucker's hats. Eyeglasses in heavy metal frames. Stirrup pants. Mall bangs. Stonewashed denim. Shoulderpads. Side parts and mullets. She grabbed a copy of the *Daily Cardinal* student newspaper on her way through Chadbourne's lobby, and let herself into room 710 – with LAUREN and SARA on the door – using one of the three keys she carried on an unfamiliar metal Harley Davidson keychain. She felt gut-punched again when she looked at the newspaper and saw the date printed on it: Tuesday, September 5, 1989.

Holy. Shit. Sara's hands, still holding the paper, dropped to her thighs and she stared out the window; all she could see at this height were a few treetops. *So it's true. This is 1989.*

Overwhelmed, Sara sighed shakily and sat on the bed in this unfamiliar room with her name on the door.

She now knew *when* and *where* she was.

But the *why* still eluded her.

And *how* on earth did she get here?

Also, she wasn't sure exactly *who* she was. In September of 1989 Sara had been just seven years old, not yet indoctrinated into the lonely life of an alcoholic's kid. She would not go to college until the year 2000, eleven years from now – and she would attend the University of Minnesota, not the University of Wisconsin. She had never set foot in Madison until she moved here in 2009. This room and these possessions were not hers. She didn't know the elderly couple in the photo on the desk.

Was she somehow living another Sara Sullivan's life? What were the odds of that?

What the hell am I supposed to do?

Sara sighed and slowly paged through the *Cardinal,* absorbing the news and opinion pages. George Herbert Walker Bush was president, with the mousy young Hoosier Dan

"Potatoe" Quayle as his vice president. Michael Moore's influential documentary *Roger and Me* premiered at Telluride. Britain's Princess Anne had finally separated from her husband after years of living apart. Sara got to the movie listings and marveled that her favorite comedy film of all time, *Uncle Buck,* was sitting at the top of the box office for the third week in a row. She'd seen it at the age of nine on a rental VHS – her trusty babysitter when her mother went out partying at the bar. "Here's a quarter. Go downtown and have a rat gnaw that thing off your face" was one of the best lines in all of filmdom, as far as Sara was concerned. She appreciated how Buck had stood up for his little niece with the evil school principal – exactly the kind of support she'd longed for from her own mother. *I can't believe it's actually in the theaters right now, original release. Maybe I should go see it.* She almost smiled for the first time today.

An hour later, Sara was absorbed in a Daily Cardinal opinion article titled "Does Greek life do more harm than good?" when the door blew open and Lauren walked in. She closed the door behind her and threw her black cotton tote bag – ESPRIT spelled out in rainbow letters on the front pocket – on her bed. She sat next to the bag and stared earnestly at Sara.

Sara put down her newspaper. "What?"

"What is going on with you?"

A warm flush crept up Sara's neck. "What do you mean?"

Lauren started untying her white canvas Keds. "I know we haven't known each other but a week, but you're different today."

"How am I different?"

"Well, for starters, you've been acting like this morning was the first time you've ever laid eyes on me. You didn't know where the ice machine is. You didn't know what today's date is, even though we've been talking nonstop about the first day of classes. You haven't once called me by my name." Lauren threw her shoes in the general direction of her overflowing closet.

"And, even though we'd already agreed to be Bio Lab partners, you ditch me for the dweeb?"

Sara dropped her eyes and stared at her hands, debating whether or not to let Lauren in on her secret. *What the hell — it's not like I have anything to lose. Maybe she can help me.* She sighed. "I should probably tell you something."

Those perfect eyebrows went up, and concern clouded Lauren's espresso eyes. "Okay. What is it?"

Sara took a deep breath. "I'm not the Sara Sullivan you think I am."

"What do you mean? You look like the same Sara to me."

"I am Sara Sullivan. I'm just not the Sara Sullivan who is actually supposed to be here."

Lauren stared for a few beats, trying to absorb the words Sara was saying, then shook her head. "You lost me."

"I am actually thirty-five years old," Sara said. "Yesterday I was living my normal life in 2019, and this morning I woke up here — in a strange place, and apparently in a different time. The thing is, this isn't my life. The real me is seven years old and starting the second grade at Loring Elementary in Minneapolis right now."

Dumbfounded silence from Lauren. Then: "If you're a different person than my roommate Sara, how come you look exactly like her?"

Sara's eyes prickled. "I don't know. When I look in the mirror, I see me. I guess you see the other Sara. I couldn't tell you why that is." Sara's throat tightened with frustration, making her voice crack. "All I can tell you is that I'm not making this shit up. And I have no idea why, or how I got here." Sara blinked back tears.

Lauren collected herself. "Okay. Let's pretend that what you said was not the craziest thing I've ever heard. If you're Sara Sullivan from 2019 (she pronounced this "twenty-nineteen"), I'm going to need you to tell me a few things."

"Okay," Sara said.

"Who's the President of the United States in 2019?" Lauren asked.

"Donald Trump." Sara rolled her eyes.

"Donald –" Astonished, Lauren burst out laughing. "Donald Trump? That douchebag rich guy out East? Mr. Gold Plated? Are you kidding?"

"I kid you not," Sara said.

"He was all over the news last spring after that jogger was raped in Central Park," Lauren remarked. "Pushing to bring the death penalty back to New York. Does he still talk and write like an uneducated buffoon?"

"Of course he does," Sara said. "Except he's in his seventies now, fat, fake hair, orange spray-tan skin, and more than a little unhinged. You know what he said once while he was campaigning?"

"What?" Lauren asked.

"He said, and I quote, 'I love the uneducated!' I posted that article to Facebook and said, 'I weep for my country.' That was when I finally realized his campaign might be more than just a publicity stunt. What's crazy is that the uneducated love him too, no matter what he says or does. It's gross."

"Oh," Lauren said, looking a little confused. "Um, what's a face book?" She pronounced it just like that – two separate words.

Sara stared at Lauren for a moment, not sure she heard the question correctly. "What do you mean?"

"I don't know," Lauren said. "You said you posted something to a face book, but I don't know what that is. Is it like a bulletin board or something?"

Sara finally understood what Lauren was asking. "Oh, no no. It's not a bulletin board, it's a website."

"A what?"

"You know, the internet."

Lauren shook her head. "Never heard of it."

Sara gaped, astonished. "Do you know what a computer is?"

"Of course I do," Lauren said, indignant. "My parents have an IBM computer at home. The computer lab downstairs has three Apple Macintosh computers, and a printer. I use them to type up my College Comp papers."

Sara had forgotten that she was in a time before the internet was widely available, when personal computers weren't much more than very expensive word processors.

"So where did my Sara Sullivan go? From 1989?" Lauren asked.

Sara shrugged. "I don't know."

"Maybe she's seven-year-old you in Minneapolis right now?"

Sara wasn't sure, but she was impressed with Lauren's leap of logic. "Maybe. I don't know. I don't know much of anything right now." She felt helpless.

Lauren moved to Sara's side and tentatively placed her arm across Sara's shoulders. Almost unconsciously, Sara scooted away from Lauren just enough that she had to drop her arm. A new awkwardness filled the space between them.

Lauren folded her hands in her lap. "Sorry," she offered.

Sara shook her head. "It's not you, it's me. I – I don't much like to be touched."

"I grew up in a family that is always touching and hugging each other; my mama has been known to force a hug on someone she thinks needs one. Whether they want it or not." Lauren smiled. "Her heart's in the right place. And she has taught me well."

"It's all right," Sara said. She stared at her hands.

They sat in silence for a moment. Then Lauren said, "The thing is, Sara is also a hugger."

Sara's head snapped up and she looked at Lauren with wide eyes.

"I shouldn't believe your crazy claim that you're some time traveler from the future. I mean, you look the same. But. You've been acting so strange all morning; you're like a completely different person. So…serious. That, along with the fact that you prefer not to be touched, sort of means that even though you look like her, you can't be my Sara."

Relief washed over Sara, bringing with it uncontrollable tears. *She believes me.* She covered her face with her hands and sobbed.

"Don't worry, love. I don't know if you're some kind of body snatcher or what, but we'll figure this out. One way or another. Until we do, it's probably best to not tell anyone about this, don't you think?"

Sara wiped her face with the hem of her shirt and nodded. "Yes."

"I'll help you learn your schedule, and show you everywhere you need to go. I don't know, maybe living the other Sara's life for a while will help," Lauren said.

Lauren was right, Sara realized. She couldn't hole up in this dorm room; she needed to get out there and act as normal as possible. To look for clues that might point her to the answers she needed: why she was in 1989, and how she got here. "That would be great. Thank you."

Lauren smiled. "Well, what are roomies for?"

CHAPTER FIVE
Thursday, September 7, 1989

Sara

The University of Wisconsin – Madison could trace its origins to the year of Wisconsin's statehood. Founded in 1848, "the UW," as the locals call it, is the oldest public university in the state. Its first building, North Hall, was constructed atop Bascom Hill in 1851; it contained classroom space and a men's dormitory. It was soon followed by South Hall and then Bascom Hall, which still stand and together form the three-sided crown of the university.

The university grew steadily over the years, its campus eventually encompassing 388 buildings on over nine hundred acres of land on and to the southwest of the Madison Isthmus – making it the largest public university in Wisconsin, and one of the top 20 largest universities in the United States. In various collegiate surveys, the UW is consistently rated a "most beautiful campus" and a "top party school."

Sara's previous experience at the University of Minnesota, also a large state university and bitter athletics rival to the UW, came in handy as she learned the other Sara's class schedule. With Lauren's help, it didn't take her long to learn where all her classes were and when she was expected to attend them, where the dining hall was, where the computer lab was, who their Housefellow was, where to find the laundry facilities, and how to order a Tombstone pizza from Chad's front desk. She even knew her declared major: Psychology. *Yeah, right,* she'd thought. *I'll become a psychologist, because clearly I need one.*

Her first two nights in 1989 had been rough. Her head was so full of questions and uncertainties that sleep was impossible. So she'd spent most of both nights in the commons room to avoid waking Lauren.

She laid on a mauve and gray couch in the darkened room, TV flickering in the background, and mostly thought about the other Sara. It felt strange to wear someone else's pajamas and lie in their bed. It felt weird to lace up a pair of white Reebok hi-top sneakers that weren't hers, but fit her perfectly. She felt like she was living in a neverending charade. She wondered if the older couple in the photo on her desk were the other Sara's parents, or maybe her grandparents. It was clear that, like herself, the other Sara wasn't really the sentimental type; besides the photo and the Einstein poster, her side of the room was devoid of decoration. It sort of felt like home. It looked stark and bare compared to the jumbled shrine to the 1980s Lauren had going on. It was like an invisible vertical plane cut their room perfectly in half.

Sara read every newspaper and magazine in the racks, and watched Nick at Nite reruns and news programs on the TV, trying to figure out how to fit her 21st century self into 1989 culture. She also hoped she would find a clue or two. Unfortunately, neither the Cleaver family nor Ozzie and Harriet had the answers she needed.

She attended her classes on Thursday, and felt like the walking dead when she finally got back to Chad that afternoon. The seventh floor was all abuzz; the University of Wisconsin's sororities had finally sent invitations to Saturday night's rush parties to all the freshmen who had indicated interest. Girls who had received invites gathered in the commons room to discuss and compare. Sara found Lauren sitting on a couch and collapsed next to her.

"Sara!" Lauren squealed. "Check it out, I got invited to Kappa Delta's rush party on Saturday!" She waved the piece of paper in the air as if Sara needed to see proof. "Come with me!"

"Yeah, no thanks. I'm not interested." Sara said, and yawned. *I need to catch up on sleep.*

"Come on, Sara," Lauren pleaded. "I really want to check out Kappa Delta, but no way I'm going by myself. Pleeease?"

"I'm going to Tri-Delt," Monica Katz sat in the matching chair on the other side of Lauren. Groups of girls mingled and chatted all around the room. Monica's bleached blonde bangs – with dark brown roots – had been carefully sculpted to stand straight up from her forehead; Sara found their height to be nothing short of amazing. "I got one of, like, six invitations to their party."

"Tri-Delt?" Sara asked.

"Yeah, it's short for Delta Delta Delta. Only the most exclusive sorority on campus." A smug smile creased Monica's pale face.

"That's not what I heard," Lauren remarked. "Skanks and hos, Tri-Delt will let anyone in. The only requirement is that you are down to party at all times."

Sara used her thumb and pinky as a mock telephone and held it to the side of her head. "Oh. Mah. Gawd. Delta Delta Delta, can I help ya help ya help ya?" She grinned, remembering her favorite *Saturday Night Live* skit; at ten years old, she'd snuck out to the living room to watch while her mother was passed out drunk on the couch.

Lauren and Monica stared at Sara as if she'd popped a third eye on her forehead. Her attempt at humor had been lost on them. *They'll realize that's funny in about three years,* she thought.

"As I was saying," Lauren said as she turned back to Monica, "Any invite to a Tri-Delt party is not exclusive. Trust me. Come with us to Kappa Delta."

"I'm not going," Sara objected. The name of the sorority tripped something in her brain. Had she heard it before?

"On the contrary, love, you are going. With me. End of discussion." Lauren turned to Monica. "You coming too?"

Monica rolled her eyes. "Gag me with a spoon."

"Fine," Lauren said. "Go hang with the rest of the skanks and hos."

Charlie

Charlie got back from his last class – Accounting 101 – around 3:00 in the afternoon, and he was hungry. After letting himself into the house, he threw the mail and his red backpack on the chrome dinette table on his way to the kitchen and the refrigerator.

He stood in front of the open fridge, chilly air wafting over his legs, staring at a couple of hot dogs, a half-empty jar of salsa, and a wilted apple. *I have got to get some groceries,* he thought.

That you, Charlie? Ruth's gravelly voice asked. He knew she was only in his head, but he always swore she could be just in the next room. She sounded that realistic.

"Yeah, Gram. Just got home from class."

I don't know why you bother with college. You couldn't hardly find your way out of a paper bag your whole life.

Charlie hung his head and closed the fridge door; he no longer had an appetite. "That's not true," he mumbled.

Of course it is, Ruth insisted. *Dumber than a box of rocks, just like your worthless mother.*

Charlie shuffled into the living room and sat on the green easy chair under Ruth's handmade macramé lampshade. He looked at her portrait on the wall above the television and asked – whined, really: "Why are you so mean to me?"

I'm just doing my job, Charlie, Ruth croaked. *Your parents decided that getting high was more important than raising you right and making sure you mind your place in this world. Those selfish assholes left me to do it.*

Charlie slouched and crossed his arms over his chest in his familiar defensive position.

You're wasting my money on college. You don't belong there.

What Charlie wanted to shout at the photograph on the wall: *I do belong there! I'm going to graduate and make something of myself! No thanks to you!*

What Charlie actually said, rather meekly, to the photograph on the wall: "But…but I'm making friends." He had never stood up to his grandmother in his life; the fact that she was dead didn't make the prospect any less scary for Charlie now. In her portrait, Ruth's small, deeply lined smile and bleary gray eyes didn't change, but Charlie thought she was watching him all the same.

Friends? Ruth cawed like a crow with laughter, then launched into a violent coughing fit: wheezy barking sounds that came from deep in her chest. Charlie thought it was a miracle she'd lived as long as she had; those lungs would have taken her if her heart hadn't given out first.

"Yes. Friends." He pulled his folded arms closer to his chest. A mental picture of Sara's face popped up behind his eyes; he still couldn't believe that beautiful girl had *wanted* to be his lab partner.

You've never had a friend in your life, Ruth pointed out. *Sorriest little sack I ever saw, you were.*

Charlie slouched further down in his chair. His knees were now about level with his forehead. "Leave me alone," he said darkly.

Shut it, Charlie, you don't know what you would do without me, Ruth croaked.

Charlie hated to admit it, but she was right. She was all he'd had his whole life – and even though she plainly resented him for being stuck raising him, he was devoted to her. He'd been devastated when she died in her sleep last year; a heart attack, the coroner had said. The cigarettes, he'd said. "I know. I miss you, Gram."

Ruth fell silent, and Charlie's stomach growled. He remembered the hot dogs in the fridge and pushed himself up off the chair, thinking one might be good with a little mustard; maybe he could scrounge up some potato chips in the cupboard. He grabbed the mail from the dining room table on his way to the kitchen. He had received two pieces today. One was from Ruth's estate attorney, Jerry Harper; he had been bugging Charlie for months to transfer the deed to the house from Ruth's name to his. *Yeah, yeah, I'll get to it*, Charlie thought and tucked the letter behind the other piece of mail, a white envelope with a return address that said Sigma Alpha Tau. Charlie stopped dead in his tracks, his anxiety ramping up with this whole new thing to worry about.

Oh god, Charlie thought, his heart racing. He opened the envelope and skimmed the letter; it was an invitation to the fraternity's rush party on Saturday night. *Oh god, I never should have filled out that card. I didn't think they would actually invite me,* he thought, starting to panic.

He pulled out a chrome dinette chair and sat, taking deep breaths and using the letter to fan himself. Last week he'd gone to the University Book Store on State Street to purchase the required books for his classes. As usual, he kept his eyes on the ground as he walked, and didn't notice the table set up on the shady sidewalk outside the store until one of the two young men standing behind it said, "Hey buddy, want to fill out a card?"

Curious, he walked over to the table and took the card. He looked at it, and then looked at the tall guy in the red Coca-Cola t-shirt who had given it to him; Charlie thought he looked a lot like Ted "Theodore" Logan from *Bill & Ted's Excellent Adventure*. "What's it for?"

"It's just for more information about our fraternity, Sigma Alpha Tau. We're gearing up for recruitment, you should toss your name in the hat." The guy pointed at a literal black tophat sitting upside down on the table. *It's not just a saying after all,* Charlie thought wryly.

"I just fill out this card, and that's it? Are you going to send me anything?"

Tall Guy shrugged. "You might get an invitation to our rush party. If you get one it means we're interested in maybe seeing if you're a good fit for Sig Tau. You don't have to come if you don't want, totally up to you."

Charlie considered this for a moment, and then asked for a pen. He filled out the card and dropped it in the hat, and then continued on his way into the bookstore. He figured he was helping Sig Tau's recruitment efforts; it never occurred to him that they might actually send him an invite.

But they did. *I don't look anything like Tall Guy; I'm short and skinny, and my ears stick out. Why would they invite me to their party?*

He didn't know – and he didn't know what to do.

CHAPTER SIX
Saturday, September 9, 1989

Sara

"I look ridiculous," Sara protested. The hems of her acid-washed jeans had been folded tight around her ankles and fastened with four safety pins on each leg. Her fluorescent tie-dyed tunic-length shirt had shoulderpads, of all things. Big ones. She looked like a defensive lineman. Half of her hair had been pulled into a ponytail on the top of her head with a bright pink scrunchie. And there was so much blue eyeshadow. "I look like I walked right out the movie *Heathers*."

"You, my love, are no Martha Dumptruck. You look awesome!" Lauren jumped up and down, clapping. She wore a purple Multiples tube dress with a wide blue cloth belt and striped leggings. "Let's go, let's go!"

They walked out of Chadbourne Hall and moved east on University Avenue. The evening was warm and the sidewalk was crowded with freshmen dressed to the nines, headed for Greek Row. As Sara and Lauren approached Lake Street, Sara wondered if the Karaoke Kid, her favorite hole-in-the-wall karaoke bar where a song could be had for a buck and the sake flowed like a river, was there yet. More than once she'd gone there by herself to belt out Alannah Myles' hit *Black Velvet* — usually receiving a standing O for her performance. It was the closest thing Sara had to a social life.

Has that song even been released yet? she wondered. Fully intending to ask Google, she stuck a hand in a rear jeans pocket to grab her phone. She didn't feel the familiar rectangle shape and remembered with a grimace that cell phones – and Google, for that matter – were not yet a thing in 1989. She rolled her eyes and thought, *But I can get a disposable camera, record Kodak moments on 35mm film, and have the film developed at Ritz Camera next time I go to the mall. So there's that.*

The group turned onto Lake Street, walked past the University Bookstore and Walgreens, and then found themselves on Langdon Street. Starting at Park Street in front of the Memorial Union and hugging Lake Mendota for seven blocks east, Langdon was lined with apartments, a few bars, two hotels – and many stately houses adorned with Greek letters. This was the UW's Greek Row.

As they walked, Sara stared in awe, as she always did when on Langdon. The oak, ash, and maple trees still majestically shaded the street, giving it somewhat of an Old South plantation feel. Many of the beautiful houses' limestone or brick facades were carpeted in green ivy. Some boasted rounded balustrades and white pillars. Others had expansive steps leading to wide front porches and heavy wooden doors, which had been thrown open to welcome the warm September breeze.

It's definitely party time, Sara thought. Lights blazed in every window, through which she could see people holding plastic cups full of beer. More people milled in the street, and others sat in yards and on porches, balconies, and roofs with their woven lawn chairs and plastic coolers. All had beers in their hands. Music blared from every house. Cups already littered the lawns and the street, and nobody seemed to notice.

"…Henry Street," Lauren's voice cut through Sara's thoughts.

"Sorry, what?"

"I said, the Kappa Delta house is on the corner of Langdon and Henry Street. Just a couple blocks, I think," Lauren pointed straight ahead.

"Great," Sara muttered. *What the hell am I doing here? I wanted nothing to do with sororities the first time I went to college.*

"Lauren! Over here!"

Sara turned and saw Lauren's Bio Lab partner – his name escaped Sara – galloping down the front steps of the Sigma Alpha Tau house. He was smiling. His white teeth were a perfect contrast to his floppy dark hair and tanned skin. He reminded Sara of Johnny Depp, circa *21 Jump Street.* Very easy on the eyes. *Another untouchable, like Luke.*

"Hi Ben!" Lauren waved.

"Where are you guys headed?" he asked. His black t-shirt was tucked into a pair of Girbaud jeans, and his white Chuck Taylors glowed in the dusklight. He looked at Sara and his smile widened. "Hey."

"Hey," Sara said. She couldn't quite meet his eyes.

"Ben, this is my roommate Sara Sullivan. Sara, I believe you've already met Ben Packard, who is now my Bio Lab partner thanks to you."

"Yeah, sorry about the confusion," Sara said, blushing furiously. She kind of wished she could disappear.

"Packard!" The gravelly voice came from a crewcutted guy the size of an NFL linebacker on the porch, where he sat with a full-sized keg between his beefy knees and the tap nozzle in one hand. "Get your ass up here man, we got a party!"

Ben waved behind him. "Yeah, Scott, just a sec." He flashed his remarkable smile again. "No problem," he said to Sara. To Lauren: "You guys going somewhere?"

"We're going to check out Kappa Delta. You looking at Sig Tau?"

"This is my second year," Ben said, sweeping an arm at the brick house packed with fraternity members and hopefuls. "Just making an appearance. Trying to recruit committee members for the Paws for a Cause benefit in October before everyone gets too wasted."

"Packard!" Scott shouted again.

"Cool, good luck with that," Lauren said and pulled Sara along. "We gotta go, but have fun tonight!"

"You too." Ben grinned. "See you in Bio Lab."

Sara was bored out of her mind and trying not to fall asleep in spite of the loud music; Roxette's "The Look" — a maddening earworm that made Sara want to slowly pull her brain out through her ears with a bent paperclip — was currently playing on loop. The first thing she did upon arrival was use the scrunchie to pull her hair back into a simple ponytail, then went to the bathroom and used dampened paper towels to wipe off the 80s clown makeup. Once she felt human again, she'd found an open spot on a pale blue damask settee and spent the next two hours nursing a single beer and watching Lauren work the crowd in the cavernous parlor. The formality of the room was absurd — with its heavy blue drapery, dark Queen Anne-style furniture, and ornate lamps — considering the nature of the parties held here. Sara had seen two girls throw up into their purses so far. Another was unconscious, propped in the corner behind a faux ficus tree. One Kappa hopeful had stumbled to the couch over an hour ago and promptly passed out next to Sara without so much as a hello. Sara's quick thinking had kept her nearly full beer from spilling all over herself, the couch, and the polished wood floor. Now she was snoring.

Sara missed her 5G iPhone; anything on Instagram would be more entertaining than this. Especially her favorite funny cat memes.

She set her half-full beer on the nearest lacquered wood table — without benefit of a coaster — and stood up. *I need to go to bed. Time to find Lauren and boogie.*

Lauren was standing in the kitchen, surrounded by sorority sisters, white cabinets, and countless plastic cups on the counter. Sara couldn't hear her over the music, but judging by Lauren's animated face and waving arms, she was regaling them with some story. She sidled up to her roommate, ducking to keep one particularly aggressive set of mall bangs from poking her eye out.

"Excuse me. Lauren?"

Lauren abruptly stopped talking and turned toward Sara. Her face lit up. "It's my roooomie!" She pulled Sara in for a drunken hug, apparently forgetting the conversation they'd had just the other day. Or maybe the impulse was just too strong. *Her mama really did teach her well*, Sara thought as she gently extricated herself from Lauren's grasp. "I'm ready to go. Let's get out of here."

"Noooo, we can't leeeeave yet!" Lauren protested. "I'm talkin to my freeeends!"

"It's cool," said one, who wore a black flat-brimmed porkpie hat and had a HI MY NAME IS AMY, SOCIAL CHAIR tag stuck to the front of her black vest. "She can hang out."

"Yeah," HI MY NAME IS HOLLY, CHAPTER PRESIDENT and her shaggy perm chimed in. "She's welcome to crash here. I have an extra bed in my room."

Sara looked at Lauren. "Are you sure? I'd rather you came home with me."

"Sure I'm sure," Lauren slurred. Then, in a dramatic loud whisper: "I think they want me to pledge Kappa!"

Everyone laughed. Sara said, "That's great, Lauren. Stay here, be safe, and I'll see you in the morning, okay?" To Holly: "Thank you."

"No problem," Holly said. "She's a blast! She'll make a great Kappa."

Sara left the Kappa Delta house and walked down Langdon Street through the warm night, ignoring catcalls from the frat houses and thinking about the last time she was a freshman in college. That was in 2000, and her clearest memory was the feeling of overwhelming relief when she'd finally left her mother's shitty apartment.

Not that Melinda had made that easy for Sara.

On moving day, Melinda followed Sara around the trashed apartment, limping, vodka bottle in hand, while Sara finished packing and loaded the

trunk of her Celebrity. Melinda clearly hadn't showered in a few days; her
dark blonde hair fell out of an old bun on top of her head in greasy chunks.
Her face was at the same time gaunt and puffy, her eyes watery. The
stained men's pajama shirt she wore was haphazardly buttoned over her
distended belly, so the shirt pulled up enough on one side for Sara to see
that she was not wearing underwear. "Jesus, Mom," *Sara said, throwing*
her shower stuff into a plastic Walmart bag. "Go put on some damn
pants."

Tears spilled down Melinda's ragged cheeks. "You always yell at me,"
she slurred.

"I'm not yelling," *Sara said, leaving the bathroom and walking down*
the hallway to her bedroom.

"You can't leave me," *Melinda wailed, throwing her head back. She*
cried out and lost her balance, tipping backward and falling against the
hallway wall. Too drunk to be ashamed, Melinda allowed herself to slowly
slide down the wall until she sat on the floor, her skinny bare legs straight
out in front of her. Her left foot, injured in a workplace accident over a
decade ago, was scarred and distinctly flatter than the right. She took a swig
of Stoli — her "pain medicine" *of choice — right from the bottle.* "Who will
take care of me?"

"I guess you'll have to finally learn to take care of yourself," *Sara*
stepped over Melinda's legs and carried her last duffel bag to the door.

"Will you leave me a few bucks, at least?" *Melinda cried from the*
hallway. When Sara did not answer, she screamed "You ungrateful fucking
brat!" *as the door closed behind Sara for the last time.*

That's the alcohol talking. That's not my mom. Sara had to remind
herself of this often.

Sara had escaped, shed a few more tears for the soulless,
addicted husk that her mother had become, and moved into her
own little subsidized place near campus. She'd felt…free. She
was a scholarship kid, attending the University of Minnesota on
excellent high school grades and a waitress job at the Big Ten
bar, which was famous for its grilled cheese-and-tomato
sandwiches. *Man,* she thought, *I couldn't wait to prove to the Mandy*

Hubers of the world that I was so much more than just my Salvation Army clothes.

She had enjoyed the anonymity that came with attending a large university; she was just a number, one of nearly 50,000 students on the Twin Cities campus. She focused on earning her business degree with an emphasis in marketing. *A practical choice,* Sara had thought, with an eye to her future.

She kept herself busy and really didn't have friends, which suited her just fine. Nobody at the "U of M" – as the locals called it – cared what she wore. Nobody tried to spit in her lunch. She was finally free to speak in class without having to endure cruel giggles and whispers. And nobody made her believe that the captain of the basketball team wanted to take her to a school dance. Kirk Brockman's deep voice echoed in her head: *Pathetic. Loser.*

Walking under the lights of Langdon Street, she approached the Memorial Union and thought about the time Luke had invited her to join him and his team for a beer at Der Rathskeller after work one Friday. He'd had to do some fast talking, but eventually she relented. She didn't engage in the conversation; she sat in the chair closest to the door, and she focused on her beer. Luke didn't seem to mind; he kept smiling at her from across the table, which made her profoundly uncomfortable. She only stayed long enough for one drink, but had enjoyed the atmosphere of the cavernous German-themed pub inside the Memorial Union.

She was disappointed to find Der Rathskeller closed for the night. She wandered to the dark Union Terrace and found a table close to the lakeshore. She sat in a metal sunburst chair and looked out on night-cloaked Lake Mendota. The lights around the lake reflected on the black water like tiny spotlights. Frogs chirped their throaty lullabies. She was exhausted, but she appreciated the darkness and solitude and let her thoughts turn to her current situation.

Why am I here in 1989? What am I supposed to do? Does Bat know I'm gone? Does he miss me? How will I get back to him? How will the other Sara get back here? Is she pretending to be a second grader again, like I'm pretending to be a college freshman again? I bet she's crushing it. I wonder what she and Melinda are doing right now. It's late, they're probably sleeping.

Her heart heavy, Sara listened to waves gently lapping the shore. Like the Cleavers, the lake didn't offer up the answers to her questions. She sighed.

Thank god for Lauren. If I didn't have her, I have no idea what I would do. The irony of this was not lost on Sara; she'd spent so much of her adult life keeping a careful distance between herself and other people that all she really had were acquaintances. In Lauren she thought she might have a real friend. *I wish I could talk her out of joining Kap—*

Suddenly she made a connection. *Kappa Delta! Oh my god – the name sounded familiar because I read about it in the Journal! Kappa was the sorority that was wiped out in the Library Mall bombing! Holy shit! I wonder –*

"Hi."

Sara jumped no less than 6 inches in her chair, her thought cut cleanly off. Adrenaline goosed her poor heart so hard that she thought it would burst right out through her throat. All she could see was a lanky silhouette against the lights across the pitch black lake. "Who's there?"

"It's me, Charlie Anderson," the silhouette said in a slightly adenoidal voice. "From Bio Lab? Sorry, didn't mean to scare you."

"Holy shit, Charlie, you scared the bejesus out of me," she said, her heart galloping in her chest. "What are you doing out here?"

"I was going to go to the Sig Tau party, but I chickened out. Came here instead." Sara saw his shadow shoulders slump a bit more with the admission. She could relate.

"Have a seat," Sara pushed a sunburst chair toward Charlie with her foot; it made a rusty scraping sound against the concrete. Her heart was still pounding.

Charlie sat. "Thanks."

"You're welcome," she said. After a few beats: "Fraternity parties not your jam?"

Charlie's voice floated through the dark. "Huh?"

Damn it – need to avoid the 21st century slang. "Sorry – I just meant, why didn't you go to the frat party?"

"Oh," Charlie said. "Um, I guess you could say that I don't go to many parties."

"Why's that?" Sara had an idea it was because he was what the experts called "socially awkward."

Charlie's silhouette shrugged. "I dunno…I tend to come down with panic attacks if I'm nervous or overwhelmed. Which happens a lot. Especially in social situations."

"I get it," Sara said. "I have a hard time making friends too."

Charlie didn't say anything for a moment, then: "I doubt that. You seem like a really nice person."

"Thanks," Sara said. "I try to be nice, but…well, let's just say I find it hard to get close to anyone."

"Me too," Charlie's voice sounded a bit like the back of his throat was packed with cotton. "I've never fit in."

Sara had a flash of intuition. "Have you ever been picked on by a classmate because your mom couldn't afford to buy your clothes from anywhere but the neighborhood thrift store?"

"Yeah," Charlie said. "Except it was my grandma. My clothes never fit, and they were dirty too because she wouldn't wash them. I had to wear them over and over. My shoes always had holes in them."

"What did they do to you?" Sara asked gently.

Silence from Charlie. She could almost feel him debating how much to tell her. "The usual stuff. I got picked last for teams in gym class. I never had anyone to play with at recess. I got shoved into the lockers as I walked through the halls, for no reason. That's why I walk as close to the wall as I can, so nobody can blindside me. Everyone called me Pigpen, after the *Peanuts* character who is always surrounded by a cloud of dirt. That one hurt. But you want to know the worst part?"

"What's that?"

"My grandma Ruth could have bought me new clothes. She could afford it. I didn't know it until after she died, but she had plenty of money. The miserable bitch just refused to spend any of it on me." His voice was bitter.

"Why?"

"She hated me," Charlie said. "She used to tell me that she never wanted custody of me, that the state forced me on her after both of my parents died of a heroin overdose when I was a baby. They were found dead in the front seats of a car parked outside Kmart; I was strapped into a carseat in the back, diaper loaded and screaming my head off. They figured we'd been there most of a day. I was nine months old." He said this with no emotion; for him these were not memories, but simple facts. He might as well have been reciting a grocery list. "She said I was nothing but a burden, just like her no-good failure of a daughter."

Harsh, Sara thought.

"She basically ignored me," Charlie continued. "Kept a roof over my head because she was legally required to, but I had to learn how to fend for myself. I dealt with a lot of shit as a kid."

"I'm so sorry."

His silhouette shrugged again. "It is what it is," he said. "Ruth dropped dead of a heart attack last year. She didn't have a will, so everything that was left became mine after probate. At least I got a house that's paid off and a savings account big enough to live on out of all those years of misery."

"I'm glad for that," Sara said, and meant it.

"How about you?" Charlie asked. "I pretty much just spilled my guts to a stranger in the dark. Now it's your turn."

"My mom didn't hate me, but she didn't love me as much as she loved her vodka," Sara said. "She was injured in a workplace incident when I was seven; she worked at a plastics factory and her foot was crushed when she dropped a heavy steel mold on it. You know what sucks the most about that?"

"What?"

"She accidentally wore the wrong boots to work, and didn't think it would be a big deal for just one day. Turns out that if she'd been wearing her heavy steel-toed boots like she was supposed to, her foot wouldn't have been crushed." Sara fell silent when another random – yet somehow familiar – phrase pierced her thoughts: *Mommy? Shouldn't you wear these ones to work?*

"You okay?"

Sara blinked. "Yeah. Sorry, got sidetracked for a second. Anyway, my mom's foot didn't heal properly, and she suffered from severe chronic pain that painkillers couldn't touch. She had to stop working and go on disability."

"I'm sorry," Charlie said.

"There wasn't a lot of money. We had to move from a nice apartment to a dumpy subsidized apartment in the ghetto of North Minneapolis. We got food stamps and all of my clothes came from the Salvation Army. My mom spent what little was left self-medicating with booze, partying at the bars and drinking herself unconscious every night. I basically lived on hot dogs and chicken noodle soup until I was old enough to get a job. So I know exactly what you mean about being so young and having to learn to take care of yourself."

Sara stopped talking for a moment, now lost in childhood memories of spending nights alone in the apartment, and being introduced a new "boyfriend" every week or two. More than one of those creeps had tried to touch her, but she had kicked and screamed every time and scared them off. *Good riddance. To all of them.* "As I got older, I just became another person Melinda would call and beg for money to spend on booze."

Sara was so swept up in her past that she forgot where she was and who she was talking to. "It wasn't long before I'd finally had enough; moved away and changed my phone number. That was ten years ago."

"What do you mean?" Charlie asked. "How do you move away and change your number when you're, like, nine years old?"

Oh, crap. "Uh. I guess I meant that it feels like ten years since I've talked to her."

"Oh," Charlie said. "Did they give you hell at school?"

"There was a girl who did everything she could think of to make my life miserable, all the time. She and her friends tripped me in the halls or the lunchroom, stole my clothes in the locker room and threw them in the trash, made rude comments about me anytime I tried to speak up in class. The worst thing she did was make me believe that a guy I had a crush on wanted me to ask him to Snowball. You know, the girls-ask-boys winter dance?"

"What happened?"

"I completely fell for it and asked him to the dance between classes one day. He and his friends just laughed at me." *Pathetic. Loser.* The familiar anger and sadness bubbled up from her internal emotional well. The one she perhaps hadn't capped as well as she'd thought.

"Bunch of jerks," Charlie said. "I bet you had a nickname too."

"Yep, Salvation Army Sara. How original." She took a deep breath, pulling herself together. The night air, with just a hint of autumn crispness in it, helped soothe her nerves. "I will never allow anyone to treat me like that again. I would rather be alone for the rest of my life."

They sat in silence for a while, listening to the gentle waves. Then Charlie said, "It's weird and cool at the same time, having this conversation with you. I barely know you…"

"…but we have so much in common." Sara finished. "I know. It's nice to be lab buddies with someone who gets it." She couldn't see his smile, but she felt it.

"Can I ask you something?" Charlie's voice floated through the dark.

"Sure."

"Why did you want to be my Bio Lab partner?"

Sara considered this. "I don't know." Which was the truth, but she couldn't shake the feeling that she'd seen him before. "There was just something about you, I guess."

"I'm glad you did. I did not want to be lab partners with that pretty boy."

"You mean Ben?" Sara asked. "I dunno…he seems like good people."

"We'll see," Charlie muttered. His tone had turned bitter. "Those frat boys are all the same. Self-absorbed bullies."

"Yeah," Sara said, in acknowledgment rather than agreement. She wondered what time it was and patted her pants pockets, looking for her phone. Of course it wasn't there; it was waiting for her to catch up with it in 2019. "Listen, Charlie, I gotta head. It's late, and I'm tired. Will you be okay getting home?"

Charlie stood. "Yeah, I'm going to catch a bus. The stop's right around the corner."

They said goodnight and parted ways. Marvelling at finding a kindred spirit in her new Bio Lab partner, Sara walked back to Chadbourne Hall under the lights of Park Street, mulling what it was about Charlie that was so familiar to her. She could still hear Lake Mendota gently lapping against the shore, as if the lake were wishing her good night.

CHAPTER SEVEN
Tuesday, September 12, 1989

Charlie

Charlie got to Bio Lab early so he could take his seat before anyone else arrived and watch Sara enter the room. He'd spent the rest of the weekend thinking about her and everything they'd talked about on the dark Union Terrace. He had never opened up like that to anybody, never shared his secrets, and he wasn't sure what to expect now. It had occurred to him that maybe there was more between him and Sara than just two people with a few things in common. *I mean, people don't talk about stuff like that with just anyone.* He'd felt a strong and immediate connection to her; there was no way she didn't feel it too. *I honestly think there might be something there.*

His ears burned at the thought.

He was zoned out, chin on his backpack, staring unfocusedly at a spot on the chalkboard and imagining what life would be like with Sara as his…girlfriend. He'd never had a girlfriend before, so he had to make up a few of the details. He saw himself and Sara walking hand in hand down State Street — she in a cute sundress and holding an ice cream cone, he wearing a Panama hat and a white polo shirt, both with huge smiles on their faces. It was like a scene right out of a B-rated romance movie.

He was so into his fantasy that didn't see the giant guy with a crewcut walk into the classroom, scan the room for someone vulnerable, and zero in on him. Charlie snapped back when he heard the chair next to him slide out and turned to see an unfamiliar hulk of a man sit in — overflow from, really — Sara's chair. The big guy looked sideways at Charlie with beady brown eyes and a stony face — as if daring Charlie to challenge his choice in seats.

Charlie was familiar with the type. Normally he would steer clear of this guy – but he was sitting in Sara's chair. This was unacceptable. It was hard, but he made his voice work. "Sorry, that seat is taken."

"Yeah," said Big Guy in a deep, gravelly voice. "By me."

"That's my lab partner's seat."

"No," Big Guy said slowly, as if Charlie hadn't heard him the first time. "It's my seat."

Incredulous, Charlie said, "You weren't here last week, when the prof assigned us our lab partners. Mine's not here yet, and that's her seat. You have to move." He wondered where this courage came from.

Big Guy finally turned to fully face Charlie and sat up straighter. *Trying to intimidate me by making himself appear bigger,* Charlie thought. *Classic.* "You gonna make me?" Big Guy snarled.

Intimidated, Charlie searched for his next words – and was relieved to see Hilliard walk in. The professor spied Big Guy and said, "Can I help you?"

Big Guy gave Charlie a last contemptuous look before turning to face Hillard. "I'm in this class now."

"Ah, you must be Mr. Scott Schlosser." Hilliard pulled some papers out of his brown leather briefcase. "They tell me you've come over here after a brief stay in Chemistry. Mr. Anderson here already has a partner. Fortunately for you we had another student drop this class, so there's a chair at that table for you." He pointed at the table kiddie-corner from Charlie's. "Mr. Hallinan – Brent – will be your lab partner."

Schlosser got up and moved to the other table. He sat and turned back to look at Charlie again. His small brown eyes seemed to sink into his head. The expression on his face was clear: *You're mine, fucker.*

Charlie understood that he naturally inspired hostility in guys like Schlosser. He suspected that big guys with self-esteem issues were always looking for someone to pick on, making themselves feel better by making others feel bad – and he, with his skinny frame, big ears, and quiet disposition, was an easy target.

The rest of the class had begun to filter in. Ben Packard greeted him as he took his seat at the table in front of Charlie. Sara and Lauren walked in together. His heart skipped at the sight of Sara – and suddenly he was nervous. He hoped he wouldn't do or say anything stupid.

Sara sat in her rightful place next to him. "Hi Charlie," she said.

"Hi," Charlie said. His fingers shook a bit as he pulled his green Trapper Keeper out of his backpack. He opened it and readied himself to take notes, and noticed Sara staring at the green binder with narrow eyes. "You okay?"

Sara blinked and nodded, then turned to face the front of the room.

"All right class, take your seats," Hilliard said. He waited a moment for the class to settle down. "In lecture last week, you were introduced to the scientific method and the concepts of observation, hypothesis, experimentation, and conclusion." He wrote these words in a list on the chalkboard, his chalk making a clacking sound at the beginning of each letter. "Here you will start to put the scientific method into practice."

Charlie felt something land in his hair as he wrote down the four words Hilliard had written on the board. He brushed it off and continued to focus on the professor.

"Today you're going to apply the scientific method to finding out how tree leaves change color in the fall, like they've started to do now. You'll see various leaves of different sizes, shapes, and colors in front of you. You also have some rubbing alcohol, distilled water, a Bunsen burner, and other tools at your table."

A spitball landed with a tiny wet plop on the table in front of Charlie. He pushed it off with his sleeve, refusing to give Schlosser the satisfaction of a reaction.

"What was that?" Sara whispered.

Charlie shook his head.

"If you've read Chapter Two in your textbook, it should be easy for you to work with your partner to make an observation, form a hypothesis from your observation, perform an experiment to prove or disprove your hypothesis, and then discuss your conclusions. If you haven't read the chapter, I suggest you open your textbook to page twelve and refer to it as you go. Afterward each table will share their findings with the class. I'll be walking around observing, if you have any questions."

The sounds of quiet conversations and scientific work filled the classroom. Charlie was carefully placing the torn pieces of several colorful leaves – *probably picked up off the grass on Bascom Hill by some poor overworked teaching assistant yesterday,* Charlie thought – into glass containers when Schlosser's gravelly voice somehow traveled under the din and into Charlie's ear: "Don't fuck it up, twerp."

Charlie did not react, but Schlosser had hit a nerve. He felt his already tenuous confidence crumble.

"Can you hand me the rubbing alcohol?" Sara asked.

"Huh? Oh, sure." Charlie grabbed a large plastic squeeze bottle with a long tapered dispenser tube and gave it to Sara, then tried to concentrate on tearing up the rest of the red leaves.

"Wait a second," Sara muttered, closely inspecting a beaker full of yellow leaves submerged in a clear liquid. "Nothing's happening."

"What do you mean?" Charlie asked.

"Well, the pigment in the leaves is supposed to leach out into the solvent. The liquid should be yellow." She consulted her textbook, then looked at the bottle Charlie had handed her. "Oh, that's why. This isn't alcohol, it's distilled water."

Shit. Shit shit shit. Panic started to squeeze Charlie's chest.

"Do we have any yellow leaves left?" Sara asked.

Charlie's ears started to burn again. "Uh, no. That was all the yellow leaves we had." He struggled to breathe normally.

"Bummer," Sara said. "I wonder if…"

"Nice job, you fucking loser," Schlosser growled from his table, where poor Brent was conducting experiments on his own because his new lab partner couldn't be bothered.

Charlie froze, his whole face burning now. His eyes stung. He couldn't breathe. *You fucked up boy,* Ruth's voice rasped.

"What, you can't even do a simple lab experiment right?" Schlosser asked, then laughed. He sounded like a deranged troll. "What fucking good are you?"

Charlie sat frozen, tears rolling helplessly down his cheeks, wanting more than anything to simply disappear. Or die.

Sara

The look on Charlie's face hurt Sara's heart. *It's like Kirk Brockman all over again,* she thought. Snippets of old memories started flashing like a slideshow in her head.

Pathetic loser.

Go kill yourself instead.

The troll-like laughter.

Mandy Huber's Miss Mauve lips, puckered in a look of cruel smugness: she saw the same look on Scott Schlosser's face now.

Turns out assholes are assholes no matter what year it is, she thought, and something in her brain snapped. Hard. She turned to Schlosser, eyes blazing: "Excuse me?"

Schlosser feigned surprise and stood up. "I mean, come on. You can't be serious with this fucking guy."

"Scott. Chill out, man," Ben urged, mortified.

"Fuck you, Packard," Schlosser sneered. "This punk needs to be taught a little lesson."

Sara stepped away from her table and squared off with Schlosser, standing directly between him and Charlie. Schlosser stood at least six inches taller than Sara; she looked up at him defiantly, fists clenched. "Oh. I don't think so," she said. Her voice shook with controlled anger. "Actually, what you're going to do is leave Charlie alone."

"Really," Schlosser snarled.

The rest of the class had stopped what they were doing to watch the show.

"Yes," Sara confirmed.

"Move the fuck along, little girl," Schlosser said. "The men have business to attend to." His angry eyes landed on Charlie.

Sara didn't miss a beat. "Is that what you call yourself?" She raised her left eyebrow and glanced down toward his crotch for dramatic effect. "Because I'll tell you what – I'm pretty sure I wear heels bigger than your dick."

Laughter and claps erupted throughout the lab; Schlosser's massive face turned an ugly shade of red, all the way up to the roots of his crewcut.

"Picking on people smaller than you doesn't make you more of a man," Sara said. "It just makes you pathetic." She ducked out of Schlosser's swing zone and went back to her seat. Her whole body shook uncontrollably like she'd just been in a near-miss car accident. She couldn't believe she'd just stood up to this guy.

Charlie's expression had morphed from terror to utter awe. "N-nobody's ever stood up for me like that before," he stammered.

Hilliard, all feathered white hair and college professor tweed jacket, appeared and said, "Mr. Schlosser, it is clear that you have no interest in participating in this class. It would be best if you leave. Immediately. And don't come back."

Glaring at Charlie, Schlosser gathered his stuff and started for the door. He made a threatening lunge toward Hilliard as he walked by. The professor, who was nearly as tall as Schlosser and had dealt with plenty of ruffians in his thirty years of teaching high school and college Biology, stood his ground and passively watched Schlosser walk out the door. Then he was gone. The entire lab seemed to breathe a sigh of relief as the students resumed their work.

Ben turned around. "Man, I'm really sorry about that. Schlosser's in my fraternity, and he's an asshole there too."

"Are you guys okay?" Lauren asked.

"We're fine," Sara said.

Ben: "The way you took him out was really impressive, Sara. Nice work."

Sara blushed. "Thanks."

Ben and Lauren turned back to their work. Sara said to Charlie, "I wonder if Mr. Hilliard has any more yellow leaves. We'll just try this again."

She turned to look for the professor, and didn't see Charlie staring at her. If she had, she'd have seen that look in his eyes: he was starting to fall in love with her.

CHAPTER EIGHT
Thursday, September 14, 1989

Sara

Sara and Lauren left Ingraham Hall after their last class of the day, Economics 101, and headed toward Bascom Hill. As usual, Lauren wanted Sara to go somewhere, and as usual, Sara was protesting.

"Lo, I'm not even a Kappa," Sara said. "Why do I need to be at this meeting?"

"Paws for a Cause is the biggest Greek event of the year. I've never been on a planning committee for anything in my life. I need your moral support. Oh, did I mention Ben's going to be there too?" Lauren winked.

Sara gave in. "Well…okay."

They chatted as they walked down Bascom Hill and across the Park Street pedestrian bridge through the September sunshine. Sara was telling a captivated Lauren about the future.

"Wait, wait, wait," Lauren interrupted Sara's story about locking herself out of her car in the dead of winter in 2007. "Your car couldn't unlock itself?"

Sara made a noise that resembled a chuckle. "I wish," she said. "I had to call the police department to come with a slim jim because my wire coat hanger got too cold and broke off inside the door."

"Geez," Lauren said. "I always kind of imagined that cars in the twenty-first century would be smarter than humans. Drive themselves, unlock themselves, maybe even fly."

"In two thousand nineteen, everyone's trying to build a better electric car."

"Electric car? Like, it doesn't use gas to go?"

"Right," Sara said. "And you plug it in to charge it."

"Wow," Lauren said. "In twenty-nineteen, you plug in your car like you plug in a lamp. That's incredible. But…when do cars start flying?"

Sara hadn't yet set foot on Library Mall since waking up in 1989, and when they emerged from the shadow of the Humanities building and started northeast across the mall toward Langdon Street, what she saw stopped her dead in her tracks. The concrete elevated stage. The fountain. A newspaper headline flashed in her mind's eye: MADISON REMEMBERS.

"Sara? What's wrong?"

Sara stared at a spot on the concrete near the large platform that was connected to the elevated stage. *That's where the shoe in the photo was lying. Right there.* Images of glass shards, blood spatter, and concrete chunks flickered in and out around the shoe like holograms. It took her a few beats to find her voice. "What did you say this meeting was for?"

Bewildered, Lauren said, "To start planning for the Paws for a Cause Humane Society benefit in October. Are you all right? You literally look like you've seen a ghost."

Of course. I can't believe I didn't see it sooner. Sara swallowed; her throat felt like it was lined with fine grain sandpaper. She turned to Lauren, eyes wide. "I know why I'm here."

"You do? How? Why?"

Sara took hold of Lauren's arm and guided her to the amphitheater-style steps of the platform. They sat. "Look. This is going to sound absolutely nuts, but I swear to god it's the truth. During your Humane Society event, someone is going to detonate a suicide bomb and turn this platform we're sitting on into a crater. And kill a whole lot of people."

Lauren was for once at a complete loss for words.

"I read about it in the newspaper on the thirtieth anniversary, before I woke up in 1989. It'll be a huge pipe bomb, and it will kill every member of Kappa Delta, all but three members of Sigma Alpha Tau, and injure over one hundred other people. And who knows how many animals."

Lauren's eyes took up at least half of her face. "But…that means…I'm going to die?"

"That's the thing. I think that's why I'm here. I think I'm supposed to stop the bombing."

"Who was the bomber? Why would they do such a thing?"

Sara shook her head. "They never found out. Whoever did it was basically vaporized. The case was cold but still open in 2019."

Silence from Lauren. Then, "Holy shit."

"Yeah, I know," Sara said.

Eyes still wide, Lauren grabbed Sara's arm. "We have to tell somebody. Like, right now."

"How in the hell are we going to do that?" Sara asked. Lauren's rising panic was catching. "What are we going to say? 'Hi, there's going to be a suicide bombing on campus during a Greek event on October 14th, but we don't know who the bomber is. Can you get on that, please?'"

"Well…yes, basically," Lauren said.

"And what do we say when they ask how we know about this?"

"We don't have to tell them that part."

"I think we do, or they won't take us seriously. We can't say 'I heard it from someone,' because they'll want to know who that someone is. And we can't tell the truth, because the minute I say 'I've been sent back from the year 2019 to stop this bombing,' they're going to personally escort me to the looneybin."

Lauren sat, uncharacteristically silent, and pondered this. Then, stubbornly: "We have to tell the police, Sara. We can't just let this happen. I don't really feel like dying during my first Greek event."

Sara looked at Lauren's terrified face for a moment, then turned her face toward the lake. Between the buildings she caught a glimpse of the sparkling diamonds cast on the lake's surface by the setting sun; this calmed her a bit. There was something powerfully attractive about the idea of handing this burden to professionals to handle. *Maybe it's worth a shot.* She sighed. "Fine. We'll go to the UW Police Department tomorrow. See if we can file a report."

Lauren smiled and threw her arms around Sara's neck. She got a brief squeeze in before abruptly pulling back. "Sorry. I keep forgetting."

A small smile crossed Sara's face; maybe she didn't mind Lauren's hugs so much after all. "It's all right."

Lauren was serious again. "Whoever this is has something against the Greek system. Don't you think?"

"Yes, that's what my friend Luke and I thought too." *Luke,* Sara thought wistfully. *I wonder if he's noticed I'm gone.*

"I don't know of anyone off the top of my head who might have a grudge, but I'll keep my eyes and ears open at the Kappa house."

"Perf," Sara said. "I'll need to —"

"What did you say?" Lauren interrupted Sara, completely confused.

"Huh?"

"Did you say…'perf'?"

"Did I?" Sara rewound the last bit of conversation in her head, trying to remember if she had used that distinctly twenty-first century slang term.

"I don't know what that means," Lauren said.

"It's short for 'perfect'," Sara said. "All the kids shorten words like that in my time. 'Totally' is 'totes,' 'obviously' is 'obvi,' 'perfect' is 'perf.'"

"No. Way. Kids in 2019 are so lazy they can't even use complete words?"

"Pretty much," Sara said. "I'll start asking around too. The bomber has to be someone associated with Greek life, like you said. I mean, that makes the most sense. Oh, and Lo?"

"Yeah," Lauren replied; she'd been staring off into space, presumably thinking about everyone she knew and wondering if they could be a suicide bomber.

"Don't tell anyone about this."

"I won't," Lauren said. "I'm pretty sure nobody would believe me anyway." She looked scared.

Sara tried to reassure her. "They'll find him, Lo."

Lauren took a deep, shaky breath. "Promise?"

"I promise." But deep inside, Sara wasn't so sure. *I have no idea where they would even start.* "We'd better go, we're going to be late for the meeting."

They ran the last few blocks and arrived at the Sig Tau house ten minutes late. The group, which consisted of one freshman, sophomore, junior, and senior from both Kappa Delta and Sigma Alpha Tau, was debating the finer points of advertising the event as Sara and Lauren found their seats.

"Look, all I'm saying is, we should do a big splash," Graham Weatherly, senior and Sig Tau chapter president, was saying. With his dirty blond chop job and peach fuzz facial hair, he looked like he would be more at home in an auto body shop than a Big Ten university fraternity.

Holly Babcock, also a senior and Kappa chapter president, had other ideas. "Last year we ran an ad in the Daily Cardinal and the Badger Herald, posted flyers all over campus and State Street, and chalked Library Mall for a week before the event. And we had great turnout. Why would you want to spend money on more than that?"

"Because I want this to be the biggest Humane Society fundraiser yet," Graham said stubbornly. "If we can get more people from outside campus to come, we'll make all that money back on hot cocoa and coffee."

"Maybe we could rent a blimp. Like the Goodyear Blimp?" This helpful idea was offered up by Michael Keller, the other freshman on the committee.

"A blimp," Lauren said, and shook her head. "Please tell me you were not responsible for any high school dances, Mike."

"Hold on a sec," Graham interjected. "This could work, you guys."

The room erupted as all eight committee members tried to talk over each other at once. Lauren stood up and started yelling. "HEY! Settle down, you guys!" Everyone quieted. "Thank you." She turned to Graham. "I'm sorry Graham, but there definitely isn't money in the budget for a blimp. But I bet we can run a display ad in the Wisconsin State Journal or the Capital Times if we can get a student discount or something." Her face turned pink and she smiled rather sheepishly at Holly. "I reviewed the budget papers while I was at the Kappa house last night."

Grinning from under her shaggy blonde perm, Holly waved her hand at Lauren to proceed. She did. "Outside of that, though, we'll have to get the word out guerrilla style."

Sara tuned out and looked around. The meeting room in the Sigma Alpha Tau house reminded her of a church basement. Several tables had been arranged in a square so that everyone could see each other. There was a chalkboard on one wall; one of the more mature residents of the house had drawn a cock and balls in one lower corner. Sara stared at it unfocusedly as she thought about her epiphany.

It really shouldn't have been such a stretch for me to figure out the connection between that newspaper article and waking up in 1989, Sara thought. *In retrospect, it's pretty fucking obvious. I might even have wished I could come back here and save a bunch of lives. Someone or something apparently was listening, because here I am. What I still don't understand is HOW I managed to wake up in an entirely different decade.*

Something else occurred to her too. The random phrases that kept popping into her mind at the strangest moments: the recurring dream she'd been having in 2019 was trying to break forth into her conscious mind. The words made it through some invisible barrier; Sara suspected it wouldn't be long before she started seeing the pictures too. All that was missing was the clickity-clack of the hidden filmstrip player. The question was: why? What did that dream have to do with her current predicament?

She sighed, and her eyes refocused right on Ben's handsome face. He was smiling at Lauren in amazement, impressed with how his Bio Lab partner had taken control and was now running the meeting while Holly Babcock, a senior who came from a prominent Madison dairy family, wrote notes on the chalkboard. His deep brown eyes moved to Sara's and his smile widened. She blushed and pretended to busy herself trying to find a pen in her black JanSport backpack. She found one, which she didn't really need, and fidgeted with it. She kept her eyes on Lauren. *Wow, she's doing a great job,* Sara observed. *For never having been on a committee before.*

Duties were assigned to committee members, the date of the next meeting was set, and the meeting adjourned. Sara stood and slung her backpack over her shoulder. She scanned the room for Lauren and found her chatting with Holly and Graham near the chalkboard. It was fun to see her so engaged; Sara could plainly see that the event planning and philanthropy aspects of Greek life were going to suit Lauren just fine. *I'll wait for her by the door.* She turned, and very nearly bowled Ben over. "Oh my god, I'm so sorry," she said. A hot blush once again made its way up her neck and face. "I didn't see you there behind me."

"Whoa," Ben said, holding his hands up. "Sorry. Are you in a hurry?"

Butterflies fluttered in her belly. "Um, no. I mean, no, not really. I just...ah..." she stammered, trying to sound and look cool when she felt anything but. "I just thought I'd wait for Lauren by the door," she finished lamely.

"Oh. That's cool," Ben said. He seemed fidgety. "So, I was wondering if I could, you know."

"If you could what?" Sara asked, confused.

Ben laughed nervously and shook his head. "Sorry. I, uh, I'd really like to take you out this weekend. If you're free. Dinner?"

Sara's heart lurched, and then free fell; she could almost hear it make a whistling noise like Wile E. Coyote made every time he jettisoned off a cliff while chasing the Roadrunner. *Why would I want to be with a pathetic loser like you?* that all-too-familiar phantom voice whispered between her ears. She recoiled without realizing she was doing it. "I don't think that would be a good idea. Sorry," she mumbled, and ducked past him. She marched up to Lauren, face burning, and cut into her conversation with Graham and Holly. "Lo, it's time to go."

"But we're not done talking about – " Lauren looked at Sara's face and understood that it was indeed time to go. "Okay, let me just grab my bag."

Back out on Langdon Street, the sun had disappeared and dusk descended, triggering the streetlights to pop on. Lauren had to jog to keep up with Sara's determined powerwalk. She demanded to know what happened. "What's your rush?"

Sara's face still burned. "Ben asked me out."

"WHAT?!" Lauren shrieked. "That's awesome! I could tell there was something between you two! When are you going out?"

"We're not," Sara said flatly.

"You're not? Why?"

"Because there wouldn't be a second date if this bomber isn't stopped," Sara snapped.

"Oh," Lauren said softly. "Right. I forgot about that."

"Besides, he didn't mean it." Sara said quietly.

Lauren stopped walking; Sara went another half a block before realizing Lauren wasn't beside her. She stopped in front of Memorial Union and turned, looking for her roommate's silhouette. "Lo?"

"I'm sorry, what did you say?" Lauren's disembodied voice was incredulous.

Sara pushed air out between her lips in frustration. "He didn't mean it, Lo. He doesn't really want to go out with me. He wants to…oh, I don't know."

Lauren's Keds pounded on the sidewalk as she closed the distance between herself and Sara. "So let me get this straight. Ben – ultra hottie and Mr. Nice Guy in the flesh – asked you out, but you said no because you think he doesn't actually want to go out with you?"

"Well…yeah…basically."

Lauren stopped next to Sara, her hair a black puffball on her head, her face unbelieving. "Do you have any idea how ridiculous that sounds?" Lauren asked. They turned the corner onto Park Street and walked past the hulking – and downright creepy-looking and, rumor had it, haunted – Science Hall. "I mean, if you don't like him, that's one thing."

"I do like him. I think. I mean, he seems nice."

"He wouldn't ask you out if he didn't like you, love. I mean, to think that he would is just silly."

Sara stared at the sidewalk, watching the cracks pass by under her feet as she considered this. Her own experience had taught her that people did, in fact, play heartless pranks on others for the perverted thrill of watching their victims suffer. She'd been Mandy Huber's favorite victim all through high school, and that was evidence enough. Although she didn't see that innate cruelty in Ben. He seemed, in fact, to be the exact opposite of a Mandy Huber mean girl.

"It's not, though," Sara said.

"What do you mean?"

"It's not silly, Lo. People have actually done shit like that to me."

The look on Lauren's face changed from disbelief to shock – and a little bit of curiosity. "Are you serious?"

"Wouldn't lie about something like this."

"What happened?"

Sara suddenly felt tired. Exhausted, in fact. "I don't want to get into all the gritty details now. Suffice it to say that someone thought it would be fun to convince me to ask the captain of the basketball team – who I had a crush on – to the winter dance. He laughed his ass off and said some choice words to me. The whole thing turned out to be a setup meant to humiliate me, and it worked."

Lauren, nearly-black eyes wide, said, "Oh, Sara, I had no idea. Who would do that to you?"

Sara shook her head. "Doesn't matter anymore. But now, when someone asks me out – whether it be my coworker Luke or Mr. Nice Guy Ben, I just assume they have an ulterior motive because it's happened to me before. And I have no interest in going through that again."

Lauren put her hand on Sara's arm, and they stopped walking. Sara ran her hand through her hair and looked at Lauren almost defiantly, expecting some sort of challenge to her long-held beliefs. Instead Lauren wrapped her arms around Sara and hugged her. "I'm so sorry that happened to you."

Surprised, Sara closed her eyes, fighting tears. She had never gotten an apology before, from anyone. She appreciated this one – even if it was more of an expression of sympathy – more than she could possibly articulate, so she hugged Lauren back and hoped it would be enough. It felt…nice. Frogs sang to them from the direction of Lake Mendota.

Lauren gave Sara one more squeeze and stepped back. "So?" she said.

"So what?"

"What are you going to do?"

Sara sighed and wiped her eyes. "Probably apologize to Ben in Bio Lab on Tuesday."

They started walking again and Lauren slung her arm around Sara's neck. "That's an excellent first step, love."

CHAPTER NINE
Friday, September 15, 1989

Charlie

He lay on Ruth's old velour couch in a sunbeam, a flattened orange pillow separating his head from its wooden arm. The room was cold; Charlie was dressed in a brown Hershey Milk Chocolate logo t-shirt and Levi's, his feet bare, but he didn't notice the chill – he was lost in thoughts of Sara.

He thought about the first day of Bio Lab, when Sara had actively chosen to be his lab partner. He hadn't known what to make of it at the time, but after some thought he was pretty sure he knew why she'd done that.

He thought about Saturday night.

He'd agonized over Sig Tau's rush party for two straight days, fighting back an epic panic attack, before finally resolving to get over himself and go. He reasoned that it might be good for him to get a social life, and this seemed like as good a place to start as any. And besides…maybe he would see Sara there.

Forget it Charlie, Ruth warned him. *If you have the balls to show up, those jocks and pretty boys will just run your scrawny ass out.*

He ignored her and went anyway – "Why would they invite me then, Gram?" he asked on his way out the door – but as he got closer to the Sig Tau house, fear started bubbling in his chest and he thought maybe Ruth was right. He was within a block when the panic attack hit in full force and he finally turned around. The decision to spend a few minutes in the darkness and solitude of Union Terrace at night before heading home had turned out to be a fortuitous one; he recognized Sara's silhouette immediately. He approached her, heart pounding, wanting to say hi but not wanting to scare her.

The conversation they'd had, the deeply personal stories they'd told each other…well, Charlie thought he knew why someone would share all of that with him.

He thought about Bio Lab on Tuesday. She'd gotten into Schlosser's fat face on his behalf, something nobody had done for him before, ever. Charlie could ask why somebody would do that, but he was pretty sure he knew the answer.

Sara wanted him. Maybe she even loved him. That was the why. That was the answer. Had to be; there was no other logical explanation.

His innocent daydream on Tuesday had morphed considerably over the last couple of days, as he thought about Sara and became more and more convinced that he understood her motivations. What had started as a cute sundress had transformed into a transparent swimsuit much like Stephanie Seymour's in this year's Sports Illustrated swimsuit issue; it didn't leave much up to the imagination. And instead of walking down State Street, they were now arm in arm on a yacht, with Charlie himself – a much taller, buffer, more dapper Charlie wearing a captain's hat, naturally, and smoking a Cuban cigar – at the helm.

Every time his mind's eye saw Sara in that revealing swimsuit, blond hair flowing, amber eyes gleeful, pangs of excitement shot through his belly. He'd become so aroused that he'd finally had to crawl into bed, tube sock in hand, and masturbate in order to find relief. It hadn't taken long.

Now, on the living room couch, Charlie closed his eyes and thought about what to do next. A date seemed like the logical next step. *Something simple. Like ice cream. Maybe I should ask her if she'd like to get some ice cream with me.*

That girl is too good for you. Ruth's raspy voice rudely interrupted him, and his eyes snapped open. *She doesn't want no pervert.*

He sat up. "I'm not a pervert," he whined at Ruth's photo on the wall.

Ruth brayed like a donkey, laughing. *I know what you were doing up in your room.*

Charlie's face flushed miserably.

She's a nice girl, and nice girls don't want a dirty sinner like you. They want nice boys who don't touch themselves like that.

"Shut up, Gram, you don't know what you're talking about."

Your grandfather never did that nasty thing, Ruth croaked. *Your worthless father did, though — I used to find washcloths in their room that were all sticky with his…stuff. I guess you take after him that way. I never should have let your mother bring him here to live with us.*

Charlie laid back down and closed his eyes, covering his face with his hands. "Leave me alone, Gram."

Pervert.

The backs of Charlie's eyelids went from black to bright red in an instant. "I said LEAVE ME ALONE!" He grabbed Ruth's heavy glass ashtray — still dirty with year-old cigarette ash residue — off the coffee table and chucked it at Ruth's portrait as hard as he could. It hit her broad forehead with a *thunk,* breaking the glass in the frame, and clattered on top of the TV. Cracks crawled like a spiderweb across the glass over Ruth's face from the point of impact on her forehead. Her eyes never moved, yet still seemed to mock him from behind the dusty glass. "Just SHUT UP!"

Ruth did. Breathing hard, Charlie took a minute to let his nerves calm. Then he decided on his plan of action: he would ask Sara out when he saw her in Bio Lab on Tuesday. *Just ice cream,* he thought. *No big deal.* His heart fluttered, and he smiled a little. He couldn't wait.

Sara

Sara had just one class on Fridays: Psychology 101. The topic and the class bored her to tears, but she felt strangely obligated to attend; she didn't want to screw up the other Sara's grades and leave an academic mess for her to clean up when she came back.

If she came back.

Lauren was not in the room when Sara arrived back at Chadbourne Hall. She'd left a note on Sara's desk: Sorry love, I got pulled into a fundraiser meeting. Go without me – and don't take no for an answer! XO, Lo.

Sara sighed and briefly weighed the pros and cons of not going to the UWPD today. *If I don't go today, Lauren will drag me over there tomorrow. I might as well get it over with.* And with that, she was back out on University Avenue, headed for the south side of campus.

She vaguely remembered driving by the UWPD recently, when she was still in 2019 and preparing to move into her new house. *It was near some big prominent building,* she thought. *Union South, maybe? Seems as good a place to start as any.*

When Sara arrived at Union South, she thought at first that she was in the wrong place. She'd expected to see the bright, modern building she saw when she drove by a couple weeks ago. Instead she was looking at an angular, rather squat, concrete monstrosity with almost no windows. She couldn't imagine why students would want to spend time in this depressing building, yet people walked in and out of the front door and milled about on the benches and sidewalk outside. The rack next to the sidewalk was full of ten-speed bikes, all with old-fashioned drop handlebars. *Huh. I guess the one I saw in 2019 hasn't been built yet. These kids don't know what they're missing.*

She looked around for the UWPD sign she remembered seeing. It was nowhere in sight, so she decided to keep walking down Randall Avenue. When she caught sight of the boxy stone memorial arch in front of Camp Randall Stadium on her right, she knew she was heading in the right direction. The massive football stadium, built on a former U.S. Army training site for Civil War Union soldiers, sat empty and silent now – but it wouldn't be that way for long. The Wisconsin Badgers were going to host the University of Toledo in a non-conference game on Saturday, and the stadium would be packed to the rafters with nearly 40,000 fans. It wouldn't be the same as if the Minnesota Golden Gophers – bitter Badgers rivals – were coming to town, but Sara imagined the game would be a good time anyway.

Just past the stadium Monroe Street jogged to her right, heading away from Randall Avenue on a diagonal; she followed it and was soon in front of the nondescript brick building with a glass block front that served as the University of Wisconsin Police Department's headquarters. She took a deep breath and pulled one of the double doors open. *I have no idea what I'm going to say, but here goes nothing.*

She walked into a small, dimly lit lobby with a couple aging waiting room chairs, a small table holding a selection of general interest magazines, and a bulletproof window set in a cinderblock wall next to a heavy steel door. A tall plant clung to life in the corner farthest from the windows.

Behind the bulletproof acrylic window sat a pudgy woman with an old-fashioned beehive hairdo in a shade of red that could only have come from a Clairol box, heavy blue eyeshadow, perfect posture, and fingers that blurred over the keys of her electric typewriter. She reminded Sara a little bit of Penelope Garcia from one of her all-time favorite TV shows, *Criminal Minds* – only much older and not nearly as cool.

"Can I help you?" the receptionist called over the steady clickety-clacking, without looking up.

Sara positioned her mouth directly in front of the holes drilled into the thick Plexiglass in the shape of a circle and said, "Hi. Um, I'd like to speak to an officer please?" She hoped the receptionist could hear her.

Apparently she did; the clattering stopped and the receptionist gave a slightly put-off sigh. She turned in her swivel office chair and regarded Sara suspiciously. When she opened her mouth, her lips parted abruptly, making a sound that to

Sara's ear sounded like a cross between a *smack* and a *tsk* sound: *smick*. "And what would your complaint be, ma'am?"

"I don't have a complaint, I just want to talk to someone about a possible crime."

"Mmm-hmm." *Smick.* "A 'possible' crime?" Penelope Garcia rolled her chair to a desk right under the window and pulled out a yellow sheet of paper and a pen. *Smick.* "What does that mean, ma'am? Was there a crime or not?"

"It's not a crime that has already happened, it's a crime that I think is going to happen."

"Mmm-hmm." *Smick.* And how do you know that this crime is going to happen?"

"I would really rather speak to an officer," Sara said, not bothering to hide her growing impatience. "Maybe file a report if they feel it's appropriate. I'm pretty sure I don't have to justify anything to you."

Penelope Garcia gave Sara a look that said she was no different than the other assholes who come in here every day. "Mmm-hmm." *Smick.* "Look, kid. I get two or three of you a day in here, thinking it's some kind of a funny joke to file a false police report." Sara wondered if she knew that her gaudy red lipstick was smeared across her yellowing teeth. "We're busy here. Go home."

"I'm not leaving until I talk to an officer," Sara said stubbornly. "I'm dead serious – and that is not a figure of speech."

Another put-off sigh – and an eye roll to boot – from Penelope Garcia. She started writing on the piece of paper. *Smick.* "Name?"

"Sara Sullivan. That's Sara with no H."

"Mmm-hmm." *Smick.* "Address?"

Sara very nearly gave her Mound Street address out of habit – she had been training herself to memorize her new address and forget Janice's Rutledge Street address before she woke up in 1989 – but caught herself in time. "Um, Chadbourne Hall, Room 710."

"Mmm-hmm." *Smick*. "That's 420 Park Street. Complaint?"

Sara breathed deeply and said, "A suicide bombing is going to happen on campus almost exactly one month from today."

Penelope Garcia stopped writing and raised her head. The look on her face told Sara all she needed to know about the older woman's opinion of her sanity. "Mm-hmm." *Smick*. "Really." Penelope Garcia wrote something on her sheet of paper, then looked at Sara again. *Smick*. "Take a seat, someone will be with you shortly." Then she disappeared.

Confused, Sara sat in one of the old chairs. She didn't have to wait long; within a couple of minutes the heavy steel door next to the receptionist's window opened, and a tall, bald man in chinos and a black UWPD polo shirt stepped out. He was grossly overweight; the entire upper half of his body strained against his shirt and pooched out over his too-tight belt and too-small pants, as if all the fat his body stored had to settle for alighting around his stomach, back and arms because access to anything below the belt (literally) was cut off.

"Sara?" His pleasant baritone voice floated out from under his thick brown Magnum P.I. mustache. "I'm detective Jake Leonard, UWPD. Follow me, please."

Sara did, and found herself inside a drab interrogation room. It contained nothing but a table with a raised bar bolted to the middle, four well-used chairs, a two-way mirror set in one wall, and a boxy camera mounted in the corner. Suddenly very nervous, she sat in a cracked plastic chair without being asked to. She clasped her hands in front of her on the table and tried not to look as intimidated as she felt.

Leonard closed the door and sat in the chair directly across the table from Sara. The room's harsh fluorescent light reflected off his smooth scalp. He pulled a small notebook and a pen out of the chest pocket of his polo, then opened the notebook to a clean page, clicked his pen – ominously – and looked at Sara with intense brown eyes. *I bet this guy can see bullshit coming from a mile away,* Sara thought.

"So, Sara," Leonard said. "Lucille tells me you know something about a bomb." Sara thought it interesting that he used her first name instead of the more formal "Ms. Sullivan" that she typically expected from people she'd only now just met. *Probably he's doing that to throw me off balance,* she thought.

"Yes. I know that one will go off at a Greek fundraiser in October."

"I see." Leonard said, making a note.

"I also know that this bomb will kill over eighty people and injure a hundred more."

Leonard raised one eyebrow, the bushiness of which rivaled that of his impressive mustache, but otherwise seemed nonplussed. He made another note. "And where will this bombing take place?"

"On Library Mall."

"Okay. Where exactly on Library Mall? Will it be near Memorial Library? Or perhaps a smidge closer to the Historical Society?"

Sara had no trouble reading his tone. *He doesn't believe a word I'm saying,* she thought. She decided to keep trying. "It'll happen right next to the raised platform near State Street. That's where the fundraiser will take place. My roommate is planning the event." She heard the pride in her own voice.

"Uh huh. And when will this alleged bombing happen, did you say?" The intense brown eyes studied her. She tried not to fidget.

"The explosion will happen at 10 o'clock in the morning on Saturday, October 14." Sara didn't appreciate his use of the word *alleged.*

Leonard scrawled something else in his notebook. "And who will detonate this bomb?"

"See, that's the thing, detective. I don't know."

Leonard sat back in his chair – it squeaked like a mouse stuck under an obese housecat – and regarded her. "You don't know."

Sara's stomach started to churn. *I knew this was a bad idea.* "No sir, I don't know."

Leonard blinked, then consulted his notebook. "Let me get this straight. You know the where and the when, but you don't know the who."

"That's correct."

Leonard leaned forward with an elbow on the table, and propped his chin in his hand. He regarded Sara intensely. "How is it you know everything but that?"

Sara had fully expected this question, but found herself unable to come up with an answer that wasn't the truth, but with which he would be satisfied. She settled for a shrug instead.

"You have no idea?"

Sara shook her head.

Leonard sat up straight, set his pen and his notebook on the table, and leaned forward on his elbows again. "You know what I think?" His intelligent chocolate eyes snapped.

Sara shook her head again; she didn't dare open her mouth. She thought she might vomit.

"I think there is no bomb. I think you have a beef to settle. Maybe you and one of your entitled sorority sisters had a fight, and you want to ruin her party by sending in the bomb squad and police in riot gear."

We call that "swatting" in the 21st century, Sara thought but did not say. Instead she burst out, "No! That's not it at all! There really will be a bomb, detective!" Frustrated tears pulsed behind her eyes. "I'm trying to save lives here!"

"Or, maybe you're the bomber," Leonard mused, pointing directly at Sara's chest. "Of course you're not going to tell me who the bomber is if it's you, right?"

"That's ridiculous," Sara said. "If I were the bomber, why would I be here telling you about it?"

Leonard shrugged. "Who knows?" He leaned back in his chair again. "People confess for all kinds of weird reasons. I see it all the time. Maybe you don't want to do this bombing, but you don't want to not do this bombing. So you're hoping we'll stop you."

"That doesn't even make any sense!" Sara shouted. Her heart pounded. "These are real people! Whose blood will be on your hands if you don't find this bomber!"

"Listen, Sara," Leonard said her name as if it were dripping with something foul-tasting. "I can't investigate a bombing, real or not real, without all of the information. If this is a real thing like you say, then come back to me with information I can use. That does not mean bringing me names that are not credible; your ass will be sitting downstairs in the holding cell faster than you can say 'kaboom' if I find out you're accusing innocent people of this...this fantasy. Do you understand me?"

Dumbfounded, Sara just sat and watched Leonard with wide, disbelieving eyes.

"I know I won't see you about this again, because it's all made up in your pretty little head." Leonard pushed back from the table, his chair loudly scraping on the linoleum floor. "You'll be lucky if I don't charge you with filing a false police report." With that, he swept up his notebook and pen, yanked the door open so hard it bounced off the cinderblock wall behind it, and was gone.

Sara laid her face in her hands and let the frustrated tears fall. She'd known this would happen. *I'm probably already on every terrorist watchlist the government has,* she thought. She took a couple of minutes to regain her composure, then quietly left the building. Lucille didn't wish her a pleasant day. On her walk back to Chad, she made herself one promise: *I will find this bomber. I have to, because clearly I'm on my own.*

CHAPTER TEN
Tuesday, September 19, 1989

Charlie

Charlie sat in his seat in Bio Lab and watched the door, waiting for Sara to walk in. Adrenaline coursed through his bloodstream, making his heart pound and his fingers shake a bit. *Who knew that asking someone a simple question could be so nerve-wracking?* he wondered.

Ben arrived first, and then Sara and Lauren walked in together, deep in conversation. Charlie's heart soared. They took their seats, and Sara greeted him. "Hi Charlie."

"Hi," he said, trying to keep his voice from shaking. "Listen, Sara —"

Hilliard walked in. "All right, class, let's get started." The room quieted, and Sara sat at attention. Thwarted, Charlie sat back and lightly hit his fist on the table. *Damn it.*

"All right, folks. In lecture last week you learned about acids, bases and buffers, and how they influence pH levels inside and outside of cells. You and your partner are going to conduct three experiments, outlined in your textbook on pages thirty-two and thirty-three, to study these effects. Of course you will follow the scientific method. All the materials you need are on your tables. I'll be walking around the room if you have any questions."

Charlie held a glass dropper full of white vinegar, waiting for Sara to assemble the other ingredients in a glass dish. Sara worked quickly but meticulously — so efficient that it almost looked like she'd done this experiment before. Her fair hair was tucked behind her delicate ears, and her forehead crinkled a bit with concentration. *That beautiful woman and I are meant to be together,* he thought. *A connection like ours doesn't come along every day.* He didn't want to disrupt her concentration, so he decided to wait until the end of class to ask her out for an ice cream cone — *just a simple ice cream cone*, he thought, *no biggie, I can do this.* Apparently Ben didn't have any of the same qualms Charlie did about interrupting Sara while she was working. He had turned around in his chair and was also watching her. "Hey Sara," he said.

Sara stopped what she was doing, but kept her eyes and hands on the table. "Hey," she said softly.

Charlie noticed her change in demeanor. *What's going on here?*

"Listen," Ben said. "If I said something wrong the other night, I'm sorry."

Sara finally looked up, her cheeks pink. "No, I'm the one who should apologize," she said.

I'm missing something. Charlie looked suspiciously from Sara to Ben and back to Sara again, still holding his dropper full of vinegar in the air. There was something about her eyes, how she seemed to have trouble looking at Ben for too long without looking away again, that made him uneasy. He knew that look, was pretty sure he'd had it on his own face half an hour ago when Sara walked into the room.

Sara continued, "I shouldn't have pushed past you and just left like that. It was rude. I'm sorry."

Ben smiled. "No worries. At all. I'm glad you're okay; I was a little worried."

Sara's face went a shade darker pink. "I'm fine."

Charlie watched helplessly, feeling invisible, as Ben scooted his chair a bit closer to Sara's side of the table. He crossed his arms on the table and leaned a little closer to her. "So. Can I take you to dinner Friday night? Please?"

What? Charlie's heart dropped, then started to pound as he watched Sara hesitate, then relent. *No. Please God, no.*

"Okay," Sara said, simply. She was actually smiling. *Have I seen her smile yet, since I met her?* Charlie didn't think he had.

"Awesome." Ben hit the table with his fist, rattling Sara's petri dish.

"Yay!" Lauren squealed. She had watched the entire exchange out of the corner of her eye. She pointed at Sara's radiant face, laughing. "Aw, would you look at that smile!"

Sara's face gradually transitioned from pink to bright red, but the smile stayed on. "Stop, would you?"

The floor fell out of Charlie's stomach; he sat heavily in his chair as if he'd been punched. He didn't realize he'd let go of the dropper he'd been holding until it shattered on the floor, enveloping him in the sour stink of vinegar. Waves of raw disappointment and betrayal washed over him with every heartbeat. He couldn't breathe. He'd shared his secrets – damn, his whole life story – with Sara. She'd stood up for him. She'd agreed when he called Pretty Boy Ben here a bully. *I…I thought…*

See what happens when you get too big for your britches, boy? Ruth's hoarse voice chimed in.

But…we have a connection. We're supposed to be together.

His heart was broken.

Sara

Finally knowing the reason why she was back in 1989 was both a relief and a special kind of hell for Sara. She regarded everyone with suspicion, wondering if they could be the mysterious bomber.

The guy working the register at the Discount Den? Suicide bomber.

The lady serving Salisbury steak and mashed potatoes at Chadbourne's dining hall? Suicide bomber.

The gaggle of East Coast students pouring out of The Towers apartment building and down State Street, looking more than a little out of place in this Midwestern enclave? Suicide bombers, all of them.

It was exhausting.

She was also a bit troubled. Charlie had behaved strangely during Bio Lab; he'd just sat there in his chair, staring sullenly at his hands. He wouldn't help her with their acidity experiments, talk to her, or even look at her. She'd wracked her brain, but couldn't figure out what his deal was. *He looked so sad*, she thought.

Sara had filled Lauren in on Detective Leonard as soon as she'd returned from her visit to the UWPD; Lauren was both indignant and resigned.

"I cannot believe he accused you of lying about the bombing," Lauren had said. "Who makes up something like that?"

"Probably beered-up university students make shit like that up all the time," Sara had remarked.

Lauren had sighed deeply. "I guess it's up to us, huh?" She'd looked scared.

Now, as they made their way down Langdon Street, they were talking about possible suspects. Sara asked Lauren what she'd been hearing at the Kappa House the last few days.

"I don't know, Sara," Lauren said. She wore huge dangling gold hoop earrings that seemed to stick out from her halo of kinky black hair. "Nobody here seems disgruntled enough to pull something like this off. Literally all they do is tape notes to the fridge calling themselves and each other fat so that they won't eat any actual food. But drinking copious amounts of beer? I guess those calories don't count."

Sara nodded. They walked up the front steps of the Kappa house. "Remind me why I'm here again?"

Lauren, long and lean in zebra print stirrup pants and a black off-the-shoulder batwing top, gave Sara the sidelong stink-eye. "Duh, for moral support."

"You do realize I don't actually belong to this sorority, right?"

"Yeah, but you might as well," Lauren said. "Nobody is going to care."

They found seats on one of the damask couches in the brightly-lit parlor; girls were scattered throughout the room, sitting on the floor, window ledges, tables — anywhere they could find an open spot. Holly Babcock stood in front of the dark bay window and called the meeting to order. It opened with members reciting in unison the Kappa Delta pledge, which they'd been required to memorize as sorority recruits. It started with "On my honor…" and reminded Sara of the Girl Scout Promise. Sara had never been a Girl Scout, but had listened to other girls in the first grade practice the Girl Scout Promise during recess, trying to memorize it so they could earn a patch to sew on their little brown sashes. She'd wanted one of those sashes so badly, had begged and pleaded with her mom to sign her up. Melinda flat out said no. She was recovering from her foot injury at the time, money was tight, and she was already starting to drink too much. Sara had been heartbroken.

The opening ritual complete, Rachel Meyer, the secretary, read last month's meeting minutes. Lauren moved to approve them. Her motion was seconded, the entire chapter voice voted with an "aye" — and then they got down to business.

"Our first item of business on tonight's agenda is an update on the Paws for a Cause fundraiser," Holly announced. "If my fellow committee members could join me up here?" Lauren and two other girls stood and carefully stepped over their sisters to get to the front of the room. Lauren looked nervous, but smiled radiantly when Sara gave her the thumbs-up.

That girl is in her element, Sara thought. Lauren started presenting her update, and Sara tuned out and looked around the room. It looked like all of the sorority's thirty-six members were in attendance. *I wonder if the bomber is here tonight*, she thought. She examined each face for subtle signs of anger or discontent: furrowed brows, mouths turned down at the corners, downcast eyes.

Everyone was watching the presentation at the front of the room intently – except one. Sara's gaze fell on a tall, skinny girl with long, straight black hair and dark eyes who was standing in a far corner with her arms crossed over her flat chest. She watched the presentation with clear contempt on her face. A plaster cast encased her right hand.

Hello…who's this? Sara thought. She'd accompanied Lauren to several Greek functions over the last couple of weeks, but couldn't recall ever seeing Morticia Addams here. *I feel like I would remember her,* she thought, and made a mental note to ask Lauren about her.

"Oh, that's Shannon Plotnik," Lauren said later, as she and Sara made their way back to Chad after the meeting. "You've never seen her because she doesn't participate much in Kappa's activities. Holly and Pam – our House Mom, have you met her yet? You'll love her – have to keep her around because she's a legacy."

"You mean, someone else in her family was a Kappa at UW?" Sara asked.

"Yeah, I guess her mom was a Kappa hotshot twenty-five years ago. Our only member ever to be elected Chapter President as a junior and as a senior. So Shannon came in here last year already a celebrity. The only reason she stays is because her mom makes her stay. She's pretty pissed off about it."

"Huh," Sara said. "So she doesn't want to be in Kappa, and Kappa doesn't want her either – but neither has a choice in the matter."

"Pretty much," Lauren agreed. "She also has this tendency to get violent when she's mad. The other day Pam busted her hiding a guy in her room, which is obviously – I mean, 'obvi' – against the rules." She laughed. "That sounds so weird, why do people in 2019 talk like that?"

All Sara could do was chuckle and shake her head.

"Anyway, when Pam kicked him out of the house, Shannon went berserk and punched a hole in the wall. That's why she has that cast on."

Ah, bingo, Sara thought. *Someone who is already pissed at the sorority and predisposed to violence?*

She couldn't have custom-ordered a better bombing suspect.

CHAPTER ELEVEN
Friday, September 22, 1989

Sara

"Have a GREAT TIME!" Lauren shouted from the kitchen as Sara walked out the front door of Kappa house to meet Ben at the Sig Tau house. She felt utterly conspicuous in Lauren's black ruffled skirt and baggy pink shirt, Holly's black vest, a pair of pink socks, and black ballet flats. Lauren had tried to pull her hair up into a high side ponytail, which Sara flatly refused.

"Not happening, Lo. I didn't do side ponytails the first time I did 1989. And I was seven years old, the perfect age for them."

"Can I at least rat your bangs?" Lauren asked, fine-toothed comb and pink can of Aqua-Net in hand.

Sara managed to escape the sorority house bathroom with her bangs and her dignity intact, despite the ridiculous Sixteen Candles outfit. Her heart skipped as she walked westward along Langdon Street toward the Sig Tau house – more with terror than excitement. Her heart went into overdrive when she saw Ben sitting on the front porch with his feet, clad in boat shoes and no socks, propped on the railing. He looked dapper in a pair of khaki pants, white polo shirt, and brown sport jacket. He jumped up when he saw her and met her on the sidewalk, grinning. His floppy hair was swept back from his face in a way that made Sara a little weak in the knees. "Hey."

"Hey," Sara replied nervously, making an effort to look him in the eye and smile.

He offered an elbow. "Ready?"

"Ready," she said and hooked her hand in his arm. Their walk down Henry Street started out quiet. Sara didn't know how to break the awkward silence, so she stared at the sidewalk.

"You all right?" Ben asked. He smelled nice, like how Sara thought a waterfall must smell.

Sara's nerves were wound so tight that the sound of his voice made her jump a little. "Me?"

"Yes, you," Ben said. "You're kind of quiet. More than usual."

"Oh. Um. Yes, I'm fine," Sara stammered.

"Okay."

They turned the corner onto Frances Street, and Ben guided her through a cobblestone courtyard enclosed by a quaint brick-and-stucco wall. Ivy climbed on the wall and its intricate wrought iron details, giving the courtyard a Renaissance atmosphere. He opened the door and Sara stepped into a hopelessly romantic little Italian restaurant. The host showed them to a dimly lit booth. A candle stuck in the mouth of an old wine bottle cast flickering orange light across Ben's face when they sat. A waiter wearing a black shirt and a long white apron brought them both iced teas, welcomed them to Porta Bella, recited the evening's specials, and then faded away to let them peruse the menu.

"Wow," Sara said, admiring the rustic Italian décor. "This place looks just like I imagine Italy must look."

Ben took a sip of his tea. "Pretty romantic, right?"

Sara hesitated. *What does that mean?* "Um, yeah. Yes." Unnerved and desperate to change the subject, she picked up the menu. "Lasagna sounds good." The smell of freshly cooked Italian food wafted around her, and Sara realized she was famished.

"The Garibaldi sandwich looks pretty amazing," Ben remarked. "You look pretty amazing too."

This made Sara deeply uncomfortable. She didn't say anything; instead she slipped the cocktail napkin from under her glass and started slowly tearing it into narrow strips.

The waiter reappeared to take their orders and refill their teas. After he left, the silence turned awkward, and Sara avoided Ben's frank gaze.

"What's going on?" Ben asked.

"What do you mean?" Sara asked. She suddenly wished she were anywhere but here.

"Well," he said. "You are destroying that napkin. And when I complimented you, you seemed to sort of...shut down."

Sara sat, hands in her lap, and stared at her pile of torn napkin strips. Her heart pounded in her ears. She was suddenly overcome with a powerful urge to run away. *I can't do this*, she thought. *I can't let him hurt me.* "I – I'm sorry, I have to go." She slid out of the booth and ran through the restaurant.

"Sara!" Ben shouted from behind her. "Wait!"

She burst out the door and sprinted through the cobbled courtyard, not stopping until she was safely hidden among the Friday night dinner crowds on State Street and headed in the direction of campus. Once she was sure Ben was not behind her, she sat on a bench outside the midcentury concrete behemoth that was Memorial Library, covered her face with her hands, and completely disintegrated – crying like she hadn't cried in probably twenty years. *He's never been anything but nice to me, and I wrecked it,* she thought. Strong currents of shame, embarrassment, and fear kept the tears coming in a steady stream.

"Hey, are you okay?" A sob stuck in Sara's throat and she peeked up through her fingers to see a kid with a short green mohawk and a skateboard standing in front of her. His kind green eyes were full of concern. "Do you need help?"

She hastily wiped her eyes and her face with her hands. "Um, no. Thanks. I'm okay."

"Are you sure?" The kid didn't look convinced.

"I'm sure," she said, trying to sound reassuring even though her eyes were puffy, her face felt hot and stretched, and she was pretty sure snot was pouring out of her nose. "I'm okay, really."

"Okay," he said. He stepped on his skateboard and pushed himself down State Street toward the Capitol. He glanced doubtfully over his shoulder one more time, then disappeared into the crowd.

Sara sat for another minute or two, trying to regain her composure. She felt awful. She'd let her old demons get the best of her when all Ben was trying to do was take her out for a nice dinner. *If this is how I'm going to behave, I do not deserve an awesome guy like Ben. Or Luke, for that matter.* Her heart twisted a bit at the thought of Luke. *It's just better that I'm alone. I can't hurt anyone that way, and they can't hurt me.*

Another line from her recurring dream floated across her mind: *No matter what, I always have you.* Her mind's eye saw the furry face and inquisitive green eyes of Bat, the only warm-blooded being she felt safe sharing her life with, and tears welled in her eyes again. *I can't do this. I want to go home.*

Sara sat on the bench and cried until she thought her tired body couldn't manufacture one more tear. When the tears subsided and she felt a little bit put together, she decided to head back to Chadbourne Hall. The sun was going down, and the crowds were starting to get a little rowdier. She took a deep breath, stood, and made her way toward Park Street. *Lauren's probably still at the Kappa house,* she thought. *I could use a little alone time. And I need to change my damn clothes – this outfit is still ridiculous.*

She saw movement out of the corner of her eye, and glanced to her right. A tall shadowy figure moved among the trees that sprouted from the large concrete platform that would host the Paws for a Cause event in three short weeks. Sara stopped and squinted, but in the fading light she couldn't make out who it was or what they were doing. She stepped closer and caught a glimpse of a white cast nearly glowing in the dusk light; it was Shannon Plotnik. She appeared to inspect the iron drainage grates at the base of each tree. *Is she looking for something?* Sara wondered. She stepped back again and watched Shannon from the shadows of the elevated stage.

Shannon dropped to her knees next to a large concrete planter full of wilting summer foliage and started digging with her castless left hand. Her long black hair cascaded over her shoulder from her high ponytail. She moved to the next planter, and then the next. *What if she's burying something?* Sara thought. Shannon disappeared from Sara's view to the other side of the platform.

Perplexed, Sara followed and found Shannon standing roughly where the giant crater had been in the State Journal photograph, facing toward Memorial Library. Shannon then started taking deliberate steps across the sidewalk, as if she were measuring the distance between the platform and the Hagenah fountain with her feet.

At that moment Sara was convinced: *Shannon's the bomber. She has to be. She's at the site of the bombing right now starting to prepare. I mean, let's think about this. She hates Kappa but is being forced to stay. She'll have to attend and help at the event whether she likes it or not. She's prone to violence already, and anyone can build a bomb with stuff from a hardware store.* Sara lived a lonely, isolated life; her TV was her constant companion, just as it had been during her lonely, isolated childhood. She had seen enough true crime TV to understand the MMO – motive, means, opportunity – framework used in criminal investigations. *And, as if I need more evidence, with my own two eyes I'm watching her take measurements so she knows how big to build the bomb. She was probably digging in those planters to see if she wants to hide other explosives there.*

She watched Shannon close in on the fountain, and her heart started pounding. *Should I confront her?* she wondered.

She didn't have to wonder long; Shannon reached the fountain, then turned toward Langdon Street and continued walking. She must have been satisfied with her reconnaissance mission, because she wasn't coming back to the platform. She faded out of sight.

Sara continued her own journey back to Chad, her thoughts jostling for position in her mind. She felt terrible about running out on Ben. She felt proud that she'd already figured out who the Library Mall Bomber was. She felt overwhelmed that she now had to do something with this information.

She rubbed her upper arms with her hands to ward off the evening chill as she walked, and wished Lauren were in the room waiting for her, and not at Kappa House. If ever she needed someone to talk to, this was the time.

Sara sighed. *The hard part's done,* she thought. *I know who it is. Now I have to stop her.*

Charlie

Charlie had been sitting on the scuffed wood floor with his back propped against the couch for hours, playing game after game on the Nintendo NES that was hooked up to Ruth's old console TV. He didn't care that his butt had fallen asleep; he was just trying to forget that Sara was out on a date with Ben tonight.

Super Mario Bros and The Legend of Zelda provided badly-needed distraction from his misery at first.

Then, shooting 8-bit ducks with a plastic gun in Duck Hunt had given him a perverse satisfaction. He pretended he was blowing Ben's pretty boy face to smithereens with every shot.

When he tired of that, he put in Donkey Kong. Then Elevator Action. At one point he briefly considered making a run to Software Etc. for more games, but the idea of taking the bus to East Towne Mall made his stomach turn.

So he kept playing.

Mindless video games only did the trick for so long, though. He gradually became aware that his mind was replaying, again and again, the moment during Bio Lab when Ben asked Sara out – and his heart broke anew every time. Eventually he realized he'd been zoning out on the memory and the game had stopped.

Why would she tell me all that about her past if there wasn't something there? I mean, she must trust me, to open up like that. Why would she go out with a frat boy? She should be with someone she trusts. She should be with me.

You know why she chose that other guy, don't you? Ruth's croaky voice piped up.

Charlie closed his eyes and shook his head. "Don't," he mumbled.

Because you're good for nothing. That girl is out of your league.

"I said DON'T!" Charlie shouted, and threw the Nintendo controller he was holding at Ruth's portrait over the television. It bounced off Ruth's square chin and hit the floor, breaking into several pieces. She fell silent, apparently satisfied with having gotten a reaction out of Charlie.

He sat and sulked for a while, then decided to take a walk around campus. Maybe, just maybe, he'd get a glimpse of her. He pulled on his denim jacket with the flannel lining, flipped the collar up so it touched his ears and covered the coarse neck hairs of his mullet, and headed out into the night.

State Street seems like the most likely place for a date, Charlie thought, so he headed north on Mills Street on his way to State Street. As he approached campus, the streets were filled the shouts and laughter of inebriated students hopping from bar to bar; there was a reason the UW was consistently rated a top party school. He kept his head down and his balled fists in his pockets as he walked. On Frances Street, he passed by the rustic Italian wall surrounding the Porta Bella restaurant without seeing it.

He stopped on the corner of Frances and State, outside the new State Street Brats (which Charlie would always think of as the Brathaus), and looked around. A proud teetotaler, Charlie felt justified in judging all of the sloppy drunks as they stumbled down and across State Street, sometimes falling off an unexpected curb or tripping over a sidewalk crack and coming up bleeding.

He decided to cross and turn right, reasoning that the eastern end of State Street, closer to the Capitol, had more nice restaurants than the western end anchored by the university. He crossed the awkward State/Broom/Gilman Streets intersection and looked in the darkened windows of the Chocolate Shoppe ice cream shop – where he would have taken Sara on their ice cream date – and Medler's Books on his way by. The building fell away to a park entrance, illuminated by a single streetlight – Peace Park.

Charlie didn't notice Peace Park, or see the group of men congregated on a stone retaining wall that encircled a young ash tree. But one of those men saw Charlie as he walked by – and recognized him immediately.

"Hey. Fucker." Scott Schlosser's gravelly voice landed in Charlie's ear like a boulder. He cringed, but kept his eyes on the sidewalk and walked faster, his heart racing. He heard Schlosser and his buddies get up and follow him. If they were trying to be stealthy, it wasn't working; under the influence of a large volume of beer, these fellows were about as quiet as a herd of sugared-up toddlers.

Schlosser, who was a head taller than Charlie, caught up to him and grabbed his arm. "I said, hey fucker. You shouldn't ignore someone when they're talking to you. It's not nice." With seemingly no effort, he pulled Charlie back and thrust him at his group of buddies. Charlie struggled to stay on his feet. The thugs surrounded him and together they moved him back into Peace Park.

Charlie tried to swallow his panic. "What are you doing?" he cried out, desperation tugging at his voice.

"Settle down, runt," Schlosser said. "We're not gonna hurt you. Too much." Like a swarm of bees, the group moved him deeper into the shadows of Peace Park. Charlie gagged at the sour stench of beer that wafted from their pores. They sat him down on another stone retaining wall, rearranging themselves so that they flanked Scott, who stood directly in front of Charlie with his massive arms crossed.

"Is this the pipsqueak you were telling us about, Scott?" asked one, a guy from western Wisconsin named Allen Bigelow, who was absolutely average in every way – save for his magnificent Mel Gibson Lethal Weapon haircut.

"Yeah," Scott rumbled. "This douchebag got me kicked out of Bio 101. What's your name, runt?"

"Ch-Charlie," he stuttered, terrified.

"Yeah. Like I was saying, thanks to Chuck here, I've been disinvited from Bio 101 for the rest of this year," Schlosser said.

Charlie couldn't let this untruth slide. "You got yourself kicked out for picking on me." He tried really hard to not sound like he was whining.

Schlosser shrugged one shoulder with his arms still crossed. "Same diff."

"What are you gonna do with this guy?" This from Ricky Jute, a skinny, jittery fellow with a flattop who stood on Scott's other side. He bounced on the balls of his feet and swung his arms at his sides front to back, occasionally clapping his hands together. Charlie wondered what else he'd consumed along with all those beers tonight.

Scott cocked his head, pretending to contemplate. "Well, what I wanna do is kick his ass from here to fuckin Tuesday. But, seeing as how we're right here on State Street before bar time with all these people around, that will have to wait until another day. Instead, maybe we just rough him up a little." Something resembling a smile cracked his massive face, revealing a gap between his front teeth. He looked more than a little like a sinister, overmuscled Louie Anderson.

Charlie's entire body broke out in a cold, slimy sweat. "C'mon, guys." He looked around wildly for an escape route. Scott and his cronies had circled around him. He felt like a rabbit cornered by a skulk of foxes.

Scott grabbed Charlie by the back of the neck. "Get up, Chuck."

"No!" Charlie shouted. He ducked and tried to scramble to his right, out of Scott's reach.

Scott, who outweighed Charlie by roughly a hundred pounds, easily pulled him to his feet and then shoved him, hard. Charlie went flying into Allen Bigelow, who stopped his momentum and spun him around before pushing him again. Back across the circle he flew; he was stopped abruptly, turned to face forward, and shoved again. And again. Scott's troll-like laugh echoed off the buildings as Charlie bounced between them like a pinball, with no control over his own body. They never let him stop long enough to gain his footing.

Finally another one of Scott's buddies, a delinquent named Jeff Nicholson – whose days as a student at the university were already numbered less than a month into the first semester – stuck his foot out as Charlie flailed by. Charlie tripped and stumbled forward, arms pinwheeling. Scott and his gang stepped back, leaving nobody there to catch Charlie this time. He went down, landing hard on his right knee and smacking his forehead on the stone retaining wall he had been sitting on earlier. Stunned, seeing stars, all he could do was roll onto his back and cover his face with his hands. He thought his head might literally explode. *Probably a concussion*, he thought, but knew he would never see a doctor. A doctor might ask questions Charlie didn't want to answer.

Scott squatted next to Charlie; his legs seemed impossibly huge – roughly the size of a side of beef. Scott said in a low voice, "I'd watch my back if I was you, Chuck." They all then faded away, leaving the park by way of Gilman Street.

Charlie was just far enough back from the sidewalk that State Street bar patrons walked – or stumbled – right by him without seeing him. He laid on the pavement for what felt like an eternity, wondering through the fog in his brain if he should try sitting up. He wasn't sure he wanted to know how badly he was injured. One thing he did know: he was cold. It was the kind of cold that starts in the bones and radiates outward, rendering his flannel-lined denim jacket, otherwise perfect for tonight's weather conditions, utterly useless.

Finally a Madison Police Department foot patrol officer sauntered into the park, ready to shoo away panhandlers and homeless people sleeping on benches and retaining walls. He spied Charlie shivering on the ground and immediately went to him, kneeling beside him. The officer's radio crackled, sending shockwaves through Charlie's head. He groaned.

"Hey, buddy. I'm Officer Daniels. Are you all right? What the hell happened to you?"

Charlie slowly moved his hands from his face and peered up through heavy eyelids. Officer Daniels was fresh-faced, probably five or six years older than Charlie himself, and had kind gray eyes and a black mustache. "Uh."

"You're bleeding everywhere, buddy. Let me call you an ambulance." Daniels reached up to the CB radio on his shoulder, ready to call dispatch.

"No!" Charlie said, and grimaced. "I mean, uh, no thank you." He very gingerly sat up with Officer Daniels' help.

"Are you sure? That gash on your forehead is pretty nasty," Daniels observed. "Your face is going to be all shades of black and blue tomorrow."

"I'm sure," Charlie mumbled. His head pulsed and his stomach roiled.

"Who did this to you?" Daniels asked, pulling a pen and pad out of the front pocket of his stiff navy blue police uniform shirt. Charlie could see the outlines of a bulletproof vest underneath. The shirt pocket was embroidered with the officer's name: M DANIELS.

Charlie had to think quickly, and it hurt like hell; it felt like bolts of hot lightning flashing across his brain and back again. "Uh, nobody. Nobody did this to me, sir. I was, uh, I was running and tripped over my own feet in the dark. Took a header into the retaining wall." He closed his eyes.

"Mmm-hmm," Daniels said, unconvinced. He made a few notes on his pad. "Is that the story you're going to stick with?"

Charlie nodded miserably.

"Well, I guess I can't make you file a report," Daniels said. "But I would reconsider if I were you. Whoever is responsible for this should be held accountable."

Charlie didn't say anything; he also didn't realize he was swaying on his feet.

"Where do you live, buddy?"

Charlie recited his address, and Daniels also collected his name, birthdate, and phone number. Suddenly Charlie's stomach turned inside out, and he vomited at the base of a tree.

Officer Daniels patted his back. "I understand that you're refusing medical treatment, but will you at least let me call you a ride home?"

"Thank you," Charlie said. Home. That sounded good. All he wanted was to crawl into his own bed and go to sleep – and never wake up.

CHAPTER TWELVE
Tuesday, September 26, 1989

Charlie

Charlie spent a good twenty minutes in the morning standing in his darkened bathroom – his eyes were still sensitive to light – examining his reflection in the mirror and debating the wisdom of going to Bio Lab. His face really did look atrocious; he had a four-inch gash across his forehead that had scabbed over in a topography of reds and browns, and the black bruising that spread outward from the wound, covering his forehead and giving him two prominent black eyes, had started to turn green around the edges. He knew from experience that if he touched that bruise, his eyes would immediately tear up from the pain. To be honest, he would probably benefit from another day in bed to heal.

Ultimately, his desire to see Sara won out. *Maybe their date was a bust,* he thought hopefully. *Maybe it was so bad, she decided that it's me she really wants. It happens.* He wasn't sure who exactly it happens to, but figured it must happen to someone, so why not him? He dry-swallowed several ibuprofen and slowly got dressed – carefully pulling his jeans over his scraped and swollen knee – laced up his sneakers, and shouldered his backpack. He felt like he'd been hit by a runaway train as he limped down the stairs, out the door, and over the half mile or so to Noland Hall.

Sara was already there when he arrived. She watched him slowly limp toward their table with wide eyes. "My god, Charlie, what happened?" she asked as he gingerly lowered himself into his chair. He tried not to wince. He looked at her and watched her eyes move rapidly back and forth, up and down as she examined the damage to his face.

"It's nothing," Charlie said. He folded his arms into his body and slouched, feeling like he might know how Barnum's Bearded Lady must have felt.

"Nothing? That's not nothing," Sara said in disbelief. "You look like you just walked out of a bar fight. Are you okay? Have you seen a doctor?"

Oh, I was out looking for you while you were on your date and I got beat up by a bunch of fraternity thugs, it's no big deal. Charlie's blood pressure shot up, sending sheets of white hot pain through his head with every heartbeat. His peripheral vision was ringed in pulsing bright red. "I said," he hissed through his teeth, then slammed his fists on the table and turned to Sara with blazing eyes. "DROP IT."

Sara physically recoiled, eyes wide, her hands instinctively protecting her chest. "Okay," she said timidly.

Charlie could see that he had scared her, but he was too angry and in too much pain to care. Without another word, he pulled a pair of neon green wayfarer sunglasses from his backpack and carefully slid them onto his face, covering his black eyes, and resumed slouching. *Jesus Christ, Charlie,* Ruth's gravelly voice piped up. *You just flushed whatever chance you had right down the fuckin toilet. You worthless piece of shit.* His ears burned.

Ben Packard arrived and took his seat at the table in front of them. He did a double-take at the sight of Charlie. "Holy shit, dude. What happened to you?"

Charlie ignored him.

"Okay," Ben gave up on Charlie and turned his attention to Sara. "Any idea where my lab partner is?"

From behind his sunglasses Charlie saw Sara glance quickly at him before speaking to Ben; she clearly did not want to set him off again. He started to feel guilty for lashing out at her. *This is why you don't have any friends, you know,* Ruth croaked, reminding him once again that as far as she was concerned, all he did was pollute the Earth with his presence.

130

"Um." Sara seemed to have trouble rebalancing. Finally she collected herself enough to reply. "She's not feeling well."

"Bummer," Ben said.

A decidedly awkward silence followed this. Charlie turned his head – slowly – and looked at Sara, and then at Ben. Sara's eyes were on her folded hands, Ben's were on Sara's downcast face. Even in his state, Charlie could see that something was off between them. A spark of hope ignited in his chest.

"Listen, Sara…" Ben began.

Sara raised a hand to stop him. She looked at Ben with sad eyes. "No. You don't get to apologize."

"Okay," Ben said, then waited.

It took a minute or two for Sara to finally speak. "You have nothing to apologize for," she said. "You didn't do anything wrong. I'm the one who messed up. And I've been feeling like shit ever since for running out on you like that." Her voice cracked, and she blinked tears back. "I'm really sorry, Ben. I freaked out."

What the hell happened? Charlie wondered. He looked straight ahead again, but couldn't help watching the drama unfold in his peripheral vision.

Ben maneuvered his head so that he could look her right in the eyes. "Sara. It's okay."

Sara shook her head. "No. It's not okay." A small sob escaped her. Charlie's anger drained away with each tear that rolled down Sara's cheek. He now fully regretted his angry outburst at her. *I'm a Grade-A asshole,* he thought.

Sure are, Ruth agreed.

"It is okay," Ben insisted. "This is all my fault. I pushed too hard. I was really excited to take you out, and I wanted to give you the best, most romantic first date I could think of. It didn't occur to me that a grand gesture like that might make you uncomfortable. That wasn't my intention."

"I know," Sara said. "Thing is, I don't think you could have done anything any differently. I would have found something to freak out about no matter what."

"Then next time we'll skip the fancy dinner and just go straight for dessert," Ben joked. "This is nothing a little ice cream can't fix."

This brought a small smile to Sara's face.

"What do you say to a do-over? I promise we don't have to do anything you're not comfortable with. I'd love a second chance to do this right."

"Okay," she relented. Her small smile tightened only slightly when Ben laid a hand on hers.

Ice cream? That was my idea! Enraged all over again, Charlie's heart started to pound, which in turn made his head throb, which only served to compound his anger. His head felt like a pressure cooker; steam was building up inside, any minute it was going to blow.

Nobody had noticed that Hilliard had entered the room until he boomed, "Mr. Anderson."

Startled, Charlie jumped; the abrupt movement sent a white hot bolt of pain through his head, making him cry out and grasp his head with his hands. The entire class turned to look at him. He felt Sara put a soothing hand on his shoulder; he violently shrugged it off.

"Mr. Anderson," Hilliard said again, more softly. "It is clear to me that you are not feeling well today. It would be best if you took the day off and visited Student Health Services. Or went home to rest."

The pain in his head now at roughly a high C, Charlie closed his eyes and nodded.

"Mr. Hilliard, would it be all right if I walked Charlie home?" Sara asked. "I don't think he should go by himself."

"Yes, of course," Hilliard said. "You both will have the chance to make up today's assignment. Thank you, Ms. Sullivan."

Sara helped Charlie gather up his belongings, shouldered her own backpack, threw his red backpack over her other shoulder, and they slowly made their way to the classroom door. Several people, including Ben, said "Hope you feel better soon" as they walked by.

Charlie kept his sunglasses on and his eyes on the floor.

Sara

Neither Sara nor Charlie said anything as they slowly walked south on Mills Street. She was quite sure he had a concussion, in addition to the giant gash on his forehead, and he was favoring his right leg in a big way. He had scared her with his angry outburst, but she found it easy to forgive him; she couldn't imagine the pain he must be in. *What on earth would cause injuries like this? And why would he come to Bio Lab today?*

After a few moments, she decided she couldn't take the silence anymore. *He might get mad again…but I have to ask.* "Charlie? What really happened to you?" The question sounded much more tentative than she had intended.

Charlie didn't say anything.

"Charlie?"

Charlie still didn't reply, but Sara didn't notice. She had suddenly realized where she was. They were approaching Regent Street. There was a Hardee's coming up on their right, on the corner of Mills and Regent. *Oh my god, that's my McDonald's! I didn't know it used to be a Hardee's!* Although the trapezoidal angles of the hipped roof suddenly made a lot of sense to her; every Hardee's looked like that back in the day. The building that housed the Hong Kong Café in 2019, serving some of the best dim sum in town, had label scars on the dark red brick and a For Sale sign in the window. Some of the old houses were different colors, but otherwise familiar. She wondered if the Greenbush Bakery and the 7-Eleven would still be there if she walked a couple blocks to the west.

"Do you live in this neighborhood?" Sara asked.

"Yeah, just three blocks past Regent," Charlie mumbled. "We're almost there."

They crossed Regent, and the ghosts of Sara's real life continued to haunt her. There was the Neighborhood House Community Center, in the same deceptively small brick building, as busy and vibrant in 1989 as it was in 2019. At Milton Street they turned west and cut diagonally through the rear parking lot of the St. James Catholic Church and School, which – save for the steel playground equipment that would be replaced with much safer brightly colored molded plastic for students by 2019 – looked the same. When they rounded the corner at Orchard and Mound, she was surprised to see that the Mound Street Laundromat was a laundromat in 1989 too. She'd always wondered what had originally been in that old building; with its glass storefront and vintage brick exterior, it looked like it could have been a dry goods store or maybe a bakery in the early 20th century. The cars parked along the curb were bigger and consumed more gas in 1989, but that was the only clue to remind her that she was not in her own time.

Half a block ahead was 1322 Mound Street – her house in 2019.

Her heart hurt as they approached the story-and-a-half red brick cottage; it looked exactly the same with its rounded green front door, four-season porch room, and single-stall tuckunder garage. She so badly wanted to run up the front steps, let herself inside, hug her cat, and forget this entire time-traveling nightmare. But she knew Bat was in 2019 – and she would be trespassing in someone else's 1989 home.

"Is this your street, Charlie?"

"I live just up ahead," Charlie mumbled. His pockmarked face had gone pale with the effort of walking just over a mile already this morning, and his limp had grown more pronounced. Beads of sweat stood out on his forehead.

Charlie stopped in front of 1326 Mound – the house right next door to what would be Sara's house in 2019. It looked much better than it would in thirty years: the grass was cut, the siding was white, and the front porch stairs were intact. Sara gaped in utter disbelief. *Oh, you can't be serious.*

Charlie took a few seconds to catch his breath and said, "Here we are." He swept an arm in a *ta-daa* motion. "Grandma Ruth's house."

The house next door…is Charlie's house? Some forgotten memory lurked just outside her consciousness, but she couldn't quite get it.

"Thanks for walking home with me, Sara." She blinked, snapping out of her reverie. Angry Charlie was gone. He looked exhausted and defeated. And…broken. Sara felt for him.

"Of course. Do you need help with anything inside?"

Charlie slowly shook his head. "No thanks, I'm good from here."

"Get some rest." She unshouldered his backpack and gave it to him. He took it and carefully climbed the front porch steps. When he reached the top of the porch steps he turned around; the look of shame and regret on his face broke Sara's heart.

"I – uh, I'm sorry I got mad," he said without meeting her eyes. Then he unlocked the front door and was gone.

Sara stood there for another minute or two, trying to process. *The house next door is Charlie's house. That has to mean something. Doesn't it?*

She had two and a half weeks to figure it out.

CHAPTER THIRTEEN
Friday, September 29, 1989

Sara

It was a perfect late September evening on State Street. Ben proposed a double scoop cone, an offer that Sara simply could not turn down. Ben was casual and comfortable in jeans and a plaid flannel shirt. Sara also wore jeans, and an oversized gray UW sweatshirt. Her blonde hair was pulled back in a simple ponytail, and her bangs brushed against her forehead.

They arrived at the Chocolate Shoppe; Ben opened the door for her, and they went in. Sara shivered. *It's always so cold in ice cream shops.* Sara placed her order, and then Ben placed his.

"I'm sorry, what did you just order?" Sara asked, aghast and more than a little grossed out.

"A scoop of cinnamon and a scoop of black licorice in a waffle cone," Ben said proudly. "It sounds terrible, but it's actually so good."

"If you say so." She took her two scoops of pralines and cream in a waffle cone from the pimply guy behind the counter, and they reemerged into the bustle of State Street. They turned left and walked past Peace Park, too engrossed in their ice cream to notice the disheveled panhandler playing *Cats in the Cradle* on an out-of-tune acoustic guitar; his open guitar case was empty save for a few scattered coins.

Sara had never been to New Orleans – never been outside Minnesota or Wisconsin, as a matter of fact – but she'd learned from watching an episode of *How It's Made* on cable one lazy Saturday morning that pralines were the pecan-based confection of choice in Cajun country. The ice cream tasted like what she'd always imagined New Orleans was like: sweet and creamy, but also a little salty and nutty.

They walked in comfortable silence for a while, enjoying the mild evening, the pre-party crowds, and each other. Sara's anxiety was noticeably absent, much to her relief. Then a thought occurred to her. "How are things going at Sig Tau?" she asked.

Ben shrugged. "Fine, I guess."

"Is everyone happy and getting along?"

Ben's forehead crinkled and he glanced sidelong at her. "I don't know. They seem to be. I guess."

She leaned into his arm in a soft nudge. "Are there any unhappy campers?"

"More than the usual, you mean? Why do you ask?"

"Humor me," she replied.

Ben sighed and took a taste of his ice cream. "Just the normal stuff," he said. "Guys stealing each other's food out of the fridge, guys clogging the toilet and not cleaning up, guys fighting over who gets the Nintendo next, guys bragging about sexual conquests and the number of beers consumed during any given time period."

Sara nodded and wondered what it was about ice cream that made the taste buds sing.

"Although..." Ben paused, considering. "Schlosser has been a bigger pain in the ass than usual lately. He regularly gets drunk and picks on the freshmen. I think he spends more time doing that than actually going to class."

"Like what does he do?" Sara asked.

"Well, last week he had two freshmen make a beer run for him, knowing full well that they are underage. He convinced them that he knows the owner of Riley's Wines of the World and they wouldn't get in trouble if they dropped his name. The owner happened to be behind the counter that day, and when he asked for ID and all they had was Scott Schlosser's worthless name, he called the cops. Thanks to that little stunt, the entire chapter is on warning with the Council now. Scott's been racking up discipline since the beginning of the year; one more strike and he'll be kicked out of Sig Tau. You can imagine how that message was received."

Interesting. "Did the freshmen get in trouble?"

"I mean, they both got citations from the Madison PD, and Graham put them on probation, but if they keep their noses clean and stop falling for Schlosser's shit, they'll be okay."

Probably not enough to push those two kids to commit a mass suicide bombing, Sara thought. A tiny laser beam of fear pierced her heart at the thought of Ben dying in such a horrific violent manner. *Schlosser, though. Might be some potential there. Could he have worked with Shannon, maybe?*

"Why so concerned, babe? We're the manly men of Sigma Alpha Tau; we can take care of ourselves." He growled and pretended to beat his chest like Tarzan, dripping cinnamon ice cream on his flannel shirt.

Babe? Sara thought. Ben had just given her a whole new set of things to worry about. *Why would he call me that?* The anxiety that ruined their first date started creeping at the edges of her mind; she tried to ignore it – but it was persistent.

Ben noticed a change in her demeanor. "Are you all right?"

Sara couldn't find words at first. She focused on her melting ice cream as she walked and debated how to answer that question. Finally she opted for the truth. "I don't know. Kind of. Not really."

"Okay," Ben said in a tone of voice that said *Tell me more.*

A couple more licks of ice cream. It tasted like cigarette ash. "I guess when you called me "babe," I just sort of freaked out a little."

"Why?"

"Because I don't know why you would call me that when we're only on our second date. Are you just saying something nice so that I might start to trust you? So you can then set me up for some future humiliation?" She tossed the rest of her ice cream in a nearby garbage can; she was sure she would throw up if she had even one more taste.

"I call all the ladies 'babe,'" Ben joked. When Sara didn't react, he grew serious. "There you go again, thinking that it would even occur to me to do such a thing. Intentionally hurt you? My god, never. I just want to spend some time with you." Having also disposed of his ice cream cone half eaten, he gently took her hand. She didn't know what else to do, so she let him hold it. She appreciated his warmth. "What happened to you to give you such a low opinion of humanity?"

They were now approaching the Lakeshore Path. The sun, a magnificent shade of orange, approached the horizon and winked at them between the gnarled trunks of the old oak trees shading the wide gravel path that hugged the shore of Lake Mendota. Joggers and bicyclists zipped by, shouting "On your left!" as they passed.

Sara's entire being screamed *Don't open up to him! Don't trust him!* – but she found herself saying, "There was a group of girls at my high school. Mandy Huber and her "cool girls." Sara made air quotes with her fingers. "They would steal my clothes from my gym locker, then wait until I came out of the shower, wet and naked, so I could watch them throw my stuff in the garbage can while they chanted 'Trash goes in the trash can.' They would trip me in the cafeteria while I had a reduced-lunch green tray in my hands, and of course everyone laughed, every time. Then I'd get hauled to the principal's office for making a mess in the lunchroom. Anything those bitches could do to make me look like a fool in front of everyone, they did it."

Ben said nothing, just held her hand and listened as they walked.

"The worst part was when Mandy made me believe that the captain of the basketball team, Kirk Brockman, wanted to take me to the senior winter dance, which we called Snowball. She said he was too chicken to ask me, so I had to ask him. She worked on me for weeks, and she had me completely convinced. I was super excited because I had a bit of a crush on him." There was the familiar prickle behind her eyes.

"Like an idiot, I approached him in the hallway between classes one day and asked him to the dance. He and his basketball buddies laughed and made fun of me in front of everyone. He wondered what would make me think he'd ever go out with a pathetic loser like me. Invited me to kill myself instead." Sara had never repeated these scarring words out loud; she couldn't stop her voice from cracking. "I took one look at Mandy's face and realized that she had set me up."

"Oh my god," Ben said softly.

"Oh, it gets better. She kept the rumors circulating too; for about a month during the spring of my senior year everyone at school believed I slept with older men for money because my mom and I were so poor. I had no friends." She sighed. "Who needs friends when you have an enemy like Mandy Huber?"

"Okay, but why? Why would she treat you that way?" Ben asked.

Sara shrugged. "In the ninth grade I told my math teacher when I caught her trying to copy from my test. I was her favorite target after that. Looking back, it seems so trivial, but she succeeded in completely ostracizing me."

"And so you walk around believing that everyone you meet is setting you up to hurt you," Ben said.

"Pretty much," Sara said. "Wouldn't you?"

The evening had taken on a dusky quality, and there was less traffic on the path. They walked for a while longer in silence, still holding hands. Her anxiety had subsided a bit; it felt good to talk about it. Even if she didn't know what to expect from Ben now that she'd shared some of her deepest, darkest secrets. *Maybe I said too much. I'm such damaged goods now that he'll just give up and disappear. Start going to Biology Lab on Thursdays instead.*

"Couple things," Ben said, breaking the silence. "First, I want you to know how sorry I am that you went through that. You didn't deserve it. I couldn't imagine anyone being so cruel to such a sweet, goodhearted person." He squeezed her hand. "That's you, you know."

Sara listened, but didn't say anything. She wasn't sure if he was telling the truth or not.

"Second, I know what you're talking about, I've seen it happen."

"You have?" Sara stared up at him with wide eyes.

"Yes," he said. "I dated my high school's Mandy Huber. Her name was Cecelia Bundy, and I spent three years watching her treat people like you were treated." He shook his head. "But I never said anything. I just chalked her behavior up to typical high school drama and ignored it. Even laughed along with her because…well, because the football star and the cheerleader are supposed to be together, right?"

Sara's entire perception of Ben had changed in a flash. More than a little repulsed, she let go of his hand and allowed a bit more space between them. He gave her a brief sideways glance, but didn't make an issue of it. He slipped his hand into a jeans pocket.

"The last straw was when I watched Cece start a rumor that Megan Vanover slept with the band teacher and got pregnant. That rumor flew around school like wildfire." He paused. "It was a huge deal. Parents lined up outside the principal's office and packed school board meetings. Mr. Cozine eventually resigned, even though none of it was true. And Megan, who was a sweet girl, just quit school. She left for winter break and never came back." His voice cracked a bit. "I'll probably never forget her eyes on that last day before break. They were…duller. Almost dead. Cece had killed her spirit with this one vicious thing she did."

141

Sara could relate. Understanding that he felt terrible about what had happened to poor Megan Vanover, she tentatively touched Ben's wrist; he pulled his hand out of his pocket and squeezed her fingers gratefully.

"Cece had a tough home life; her dad was always gone and her mom was too busy carrying on extramarital affairs to spend any time with her. That's not an excuse, but it explains a lot. In my experience, hurt people hurt people. "

Sara pondered this.

"Anyway, the thing with Cece and Megan made me realize that I was part of the problem. By ignoring Cece's behavior, I was condoning it. Allowing it to become normal. I could have stopped her." He ran his other hand through his hair. "I broke up with her as soon as we got back from winter break. And I promised myself I would never stand by and let someone treat someone else so badly ever again." He looked at Sara and grinned. "I was all set to kick Schlosser's ass that day when he was picking on Charlie, but you beat me to it. You are a complete badass."

Sara's smile reached all the way to her eyes.

"It's probably a safe bet that your Mandy was dealing with some issues of her own, and the only way she knew to make herself feel better was by making you feel bad. You didn't fight back, so you became an easy target that she could victimize again and again."

It had never occurred to Sara that Mandy's behavior could have been a symptom of troubles in her own life. In fact, Sara so completely believed that that she was the one with the problem that she had invested all of her energy into self-protection: minimizing interactions at school and later at work, turning down invitations to social events and dates, hanging out with her cat instead of with people.

No matter what, I always have you. A phrase she'd whispered into the soft black fur just below Bat's ears many times. She remembered saying to Charlie, *I will never allow anyone to treat me like that again. I would rather be alone for the rest of my life.* This had always been her guiding principle. She was lonely, but she was safe. That was all that mattered.

Now, Ben's words swept open a heavy curtain in the part of her mind where self-worth, self-esteem, and self-confidence had lived in darkness for most of her life. The light hurt, it made her want to scramble for the comfort of darkness like bugs abruptly exposed when a rock is turned over, but there was potential here. Sara wondered if it was possible to heal.

"Remember what I said last week?" Ben asked.

"'Let's go straight for dessert?'" Sara's impression of Ben was better than passable; it was dead on.

He threw his head back and laughed, long and loud. His deep voice echoed in the trees around them. Her response had surprised and delighted him. She couldn't help but laugh with him. He pulled her to a bench next to the water. They fell more than sat on the bench, trying to regain their composure.

"I guess I did say that —" Ben started.

"You're always talking about food," Sara interjected, still giggling. It felt good to laugh. She did it so rarely; she never really had much to laugh about.

Ben touched Sara's chin, forcing her to look him in the eye. "Last week I told you that you are beautiful. And amazing. And that I would never hurt you."

Sara, her throat choked with sudden emotion, simply nodded.

"I meant every word," he said, and kissed her.

Surprised, Sara's eyes closed instantly and she drew air in through her nose. His lips were soft and warm, and tasted like cinnamon and black licorice. *He's right, not a terrible combination after all,* she thought. They explored her lips slowly and gently, and she tried to respond in kind. Thanks to her major trust issues, she'd made it to the age of thirty-five without ever being kissed — and a little part of her brain wondered why she would deny herself this experience. *I had no idea this would feel so...so good*, she thought. She hoped she was doing it right.

He broke away and gently rested his forehead against hers. She swam in his deep brown eyes. Whatever defenses she thought she had left were gone; her protective walls had crumbled under the weight of Ben's kindness. She felt naked. Exposed.

He cradled the side of her face with one of his hands; she couldn't help but turn her cheek into his warm palm. Much like her beloved Bat would do.

"Oh boy, I've been wanting to do that for a long time," Ben said softly, his deep voice pouring into her ear like melted butter.

Sara closed her eyes and focused on how she felt being this close to Ben in this moment. She felt...absolutely terrified. She felt...overwhelmed. She felt...deliriously happy. This foreign combination of emotions threatened to burst her heart. She knew she was opening herself up for heartbreak and humiliation, but in this moment she did not care.

He kissed her again and then wrapped her in his arms. "I will never, ever hurt you," he whispered.

She hugged him back fiercely, squeezing her eyes shut against the tears. *But can I keep you from getting hurt?*

CHAPTER FOURTEEN
Saturday, September 30, 1989

Charlie

After Sara walked Charlie home on Tuesday, he'd limped straight upstairs to his sparsely furnished bedroom, pulled the curtains closed, and fallen into bed. Over the next four days, the only reasons he got out of bed were to (slowly) fetch a glass of water and use the bathroom.

His head felt like he had the world's worst migraine headache. Any light, sound, or movement sent firecrackers of white hot pain through his head. Opening his eyes and looking around the room caused powerful waves of nausea; twice he'd thrown up into the small trash can sitting next to his bed. His darkened room stank of acidy vomit.

He'd slept a lot, taken a lot of ibuprofen, and basically wished he were dead.

Today he finally felt a little bit better. He was still sensitive to light, but the nausea had subsided. He lay in bed, eyes closed, thinking about Sara. *I love her more than he ever could. I would treat her like a goddamn queen.*

Watching Sara and Ben hit it off was making him crazy. Every time he worked up the courage to make his move, Pretty Boy swept in and stole his chance. Every. Single. Time. A dull throb started up in his head, pounding to the rhythm of his heartbeat.

One thing Charlie was absolutely certain of: he and Sara were meant to be together. She just didn't realize it yet.

But somehow, some way…she would.

Sara

She had the dream again, for the first time since waking up in 1989. It still played like an elementary school filmstrip, only now it seemed to have more…clarity.

145

"Mommy? Shouldn't you wear these ones to work?" Her little arms holding up a pair of steel-toed work boots. The boots her mother had declined to wear the day she hurt her foot – the first in a chain reaction of events that culminated in Sara's profound fear and mistrust of people. Even in her dream, her heart hurt.

Clackity-clack. Scene change.

"He just…he looks so sad. Now I kind of wish I'd said yes when he asked me to be his Bio Lab partner. I really am some kind of jerk." The face that had been blurry and out of focus before was crystal clear now; it was Lauren, and Sara now understood that the voice belonged to the other Sara. She also realized this part of the dream was what had unconsciously compelled her to ask Charlie to be her Bio Lab partner.

Clackity-clack. Scene change.

"No matter what, I always have you." Bat's furry black face. She wanted to kiss it and love him up – but noticed a change in her reaction to seeing his image. Before 1989, he was literally all she had. Her only family, her only confidant. She held onto him like a life preserver. Now, she saw…her pet. Her companion. Just one of several now.

Clackity-clack. Back to Scene 1.

Hours after waking up, Sara was still curled up in the other Sara's bed, covers over her head to keep the world out. She was struggling today, no way around it. Her date with Ben last night had been amazing. Her first kiss had been amazing. She'd floated home on clouds afterward, and fallen asleep smiling.

When she awoke this morning, however, she realized that her recurring dream had somehow foreshadowed her trip back to the past – a fact that troubled her greatly. After turning that over and over in her mind for a while, her thoughts turned to analyzing last night with Ben – and the old self-doubt came crashing back in. She began to wonder if she'd made a mistake telling him so many of her secrets. She'd broken her own rules for a moment of pleasure – but at what cost? She'd left herself wide open to the hurt and humiliation she'd spent her entire adult life trying to avoid.

Her breathing sped up and she squinched her eyes shut; it was everything she could do to keep the panic at bay. *What have I done?*

It wasn't often that Sara thought about her mom anymore, but right now, during her current emotional crisis, she missed Melinda desperately. *Every girl needs her mom,* she thought. *Even me, I guess.*

The last Sara had heard of her mom, probably close to a year before her journey back in time, Melinda was still drinking heavily and shacked up with some crack addict in a rundown old house in north Minneapolis.

An unknown number flashed on Sara's phone one Sunday night while she was watching 60 Minutes, Bat curled in her lap. She didn't usually take calls from unfamiliar numbers, but for some reason felt compelled to answer.

"Sara? It's your mother," the familiar voice had slurred. Sara could hear several loud voices in the background.

Taken aback yet not completely surprised, Sara said, "Hello Mom."

"Listen, baby, I need some money. Larry hit me again last night, broke two of my teeth, and I gotta get out of this shithole."

"I'm not sending you money, Mom." Sara pressed her fingers into her eyes. The voices in the background grew louder; it sounded like an argument was brewing.

"You always were an ungrateful brat," Melinda's words ran into each other; she sounded sloppy drunk. "Too selfish to take care of your own mother."

"Yeah. Except we both know I took care of you for years, when it should have been you taking care of me." Sara tried to keep her voice even so Melinda wouldn't know she'd hit a nerve. "Why don't you stop trying to

feed me this line of complete bullshit, and admit that all you want is money to spend on booze."

Melinda hung up on her. Sara changed her number again.

Now, safe under the other Sara's covers, eyes closed, Sara sighed. Another memory suddenly came to life in her head: she was six years old with Melinda at the Como Zoo in St. Paul on a beautiful September day in 1988. *A little more than a year ago from right now*, Sara thought. *Mind blown.* They stood in front of the gorilla enclosure, watching and laughing as the giant primates wrestled with each other under a misting fan. This was one of Sara's earliest and most treasured memories; the zoo visit happened about a year before her mom injured her foot – and the alcohol took over both of their lives. Melinda's eyes had been clear and sparkling, her smile genuine, her body not puffy and ravaged by the effects of alcohol abuse. Sara's heart hurt. She sometimes wished Melinda was functional enough to lean on and provide motherly advice. Going through life alone as a woman without her mom was hard.

I could call her now, she thought hopefully. *I still remember the phone number for the old apartment on 42nd Avenue.* She sighed, reality sinking in. *And say what, exactly? Hi, this is Sara, I'm all grown up now, stuck in 1989 and could sure use some advice? While she's looking right at seven-year-old you watching Scooby Doo? Get real.*

Sara heard the door open and sat up, pulling her covers off her head. Some of her hair clung to her face with static electricity; some of it stuck straight up. She blinked in the sunny brightness of the room. Lauren breezed in, carrying the mail in one hand and what looked like a hastily built salad from the dining hall in the other. She had pulled her hair tightly up into a round poof on the top of her head. "Hi love," she said, setting the salad and the mail on her desk.

"Hey," Sara said. "Meeting go well?"

"It went swimmingly!" Lauren sat on her bed. "Holly pulled me aside afterward and asked if I would like to take her place as chair of the committee. Can you believe it? First freshman ever to run this event!"

"That's amazing!" Sara said, and meant it.

"Holly said I've been doing such a great job leading the meetings and getting things done, I should get the title to match."

"Good for you, Lo. You deserve it."

"That's what Graham said too. I was a little worried about him, being a senior and now he has to do what I tell him to. But he's cool. They all are. Ben gave me a huge hug and told me he's proud of me."

Sara's heart skipped a beat. She wasn't sure if that was because Lauren said Ben's name, or because Ben had given Lauren a hug.

Lauren took a closer look at Sara. "Are you okay?"

Sara ran her fingers through her hair in an effort to smooth out the static. "I don't know."

Lauren sat next to Sara on the bed. "Tell me."

Sara sighed. "Ben kissed me last night."

Lauren grinned and clapped her hands together. "That's fantastic, Sara! I've been trying to tell you he likes you."

I know," Sara said. "But…"

Lauren's full lips pursed and her eyes narrowed in anticipation of being annoyed. "But?"

"I also told him about some of the stuff that happened to me in high school. I told him about Mandy Huber. I gave him so much ammunition, Lo."

The expression on Lauren's face did not change – except her left eyebrow shot up. "Ammunition."

"Yeah. He knows all this stuff about me now, he can use that to hurt me." Tears welled up in Sara's eyes. She blinked them back.

Lauren shook her head. "Oh, Sara. How many times do I have to tell you that Ben wouldn't do that? He doesn't have a cruel bone in his damn body."

"But —"

"Listen," Lauren interrupted. She looked earnestly at Sara. "Ben is not like Mandy, love. I'm not like that. Charlie isn't either. You are surrounded by people who love you and would never, ever hurt you."

Sara nodded and dropped her eyes. Hearing it from Lauren was different than hearing it from Ben. More real, somehow. Sara had grown to trust Lauren over the last three and a half weeks. She was inclined to believe Lauren because Lauren had yet to hurt her. Sara felt a huge weight lift from her shoulders; she took a cool, cleansing deep breath. "Thank you."

"Anytime, love." With a smile, Lauren picked up the mail and thumbed through the envelopes. "Oh cool, my mom and dad sent me a new phone card," she said. "There's something for you here too." She handed a white envelope to Sara.

It looked like a Hallmark greeting card. Sara hadn't received any mail since awakening to find herself in 1989, and she was unreasonably excited that something had come for her. She examined the front of the envelope. It was postmarked WAUSAU WI SEP 28 89 54401, and according to the return address, which was written in old-fashioned cursive, it was from Mom & Dad. A pit opened in her stomach, and she stared down at the card in her hands.

"Sara?" Lauren said, concern in her nearly-black eyes.

Sara gave a watery sigh. "You know, Lo, I've grown to kind of like being here in 1989. For the first time in my life, I have friends. I have a life. It's pretty easy to forget that I don't actually belong here."

"What do you mean?" Lauren asked.

"You say I look the same to you, but really, I'm an impostor in someone else's life. And this card is a reminder of that." She

150

held up the card. "It has my name on it, but it's not for me. It's for the real Sara Sullivan, the one who belongs here in 1989, from her parents in Wausau." She ran her fingers over the smooth white envelope. "Right this moment, my mom is living in an apartment in Minneapolis, working at a plastics plant to support herself and me. The actual me is seven years old. Who knows, maybe that's where the other Sara is, pretending to be me. And doing second grade all over again, showing the class who's the boss in their weekly game of Math Roulette."

Lauren didn't say anything, just looked at the envelope in awe.

"This life isn't mine. Not really," Sara said, then started to cry. *I didn't know I had so many tears,* she thought. She had done more crying in the last month than she had in probably her entire life. Some of those tears had Mandy Huber's name on them and were long overdue. Some of them were for her mom.

Lauren wrapped her arms around Sara and hugged her while she grieved for the life she knew she would eventually have to leave behind. "Oh, love," she said, smoothing Sara's hair. "You're here to do something amazing: save a whole bunch of innocent lives. That's a huge burden for a girl to carry. But you know what? If there's one thing I've learned over the last few weeks with you, it's that if anyone can do this, you can."

The tears finally subsided, leaving gritty eyes and puffy eyelids. "Thanks, Lo. I appreciate your vote of confidence." Something occurred to her. "You know what? I just realized that this is the first time I've heard from the other Sara's parents since I've been here. Your mom calls every other day at least. Don't her parents call every once in a while to check in on their kid?"

Lauren stood, grabbed the salad from her desk, then sat cross-legged on her own bed to eat it. "I'm not surprised," she said between bites. Sara always thought that the crunching noise made by chewing fresh iceberg lettuce was weird; it sounded like short bursts of TV static.

"The other Sara's parents are a lot older," Lauren said, popping a chunk of turkey in her mouth. "When I met them, I actually thought they were her grandparents. I guess they both have a hard time hearing. She told me once that they have a telephone, but they hardly ever use it."

Sara finally noticed what Lauren was wearing: hot pink leggings and off-the-shoulder purple sweatshirt. "Good lord, woman, are you trying to make me go blind?"

Lauren laughed. "You should see my legwarmers, man. They're neon yellow."

Sara shook her head and gazed at her roommate fondly. *I don't know about your fashion choices, but damn, you're good at helping this broken girl learn how to live life.*

CHAPTER FIFTEEN
Tuesday, October 3, 1989

Charlie

His head felt much better this morning; he wasn't wearing sunglasses, and he couldn't feel his heartbeat in his temples anymore. Charlie walked into Bio Lab and saw Sara sitting there chatting with Lauren. He thought his heart would burst right through his throat, but tried not to show it. He sat next to Sara. "Hey."

"Charlie!" Sara was clearly happy to see him. She inspected his face with those amazing hazel eyes; all he could do was stare at them. "Wow, you look so much better. Did you rest this weekend?"

He nodded. Sara turned to Lauren. "You should have seen him last week, Lo. His face looked like he'd been on the losing end of a bar brawl."

"What happened?" Lauren asked.

Charlie shook his head. "It was nothing. I tripped over something and hit my head." *Yeah, I tripped over that asshole Scott Schlosser's foot.* "I feel way better now."

"I'm glad," Sara said." I was really worried about you."

Ben arrived and took his seat next to Lauren. "Hey guys." His glance fell on Charlie. "Wow, dude, you look awesome," he said. "Feeling better?"

Charlie nodded. "Yes, thanks." *Why is everyone being so nice?* he wondered. Ruth's voice answered: *Only God knows why.*

"Listen, you guys," Ben said. "We're having a big party at Sig Tau on Saturday night. We've got some legacy members coming into town. We'll have a DJ, a couple of kegs, and people from all over Greek Row will be there. You guys should come." He smiled at Sara. She smiled back. Charlie tried not to let it bother him. But it did.

"That sounds great, Ben!" Lauren squealed.

"Charlie too," Sara said. She seemed more relaxed than Charlie had ever seen her. She was even smiling – a rare occurrence, in Charlie's experience.

"Huh?" Ben and Charlie said this in unison; Ben because he'd been staring at Sara and not paying attention, Charlie because he was shocked.

"Charlie's invited too, right?" Sara asked.

"Of course Charlie's invited too," Ben said, and grinned at Charlie. "You up for it, bud?"

Charlie didn't know what to say. He thought back to the night of the pledge parties, and how he'd gotten within a block of the Sigma Alpha Tau house before his anxiety got the best of him and he retreated. *Maybe knowing a couple people will help,* he thought. *And besides, Sara's going to be there.* "Sure," he finally said.

"Excellent!" Lauren gushed. "All my favorite people will be there! This party sounds like kind of a big deal, I'll need to pick out something new to wear."

"I'm pretty sure Sara could show up in a floral yellow bedsheet and look perfect," Ben said, smiling again. *Ugh. Gag me,* Charlie thought.

"Unless it's a toga party, I definitely won't be wearing that," Sara said dryly.

Hilliard strode in and the class settled down. He started booming about carbohydrates, fats, and protein, reminding the class how these different molecules make up living cells. He gave a few instructions for the day's experiments, then set the class loose to work. He walked up to Charlie and Sara's table. "Hello, Mr. Anderson," he said. "You appear to be much improved this week. I trust you're feeling better?"

"Yes sir," Charlie said. "Thank you."

"I'm glad to hear it," Hilliard remarked. "I was quite concerned; I very nearly called an ambulance for you."

"I was worried too," Sara chimed in.

"It wasn't as bad as it looked…" Charlie said feebly.

"No, it was way worse. I didn't think you were going to make it home," Sara said.

"Well, in any case," Hilliard said, "I'm relieved to see you're feeling better. I'm going to give you both a pass on last week's assignment."

Sara thanked Hilliard. "That's very kind of you."

Hilliard nodded and walked away, inspecting the work of other tables.

Charlie felt the weight of Sara's gaze. He glanced at her.

"I really am glad you're feeling better, Charlie," she said. "And I'm glad you're coming to the party on Saturday night."

His face started to heat up. "I'm glad you'll be there too." The very idea of a fraternity party gave Charlie heart palpitations, but Sara had seen to it that he got invited. She wanted him there…and wild horses wouldn't keep him away.

Sara

Tuesdays were fast becoming Sara's favorite day of the week; she had just two classes – Bio Lab in the morning and Women's History in Van Hise Hall at 2:00; by 3:30 she was free to get on with her day. Today she thought she would wait for Lauren in their room and see if she was interested in heading over to the Union for a late lunch on the terrace.

She walked into Chadbourne Hall, rode the elevator up to the seventh floor, and found Monica Katz and Julie Morgan, her neighbors across the hall, sitting in the commons room to get their daily fix of their favorite soap opera, *General Hospital.*

"Oh my god!" Monica shouted at the television. "I knew it!"

"What's going on?" Sara asked.

"Charlene almost died in a fire at Tony's house last week – and Lucy paid someone to set it!" Julie was clearly distraught. She was the athletic type who mostly wore black or navy blue Adidas track suits and tied her caramel-colored hair back in low ponytails; she was not the sort Sara would have pegged as a fan of soap operas.

"They're my guilty pleasure," Julie had confided in Sara over a bowl of cereal – Grape Nuts for Julie, Froot Loops for Sara – in the dining hall one recent morning. "Monica watches every day and I always get sucked in."

Sara sat in an empty mauve vinyl chair and watched for a few minutes, sort of hoping to get sucked in too so she could figure out what the big deal was. She had a difficult time seeing past the dramatic movements and gestures. The closeups and pregnant pauses. The bouncing between multiple conversations and different sets of characters. Sara found it impossible to understand what she was watching. She was, however, fascinated to observe that Monica's and Julie's emotions seemed to whipsaw with every little thing that happened to any of the huge assortment of characters – many of whom were apparently related.

Finally the elevator dinged, rousing Sara from her trance-like state. She still didn't completely understand this show, wasn't sure yet what Wyndamere was and why Ned and Dawn were arguing about it, but Monica and Julie were completely invested.

Lauren strode into the commons room with her usual flair. "Hello, loves!"

"SSSHHH!" This came from Monica and Julie in unison.

Sara stood and walked with Lauren to their room. "I don't get why anyone watches that crap," Sara said. "I mean, isn't real life dramatic enough?"

Lauren laughed and unlocked the door.

"I was thinking we could go over to the Union, maybe grab a grilled cheese and hang out on the terrace. What do you think?" Sara said.

"I think that sounds like a lovely plan," Lauren said. "Let me just drop my stuff and powder my nose."

Within fifteen minutes they were on their way down Park Street toward Memorial Union and Lake Mendota. The air was crisp, promising that autumn was on its way. Sara was dressed appropriately in jeans, sneakers, and the same gray UW sweatshirt she'd worn on her date with Ben over the weekend. Lauren wore a sherpa-lined denim jacket and black stirrup pants. *Always the fashionista,* Sara thought, smiling.

They ordered grilled cheese sandwiches and drinks from the cafeteria, then took their trays to one of the few empty sunburst tables on the terrace. The sun sparkled on the lake and helped take the bite out of the autumn chill. Sara raised her face to the warmth, then looked around the packed terrace. *I guess we're not the only ones to have this idea,* she observed.

As she bit into her warm, gooey-on-the-inside, crispy-on-the-outside sandwich, her eye fell on a couple huddled over a table next to a large oak tree roughly thirty feet away. She chewed and watched….and then realized who she was looking at.

She gently kicked Lauren's shin. "Lo!"

"What!" Irritated at Sara interrupting her lunch, Lauren set her own sandwich down.

"Look over there," Sara discreetly pointed. "See them?"

Lauren squinted. "Yeah, that looks like Shannon Plotnik. With…is that…?"

"It's Scott Schlosser!" Sara whispered. The table was so wildly too small for him, he had to fold himself in half so he could rest his elbows on it. Shannon was also leaning forward, and they appeared to be deep in a serious conversation. "Did I tell you I saw her on Library Mall the night of my first date with Ben?"

Lauren nodded. "You did tell me that she was doing something super fishy. You thought she might be the bomber."

"I still think she is. She was acting too suspicious not to be, you know? But. Did I tell you what Ben told me about Schlosser on Saturday?"

Lauren picked up her sandwich again and took a bite. She shook her head as she chewed. "All you told me about your second date was that Ben kissed you." She grinned.

"He told me that Schlosser has been acting like a real jerk all year," Sara said. "He got the whole chapter in trouble, and the Council has put them on probation. One more strike and they're going to kick him out of Sig Tau."

Lauren's eyes widened. "Really?"

Sara nodded and took a sip of her Original New York Seltzer. She couldn't remember the last time she'd had one of these flavored sparkling waters in the distinctive glass bottles. The bright, effervescent peach flavor took her right back to her childhood. Which was, when you thought about it, actually right now. "Yeah. Ben said he didn't take the news well."

"Huh." Lauren stared at Schlosser and Shannon for a second, then said, "I wonder…"

"Yeah," Sara said. "I wonder too."

"Do you think he could be the bomber?"

"I do," Sara confirmed, and finished the last bit of her sandwich. "He's already an asshole, he's angry, and I think he could be violent. I mean, you saw how he threatened Hilliard that day he got kicked out of Bio Lab."

Lauren nodded. "I sure did."

"I actually think they could both be the bomber," Sara said, floating her latest theory. "I think they could work together to plan it and build it. For all we know, that's what they're talking about right this minute." She glanced at Scott and Shannon, who were still deep in conversation. "It's a perfect plan, if you think about it. They'll both die at the event, leaving no witnesses."

Sara and Lauren were both quiet for a moment, watching Scott and Shannon.

"I kind of want to throw up," Lauren said.

"Me too," Sara said. Her sandwich had turned to lead in her stomach. She was watching these two assholes plot the worst act of domestic terrorism in Wisconsin's history. Her heart pounded, and her hands were suddenly cold. "Should we report them, do you think?"

Lauren's perfect eyebrows shot up. "Well, how confident are you that it's them?"

Sara stared at Lauren for a moment. "What do you mean?"

"Do you have any proof? I mean, remember what Detective Dickwad said about falsely accusing someone. We could get in serious trouble if we don't have proof," Lauren said.

"We also don't want to die in a suicide bombing in a week and a half," Sara reminded Lauren, in a rather cruel bid to manipulate her into agreeing that Sara was right.

Lauren sat up straighter, anger in her black eyes. "Not cool, Sara."

Sara sat back in her sunburst chair and stared at the crumbs on her sandwich plate like a sulking child. Then she sighed. "You're right, I'm sorry. No, I don't have proof. But my gut says it's gotta be them."

Lauren shook her head. "Your gut isn't enough. If you report them and end up being wrong, you've falsely accused two innocent people, Detective Dumbass throws you in jail, and the bombing happens anyway. Not an ideal ending."

Sara agreed.

"You have to find some proof. You have to make sure you're stopping the right people. Or person."

Sara rolled her eyes and sat up straight; her tantrum was apparently not over yet. "Fine. I'll find some proof. But you'll see that I'm right."

"Great, I hope you are," Lauren said. "I really do. Because I don't want to die."

That tiny beam of pure fear pierced her heart again at the thought, like it had at the thought of Ben dying in the bombing. "You won't. I'm going to stop them."

"Okay, well, it won't be today," Lauren said. "It appears they've left." She pointed at Scott and Shannon's now-deserted table.

"That's all right. I'll get them," Sara said, resolving herself.

I have to.

CHAPTER SIXTEEN
Wednesday, October 4, 1989

Sara

After dinner, Sara lay prone on her bed, reading last week's People magazine. She'd seen a photo of Roseanne Roseannadanna and the headline *The Wild & Crazy Story Behind Saturday Night Live!* on the bright blue cover and snatched it from the commons room. SNL had been her weekend babysitter for most of her childhood, had helped her cope with her mother's alcoholism, so it held a special place in her heart. The article was a first-person telling of the development of the show and its first season by key players including the show's creators, producers, writers, and stars. She grinned when one producer commented that in the early days, if an NBC executive "gets on the elevator and runs into Belushi, we're all dead."

Reading about something as intimately familiar as SNL helped ground Sara a bit. It occurred to her that her budding romance with Ben might be distracting her from the fact that she was only in 1989 on a temporary visa. She had a very important mission, and by allowing herself to get too integrated here, she was in danger of losing sight of it. And she was running out of time.

She rolled to her back and sighed. *God, what am I doing? I have to focus on saving these people, not becoming one of them. They all are going to die ten days from today if I don't pull my head out of my ass.*

She sat up and grabbed a notebook and pen from her desk, intending to write down everything she knew up to this point. *Okay, let's review.*

Abandoned house next door = Charlie's house.

Woke up in dorm room with Lauren. Lauren = bombing victim.

Bio Lab with Charlie, Lauren, and Ben (also bombing victim).

Charlie not a member of Sig Tau. Bombing victim too?

Sara stopped writing and stuck the barrel end of the blue Bic between her teeth. Seeing it all in writing made it clear that there was some connection between herself, Lauren, Ben and Charlie that traced to the bombing. She knew that Lauren was certainly killed in the bombing, and Ben almost certainly, given their involvement in the Paws for a Cause event. She thought back to the article she'd read in the Wisconsin State Journal and tried to remember if it had listed the names of the three surviving Sig Tau members. She didn't think it had. *I would remember if I'd seen Ben's name on that list*, she thought.

But what about Charlie? How did he figure in all this? He wasn't a member of Sig Tau, and he didn't have the best social skills, so it wasn't likely that he would even attend the event, much less die there. The fact that Charlie lived at 1326 Mound Street in 1989 had seemed significant at first, but now felt more like a crazy coincidence; the house could have been abandoned at any point between 1989 and when she moved in next door in 2019. She considered, then wrote:

Charlie going to event? Ask in Bio Lab.

Can event be cancelled? Postponed? Ask Lauren.

It hadn't occurred to her until just that moment that postponing the event, or cancelling it altogether, might be an option. She felt a bit foolish. *It couldn't possibly be that easy. Could it?*

Sara bounced the end of her pen against the notebook paper, making a rapid tap-tap-tap-tap sound, and thought about her suspects. She wrote:

Shannon Plotnik: angry, hates Kappa, prone to violence. Mapping out Library Mall in prep for bombing?

Scott Schlosser: bully, angry, about to get kicked out of Sig Tau, maybe violent?

Working together to plan & carry out bombing? NEED PROOF.

The more she thought about it, the more likely she thought it was that Scott and Shannon were in on this together. She just had to prove it.

Then she took a moment consider some what-ifs. She wrote: Ben: come back to 2019 with me?

She stopped and reread, unconsciously chewing her pen again. That was a big what-if. It was based on some pretty big assumptions. *If* she succeeded in stopping the bombing *and* figured out how to get back to 2019, *then* maybe Ben could come back with her. But the logistical implications were enormous. If he lived past the 14th of October and traveled back to 2019 with her, would there be two of him there? She had no idea what the consequences of that would be. Or, would twenty-year-old him from 1989 simply wake up in his fifty-year-old 2019 body, wherever it was living? Based on her experience thus far, she suspected that would probably be the case. Which would make bringing Ben back to 2019 with her extremely difficult, especially if 2019 Ben did not live in or around Madison.

I really am living Back to the Future, she thought. *All that's missing is my own personal Doc Brown.* All she knew in this moment is that Ben made her feel like a real, valued person — a feeling she had never experienced before. It would be excruciatingly painful to leave him. She pushed that thought aside and jotted down another what-if: Stay in 1989?

This option seemed on its surface to be the most viable. It was certainly the most attractive. She was already here. She had friends and a life here. She could keep Ben, and he would never have to know that she hadn't been telling him the full truth

163

about herself. She could keep living like she was now, and nobody but Lauren would be any wiser. Her heart beat a little faster at the exciting, if not entirely rational, idea. Then she realized that there were two other Saras who had been displaced so that she could be here in 1989: her seven-year-old self (who was probably hanging out in 2019) and the other Sara from 1989 (who was likely reliving the second grade all over again). Maybe they didn't want to stay in their new realities. Sara sighed.

Sara heard Lauren's voice down the hall. "You girls are crazy!" Her throaty laugh preceded her into the room.

"What's going on?" Sara asked.

Lauren laughed again and shook her head. "Oh, those damn fools out there think they can stay up all night to watch a *Twilight Zone* marathon on TV." She poked her head back out the door and shouted, "It's a school night! I don't know about you, but I have exams tomorrow! A girl needs her beauty sleep!" She came back into the room and closed the door behind her.

Sara shook her head. She looked back at her notebook and reread her notes. "Oh, hey – question for you."

"Shoot," Lauren muffled through the shirt she was pulling over her head.

"I can't believe I didn't think of this before, but – do you think it would be possible to cancel the fundraiser? Or postpone it?"

"Mmm," Lauren intoned, selecting an oversized t-shirt from her dresser. "I mean, yes. We probably could cancel or postpone. But I just wonder if that would really help. If someone really wants to take out a couple of Greek houses, don't you think he'll just find another way to do it?"

"Good point," Sara said. That hadn't occurred to her, but it made sense. "He probably would. In that case, maybe it would be better to just hold the event as planned. We know that will draw them out. It's probably our only real chance to stop them."

Finished changing into her pajamas, Lauren stood. She ruffled Sara's hair on her way to her bed. "You'll figure it out, love."

God, I hope so, Sara thought.

Charlie

"What was I thinking? I can't go to a frat party." Charlie was pacing in the living room by the light of the floor lamp, moving from the green easy chair to the phone next to the door to the television set and then to the couch. And then the whole circuit would start over. He had started to regret telling Sara he would go to Pretty Boy's frat party the minute he'd left the classroom yesterday. It had been on his mind almost constantly; the nervous energy built up until he could sit still no longer.

He made his way from the phone table, where he had compulsively lifted the receiver and then placed it back in its cradle – taking an indulgent moment to admire his prized red sneakers, which sat on the floor next to the door – to the TV in the corner. He drummed his fingertips on the set's wooden case and looked up at Ruth's photo. "Did you hear me, Gram? I can't go to a fucking party." He made his way to the couch. "I can barely go to the grocery store."

Watch your filthy mouth, Ruth snapped. *If you don't want to go, why in the hell would you tell the girl you would?*

A fair question. Charlie paused. "Because she asked me to."

Ruth made a raspy dismissive sound. *So what?*

"And…and because I love her." The words felt strange in his mouth. Kind of sticky. Like peanut butter that sometimes glued his tongue to the roof of his mouth. He had never actually said them before.

You don't love her, Ruth scoffed. *You just want to get into her pants.*

That stung, but he refused to take the bait this time. "No, Gram. I love her." He moved from the couch to the olive green armchair and sat. The macramé lampshade carved funky shadows on the ceiling above him. "I loved her the minute I laid eyes on her."

Don't be pathetic, Charlie. You have no idea what love is.

Charlie stared at Ruth's cracked portrait, his mind spinning. He spoke before he knew he even had words to say. "And whose fault is that?"

Don't you talk back to me, young man. Ruth's ragged voice had taken on a slightly panicky edge. Her grandson, usually so meek and compliant, had never challenged her before.

"Seriously, let's talk about why I don't know what love is, Gram. I can think of only one reason."

Silence from Ruth.

"You never loved me, Gram. Never."

I kept a roof over your head. I fed you.

"Only because you were obligated to. Not because you wanted to. You made sure I understood this very early on."

I clothed you.

Charlie burst into surprised laughter at this. "Clothed me? Sure, in the most basic sense. You purchased items of clothing for me from the thrift store every once in a while. Never anything new because that would eat into your bingo money, god forbid." He looked at the floor and scowled. "The thing is, Gram, I was the kid who showed up at school every day in dirty clothes that didn't fit me and shoes with holes in them because you were never around. You spent all your time at the bingo hall." His voice turned bitter. "A grandmother who loves her grandson doesn't neglect him, Gram. Doesn't treat him like you treated me."

Shut your hole, Charlie. I did the best I could. If you want to blame someone for your terrible life, blame your worthless mother and that no-good bastard she was with. Their heroin was more important to them than you ever were.

Charlie crossed his arms and continued to scowl at the floor.

Besides, you should be thanking me for playing bingo. How do you think I was able to leave you with a mortgage-free house and a bank account big enough to support you for the rest of your sad little life? Hell, I even set it up so that you don't have to worry about paying county or city bills; that happens automatically. You don't even have to think about it. Ruth paused. *You can't say that I didn't take care of you.*

Charlie knew when he'd been bested. Tears of frustration prickled behind his eyes. He blinked rapidly, still staring at the floor.

What, you're going to cry now? Ruth's ruined voice was starting to sound more strained and twangy, like a cello bow being dragged across out-of-tune strings. *Like a little baby?*

Charlie stood and resumed his pacing. Moving around helped him push the tears back. "No. I'm not crying."

Good boy, Ruth rasped.

Charlie paced in silence for a minute or two, then stopped in front of the TV and Ruth's portrait again. "I don't want to go to this party. But I also don't want to disappoint Sara." He reversed direction and went back to the phone table. He lifted the receiver again; the dial tone made a distant, tinny buzzing sound before he replaced it. "She made sure Pretty Boy invited me."

I think you know what you're going to do, boy. Why do you keep hemming and hawing?

"Because I'm also a little worried about running into Scott Schlosser again." Back to the TV he went. "It's his frat house, and he hates my guts."

Just avoid him, Ruth advised. *Stay away from the places he's most likely to be.*

"The bar," Charlie muttered. "Wherever the beer is." A memory stole over him: the night he'd gotten his concussion, and how those boys had stunk like stale beer. He was sure he could still smell it.

You don't drink anyway, so that shouldn't be difficult.

Charlie nodded. "You're right." He made one more loop around the living room. "All right, I'll go. I'll go because Sara wants me to go." His heart palpitated in his chest. He would keep her face in the forefront of his mind until he got there and found her; it was probably the only way he'd be able to do this without having a record-setting panic attack. *Sara wants me to go.*

Of course he would go.

CHAPTER SEVENTEEN
Saturday, October 7, 1989

Sara

The Sig Tau house was packed wall to wall with party guests. Pop music thumped in the background. The crowd around the beer keg in the backyard was a dozen deep. People held red Solo cups in the air as they squeezed sideways through the crowd. Big guys wearing flannel, smaller guys wearing sweaters, girls in stirrup pants or miniskirts – all holding beers, many holding cigarettes – all shouted to be heard over the cacophony.

Sara and Lauren stood in a corner near the door. Lauren was a vision in a coordinating acid-washed denim skirt and jacket and blue mock turtleneck. Her kinky black hair was a perfectly coiffed cloud around her head. Sara wore jeans and a simple light pink shirt with shoulderpads. Under Lauren's supervision, she'd used a curling iron on the ends of her hair and her bangs, and forged a side part on her skull. She looked like every female character in Beverly Hills 90210. *About this time next year, all these people are going to find out who Luke Perry is. And it will be glorious,* Sara mused.

"Why again are we standing in the corner?" Lauren asked, clearly impatient to get into the crowd and mingle.

"I want to keep an eye out for Charlie," Sara said. "I have a feeling he's going to have some anxiety about this party, so I want to catch him as soon as he gets here."

"Okay, well, I'm going to go get a beer and say hi to a few folks," Lauren said, bouncing on the balls of her white canvas Keds.

"Did you see the line at the keg?" Sara asked. "It'll take you at least an hour to get a beer."

Lauren grinned. "Don't you worry, I'll get my beer right away. The guy holding the tap is in my Statistics class, and he keeps asking me out. Maybe I'll say yes this time."

Sara raised her eyebrows, and Lauren flitted away. Sara surveyed the crowd and caught sight of Ben on the other side of the room. He saw her looking at him, grinned, and waved at her. Her heart melted, and she waved back. His dark mop of hair stood straight up in random chunks in the heat and humidity of the crowded room. *He looks particularly gorgeous tonight,* she thought.

She tore her eyes away and continued scanning the front room for Charlie. The room was packed so full that a single person's movement caused a ripple effect of ocean-like waves through the entire crowd. When one flannel-clad fellow near Sara tripped over someone's foot and went sprawling, Sara had only inches of space to step against a wall in order to avoid taking his entire beer to her face. *This party is out of control,* she thought. *Fire codes? What are those?*

She resumed her post in the corner and spied a familiar tall, dark ponytail walk in the front door. Shannon Plotnik's pale face was set as she pushed through the crowd, causing more rippling waves of people. She appeared to have a specific destination in mind. Sara, only ten or so feet away, watched her closely. *She looks like a woman on a mission,* she thought.

Shannon steadily made her way toward the kitchen. Sara made a quick decision to follow her. She took advantage of the wake Shannon left behind her in the crowd, rather than pushing through the masses of people herself. She felt a little like some sort of weird waterskier, being pulled down the wide hallway behind a fast and very purposeful boat.

Sara stopped where the hallway met the industrial-sized kitchen on the right side and the massive dining room to the left. Both rooms were as packed full of people as the front living room. In front of her, the hallway ended at a pair of sliding glass doors out to the backyard, where the keg was. Both doors were wide open for easy access to beer, and the cooler air pouring in was probably the only thing keeping partygoers in the house from passing out.

Sara stood on tiptoe to see if she could catch sight of Shannon. *There she is.* Her back was to Sara, standing near a scarred wooden dining table set up in the kitchen, where several Sig Tau men were sitting in mismatched chairs, playing drinking games with a battered deck of cards. Piles of beer cans sat on every surface around them, including the floor. Sara took a few steps into the kitchen to get a better look. Shannon was standing behind an old ladder-back chair currently occupied by Scott Schlosser. His beefy legs spilled over both sides of the chair's wooden seat.

Sara's heart skipped. *They're together,* she thought. *This is my chance to nail them. I can't let these two out of my sight.*

Shannon bent over and said something into Scott's ear. He nodded, took a quick shot of something clear – *probably vodka,* Sara thought, thinking of her mom – pushed his chair back, and stood. He tossed the cards he'd been holding on the table, and together he and Shannon stepped away from the table.

Sara followed them through the kitchen and up the back stairs. With each step, the distinctly male odor of dirty socks and sweaty old athletic equipment grew stronger. Heat and humidity from the masses downstairs only made the smell more pungent. Sara took shallow breaths so she wouldn't gag.

The back stairs opened on the second floor dormitory area; a rectangular hallway opening onto roughly two dozen double sleeping rooms that encircled a central area with a large bathroom and a study. Sara caught a glimpse of Scott and Shannon before they rounded the corner at the other end of the short hallway. Sara ran quietly on tiptoes to catch up with them, and peeked around the corner just in time to see them disappear into a room about midway down the long hall.

Gotcha, Sara thought. *That must be Scott's room. I bet they've got all kinds of evidence in there. If I'm lucky, they've even got notes about the bombing and lists of supplies.*

Sara pondered her options for a moment. *Do I confront them?* she wondered. *Should I knock on the door and tell them I know what they're doing?* Panic squeezed her stomach at this idea, and she wished she'd brought Ben or Lauren up here with her.

She decided to see if she could hear them talking through the door. She tiptoed up to Scott's room, the only closed door on this stretch of hallway, and carefully pressed her ear against the solid wood. She could hear the sounds of Scott's deep voice and Shannon's quieter voice, but couldn't make out the words they were saying. Thumping bass from the music playing downstairs didn't help.

After a few minutes of hearing voice sounds but no words, Sara decided that the only way she was really going to catch them red-handed was by being bold. By confronting them. Heart pounding, she grasped the brass doorknob and gently tried to turn it. It wouldn't budge. She tried turning the knob the other way for good measure, with the same result. *Crap. It's locked.*

She gathered her courage and finally pounded on the door with her fist as hard as she could. "I know what you're doing in there!" she shouted.

Scott's voice, previously muted, suddenly roared, "Occupied! What the fuck!"

Sara ignored this and kept pounding.

In very short order the door flew open, and a mostly naked Scott Schlosser stood there, beady eyes blazing. The room was pitch black behind him. His massive body was covered with thick brown hair from his neck to his ankles. A wrinkled towel had been hastily wrapped around his waist. Sara, horrified, stepped back. "Oh my god," she blurted.

Scott recognized her from their confrontation in Bio Lab. "What the fuck do you want?" Scott snarled. "Fixing to get me kicked out of my frat too, bitch?"

"I—I'm sorry," Sara stammered. She raised her hands to chest level in an "I come in peace" gesture. "I thought you were someone else. I must have the wrong room."

"Fucking right you have the wrong room. You're not even supposed to be up here, you stupid cunt." Schlosser slammed the door in her face and reengaged the lock.

Sara stood there a minute with her hands still up by her chest. She'd had it all wrong. These two weren't planning a bombing. They were carrying on a standard, run-of-the-mill secret fuckbuddy relationship. And if she stopped long enough to actually think for a minute, it made sense.

Scott was the guy Pam the Kappa Mom had kicked out of Shannon's room.

They had clandestine meetings in populated public areas.

Sara didn't know why Shannon had been digging in planters on Library Mall, but it occurred to her now that maybe it wasn't because she was looking to build the biggest possible bomb. In fact, in retrospect, she'd looked like she was maybe searching for something she'd lost. A piece of jewelry from a fuckbuddy, perhaps.

I was wrong this entire time. I can't believe it. Completely deflated, Sara made her way back to the stairs and slowly descended to the hot and stuffy kitchen. She seriously considered leaving the party and heading back to Chad to wallow in the misery of knowing her search for the Library Mall Bomber was about to start over again at the beginning – but then she spotted Charlie.

He was standing at the other end of the wide hallway, just inside the front door, and looking terrified. He had tried to tame his coarse hair with a comb, which made his ears appear to stick out even further from his head. He wore a button-down green plaid collared shirt, a pair of khaki pants, and the red canvas

Cons he'd worn on the first day of classes. "Charlie!" she shouted over the music, waving.

Relief washed over his pitted face when he finally saw her. The big gash on his forehead was nearly healed now, the old scabs falling away to reveal pearly new pink skin. The bruises and black eyes were completely gone. Sara and Charlie moved fitfully toward each other through the crowd, finally meeting up in the middle of the front foyer. "Hey Sara," he shouted over all the noise.

Sara leaned in closer to him. *Is that…Old Spice?* "I'm so glad you came! How are you? Okay?"

He nodded.

"Good," she yelled. "Let's go get you a beer. Maybe that will help calm your nerves." She took his hand – she felt it shaking a little – and pulled him back down the packed hallway.

Finally they were outside in the backyard, where it was much cooler and quieter, and there was more room to move. Sara marched up to the keg line and stood on her tiptoes. She waved at Lauren standing next to the keg, talking to the brown-haired guy with the tap. Presumably her would-be suitor in Statistics class. "Lo!"

Lauren looked around at the sound of her name and grinned when she saw Sara. "What's up? Need a beer?"

"I need two," Sara shouted, holding up two fingers. "Charlie's here!" She pointed at Charlie, who was standing awkwardly in the corner of the yard, next to a ramshackle wooden fence.

"You got it!" Lauren held two red Solo cups for Statistics Guy to fill, then asked the crowd to pass the cups back. They did; the cups surfed their way toward her above the crowd, and she caught them deftly when they got to her. "Thanks, Lo! I have something to tell you later!"

Lauren gave her a little salute and turned her attention back to Statistics Guy. *He's kind of cute,* Sara observed. *Pretty green eyes. I hope she says yes next time he asks her out.*

Sara brought the beers back to Charlie, and handed him one. "Here you go."

"Thanks," he said, and took a tentative sip.

The look on his face made her chuckle. "Not a beer drinker?"

"This would be my first beer," he admitted. "It tastes kind of weird."

"You get used to it," Sara said, talking to Charlie but looking around at the people hanging out in the backyard. The air was chilly, but not unbearably so. "Oh, hey, before I forget – are you coming to the Paws for a Cause fundraiser next Saturday?"

"What's that?" Charlie asked, then belched. "Sorry. You were right, beer is pretty easy to get used to. I kind of like it."

"It's a pet adoption event that Kappa and Sig Tau are hosting on Library Mall. People can come and adopt cats and dogs, raising money for the Dane County Humane Society. There will be hot drinks for sure, not sure about food."

"Oh, right, I think I heard something about that last year," Charlie said and took another large gulp of beer.

That's going down awfully easily, she thought. "Yeah, it's an annual thing. It starts at nine o'clock on Saturday morning."

"Are you going?" Charlie asked.

"Of course," Sara said. "Lauren is chair of the planning committee – the first freshman ever to lead the event. I wouldn't miss it."

"Maybe," Charlie said. His cup was empty. "Can I get another one, do you think?"

Sara gave him her cup. "Here, take mine. I'll go get a couple more." Two more full cups crowdsurfed their way to her, and when she returned, Charlie's second beer was empty. She gave him another, his third in ten minutes, and wondered if she should be concerned.

"You're right, this is helping calm my nerves," he said. "I was so nervous. I almost didn't come."

"Panic attack?" she asked, sipping her own beer. It was tangy and sour, and the carbonation bubbles covered her entire tongue. She loved that sensation.

Charlie nodded. "Yeah."

"So what made you decide to brave it?"

Charlie was silent for a few seconds, then he downed the rest of his beer and looked at his cup. "I think I need another one of these."

Reluctantly, Sara got him another beer. "Maybe you should slow down, Charlie. If you don't drink much, all this beer in such a short time is going to hit you like a freight train."

Charlie shrugged and drank, then burped again.

"So? How did you talk yourself into defying your anxiety and coming tonight?" Sara asked. She detected a bit of a sway in his stance. *That's it, no more beer for him*, Sara thought.

"The only reason I came tonight is because I knew you were going to be here." The whites of Charlie's eyes were starting to turn pink.

Sara smiled, assuming he meant because they were becoming such good friends. "Oh, that's awesome. I'm glad."

Charlie shook his head, dislodging a couple chunks of his carefully combed hair. "No, that's not what I mean."

Sara was confused. "Okay, what do you mean?"

Charlie swayed a bit more dramatically on his feet; she could see the alcohol was in full effect already. "What I mean is…I mean…you are the only reason I do anything."

A pit opened in Sara's belly. *Oh, no.*

"I'm crazy about you, Sara. I've loved you from the minute I laid eyes on you," Charlie slurred. "If it weren't for you, I would fail Bio 101 because you are the. only. reason —" He hit his palm with his fist to emphasize these words. "– I bother going to class."

"Charlie," Sara started.

"I'm not done," Charlie pronounced, pointer finger of his right hand in the air. "You're nicer to me than anyone has been in my. entire. life." Fist in palm again. "I don't want you to be with Ben." His eyes were pointed in the general direction of her face, but he clearly couldn't focus them. "I want you to be with me. We should be together, boyfriend and girlfriend."

Goddammit, Sara thought. *This was not part of the plan.* Her heart broke knowing that she was about to break his heart. She took a deep breath, and then took his hand. "Listen, Charlie. I love you, too."

His entire face brightened. "You do?"

"Yes," she said. "But I love you as a friend. Just as a really good friend, Charlie."

The brightness promptly fell out of his face, and his hopeful smile disappeared. He looked crushed.

"We can't be together, Charlie. Not the way you want to be. I'm so sorry."

"Because of Ben?" he mumbled, staring at the grass under his feet. It was starting to turn brown in the crisp October air.

"No. He's not the reason why." She paused. "It's – it's complicated."

"I really don't think it is," Charlie said. "Either you want to be with me, or you don't. I guess you don't," he said and pushed past her, stumbling back toward the house. His face had turned red; Sara suspected it was because he was trying not to cry.

"Charlie!" She called after him. "Where are you going?" *Dear god, he's drunk out of his mind!*

He didn't answer her. He staggered inside – and right into the waiting arms of Scott Schlosser.

Charlie

"Another shot, Chuck?" The tinkling sound of glass hitting glass pierced Charlie's ears as Schlosser poured another round. The air was cool and damp, the noise of the party upstairs muffled. Charlie propped himself up against the bar and blinked at Scott, trying to clear his vision. The high egress windows were covered in black plastic; the only light came from several neon beer signs hung on the stone walls. He couldn't quite remember how he ended up in the basement, but he was glad to be away from the crowded party.

"Oh man…" Charlie moaned. He held his head in his hands and leaned his bony elbows on the makeshift bar's laminate surface. One elbow slid in a puddle of spilled vodka, causing Charlie to lose control of his head and bonk it on the bar. He was still recovering from his concussion and would definitely feel that tomorrow – but right now there was no pain. "OH MAN!" he moaned louder, then laughed helplessly. He looked at Scott with heavily lidded, bloodshot eyes. Pimples stood out like stoplights on his pale skin. "I think…I think I'm wasted," he slurred in disbelief.

Schlosser grinned. "I think so, buddy. Have another." He pushed a fully loaded shot glass toward Charlie. Scott picked up his own shot glass and waited. His eyes had a predatory glint to them, but Charlie didn't see that. He was busy trying to drown his misery in vodka. *Sara doesn't want to be with me.*

He slowly turned his attention to the shot glass in front of him. He focused on picking it up, his forehead wrinkled in saturated concentration. His hand was shaking, causing a little of the clear liquid to slosh over the lip of the shot glass. *Can't spill any. Gotta be cooooool.* He grinned sloppily at Scott.

Schlosser's lip curled in disgust. He held his own shot up high. "A toast," he said, his voice gravelly. "A toast to Sig Tau, the best brotherhood on the whole motherfucking campus."

"I'll drink to that," Charlie slurred again, as he had with each shot and each toast. He put the glass to his lips and swallowed the vodka in a single gulp. He didn't even feel the burn anymore. He slammed the glass back down on the bar and wiped his thin mouth with his forearm.

Scott had already taken his shot and stood looking at Charlie with clear distaste when Jeff Nicholson, he of the "beer before everything, especially school" mentality, walked into the room. "Dude. What are you doing?"

"My friend Chuck and I are having a few shots," Schlosser said. "And I was just remembering that I never did properly kick his ass for getting me kicked out of Bio 101."

"Since when did you ever care about Bio 101? Or any class?" Nicholson asked. Trying to distract Scott, he suggested, "Let's not waste our time on this twerp and go get a beer upstairs."

"Nah. This little cocksucker has to pay. I'm not gonna graduate because of him."

"It's your show, dude," Nicholson said and disappeared up the stairs.

"Oooh,...make the world stop spinning." Charlie swayed alarmingly on his barstool.

Schlosser moved closer to Charlie, putting one massive arm around his thin shoulders. "C'mon, Chuck. You need to lay down."

Charlie didn't know where Schlosser was taking him, and he didn't much care. Schlosser was right; he needed a place to lie down and cover his head. He looked blearily around, seeing only vague dark shapes around him. Schlosser's arm removed itself from his shoulders, and he stood swaying. The room would not stop spinning. *I think I need to throw up soon,* he thought.

"Feeling okay?" Schlosser stood directly in front of Charlie, a shadowy mountain in the dark room.

Charlie lifted his head with some difficulty; it seemed to weigh a metric ton. His ears buzzed. "I…"

Charlie's jaw exploded. He didn't see Schlosser's boulder-sized fist coming at him in the darkness. Charlie's head snapped back – this time the pain seared right through his muddled brain like a hot knife – and he lost his balance. With nary a sound, he landed ass-first on the cold concrete floor, cracking his tailbone.

Schlosser stood over him, his fists clenching and his biceps bulging. "I want to make sure we have an understanding, Chuck." He punctuated this with a kick to Charlie's ribs, which sent Charlie rolling like a convenience store hot dog. "You are the reason I got kicked out of Bio 101." Schlosser took a step and delivered another kick, this time to Charlie's left kidney. Charlie would be pissing blood for a week.

Charlie curled up in the fetal position, white spots floating behind his eyes. He shook his head, mumbling, "No no no no no…"

"Oh yeah, you little pussy." Schlosser squatted next to Charlie's head and grabbed a handful of sweaty straw-like hair. He yanked Charlie's head back. "Look at me. Open your fucking eyes and look at me, motherfucker."

Charlie, still not sure what was happening, forced his eyelids open. As they creaked apart, he could see Schlosser's eyes. They seemed to glow red. Terror streaked through him, making his fingertips tingle and his stomach roil. He tried to swallow.

"Now that I have your attention, I will repeat myself. You got me kicked out of Bio 101. And now…well, now I'm not gonna graduate this year because I won't have enough remedial science credits. And that, Chuck, is a major problem. For you." Schlosser still held Charlie's hair in one hand. His other hand dangled between his knees like an Easter ham.

Charlie, his eyes rolling like a horse's in terror, tried to agree. Instead he opened his mouth and vomited. The evening's partially-digested meal, a Salisbury steak TV dinner, spewed out in a mess of vodka and beer and landed squarely on Scott Schlosser's Adidas.

"Fuck!" Schlosser promptly let go of Charlie's hair and jumped back, snarling. "Oh, you're gonna pay for that, fucker. Jesus fucking-A CHRIST!" He hopped the perimeter of the dark basement room, trying to shake Charlie's puke from his shoes.

Charlie just lay on the floor on his back, dazed. His head felt a bit clearer, but the pain was intensifying. His tailbone throbbed.

One size 12 planted next to his shoulder, and then another. His eyes followed the massive legs up, over the round bulging chest, to Schlosser's wide and angrily distorted face. "Think you can puke on my shoes?" he snarled. Then he squatted and sat on Charlie's chest.

Pinned, barely able to breathe under Schlosser's weight, Charlie thrashed his legs in an effort to dislodge Schlosser from his chest. He could feel his own vomit seeping into his right sleeve, warm and slimy.

Schlosser, enraged at Charlie's defiance, started throwing punches. Each landed with a meaty thud on a different area of Charlie's head. One to the right cheekbone whipped Charlie's head to the left. Another to the left temple sent Charlie's head back to the right. Schlosser kept punching until Charlie's legs stopped moving. He sat on Charlies chest for a few seconds before standing up. He looked down at Charlie, emotionless. "Fucker," he muttered, then turned and disappeared.

After about half an hour, in the cold quiet of the dark basement storage room, Charlie stirred. He tried to open his eyes, found that one only opened halfway and the other wouldn't open at all. He groaned and sat up. His head spun and throbbed, and his body hurt from head to toe. The distinctive reek of puke wafted around him. *I have to get out of here.* He staggered to standing and felt his way to the door. Schlosser had left it open, and Charlie followed the dim light through the basement. The sounds of the party beckoned him, and he followed them up the stairs. He emerged into the packed kitchen and beelined for the front door. The music pounded, and the thick air reeked of beer, cigarettes, and sweaty bodies. His stomach turned again. He looked at nothing but the floor as he pushed through the crowd.

"Charlie!" He heard Sara shout his name from somewhere behind him. The last thing he wanted was for her to stare at him like he was a carnival sideshow. He limped through the front door and disappeared into the dark night, headed for the safety of home.

CHAPTER EIGHTEEN
Sunday, October 8, 1989

Charlie

His own eyes, bruised, nearly swollen shut, stared back at him. It was well past midnight. He'd sat on the couch for the last two hours, staring at the muted TV and gathering up the courage to look in a mirror. He was sober now, but he wished he had a beer to sip on. The pain was incredible.

Both of his eyes were hugely swollen, but he'd managed to crack them both open. There was a large scrape across his chin; it had probably dragged across the rough concrete floor after Schlosser kicked him in the ribs. *Great, it matches the gash on my forehead.* His nose, also bruised and swollen, now had a subtle flattened look to it that suggested Mike Tyson won the match. One eyebrow was split open; blood had dried in streaks over his swollen left eye and down his face. Angry bruises crawled up and down both sides of his jaw. All of his teeth appeared to be present and intact. *Thank God for small favors.*

He gingerly lifted his blood-soaked shirt, and winced when he saw the perfect red shoeprint on his skinny ribcage. He suspected one or two ribs might be cracked; every breath he took sent fresh waves of pain through his body. He pulled the shirt over his head – very slowly, very carefully, clenching his teeth against the pain – and dropped it in the bathtub. Then he retrieved the hydrogen peroxide and cotton balls from the medicine cabinet behind the mirror and went to work cleaning himself up.

Slowly, methodically, he mopped the blood from his face and disinfected his wounds, ignoring the sting. Bloody cotton balls piled higher and higher in the small bathroom garbage can. Finally he finished cleaning, and carefully placed bandages over the wounds on his eyebrow and chin. He took several ibuprofen to help take the edge off the pain, and inspected his handiwork in the mirror. *I probably should go to the emergency room, but this will do for now.*

He slowly limped his way back downstairs and sat – carefully, so as not to aggravate his bruised tailbone – on the couch again. His gaze fell on the muted television; images from old episodes of M*A*S*H flicked by on the screen (he could own all eleven seasons on VHS for only $24.95), but he didn't really see them. He turned inside himself to take a look at the real damage done tonight.

Sara didn't want him. And now their friendship was wrecked. *What the fuck was I thinking? I wasn't going to tell her how I felt. Now look what I've done.*

Ruth: *You were thinking with your dick, kid.*

He had to admit that Ruth was right on that count. "All the beer didn't help either," he mumbled.

Ruth: *I always said that alcohol is the devil's brew.*

He hadn't taken Schlosser's helpful advice and watched his back – handing Schlosser another spectacular opportunity to kick his ass. *That fucker has put his paws on me for the last time,* he thought.

Ruth: *So what are you going to do about it, Charlie?*

I don't know, Gram. What can I do? He's twice my size.

That doesn't matter, Charlie. What matters is that you're smarter than he is. If you can't solve your problem with brute force, then you have to use your brains.

But…you always say I couldn't find my way out of a paper bag.

I just told you that to keep you in line, Charlie, Ruth rasped. *A kid who believes he's stupid is easy to control. Truth is, you always reminded me of your grandfather; he was a very intelligent man. Your shit-for-brains mother, not so much.*

Charlie's gaze gradually focused on the muted Time-Life commercial. He recognized the scene in the series finale in which the 4077th M*A*S*H is attacked by mortars, and one explodes directly in front of Father Mulcahy as he tries to free a bunch of POWs – and inspiration struck.

I got it, Gram. You're right, I can outsmart this motherfucker. He and all of his fraternity buddies are going to learn a very valuable lesson: you don't get very far in life being a bully.

Ruth: *Yes. You got it. That's my boy.* The pride in Ruth's ruined voice was unmistakable.

Charlie's heart swelled. *Thanks, Gram.*

Ruth didn't respond, but that was okay. His head, his face, and his tailbone still throbbed with pain; he knew there would be no sleep tonight. Instead he would use that pain – hone it, sharpen it like a blade – to help him formulate his new plan. *They're all gonna pay.*

Sara

"They were doing WHAT?!" Lauren shrieked.

"Ssshhh," Sara shushed her, giggling.

Wide-eyed, Lauren covered her mouth and nose with her hands. "I can't believe Shannon is doing the nasty with that asshole! And you saw him naked!" She dissolved into helpless laughter.

They were sitting across from each other at a table in the Chadbourne dining hall, eating breakfast. Lauren had an entire spread of scrambled eggs, bacon, and toast in front of her, along with a big glass of orange juice. "A big breakfast is the best hangover cure," she declared before heartily chomping a piece of crispy bacon.

Sara had her usual bowl of Froot Loops – except this morning, she'd mixed in a few Apple Jacks. *That's me, living on the edge,* she thought.

"So Scott and Shannon are not the bombers," Sara said glumly.

"Aren't you glad you didn't call the police on them?" Lauren asked. "Detective Dingleberry would have had your head if you did." She took a bite of her eggs. "Mmmm…so good."

Sara nodded. "Yes, but now I'm back at square one with less than a week to go. And no idea where to look."

Lauren leaned on one elbow and waggled her fork in Sara's direction. "It's gotta be someone with a connection to the Kappa house or the Sig Tau house," she said.

"Agreed, but who? Who else is angry enough to kill eighty-something people with a giant pipe bomb?"

"I don't know," Lauren said through a mouthful of buttered toast. "There's gotta be somebody. A pledge who didn't get in, maybe?"

"Maybe," Sara said, listlessly stirring her cereal into mush.

"What else is on your mind?" Lauren asked.

"I'm worried about Charlie," Sara said.

She told Lauren about seeing the left side of Charlie's face, covered in blood, as he made his way out of the crowded Sig Tau house. Horrified, she'd tried to get to him; by the time she reached the door, he had disappeared.

"What did you do?" Lauren asked.

Sara stood there, not really knowing what to do. Finally she decided to find Ben; maybe he could help figure out what had happened. She ducked around dozens of sweaty bodies as she wandered the house looking for him. People had started to pass out where they stood; one couch had no fewer than six unconscious bodies piled on it.

Finally she found Ben in the kitchen, playing drinking games with the same guys she'd seen sitting there earlier. Without a word, she took his arm and pulled him up out of his chair, through the crowds, and into the backyard. The line around the keg had diminished considerably; Lauren and Statistics Guy were nowhere in sight. She was too agitated to notice that the air had cooled several degrees in the hour since she'd followed Charlie inside.

186

"What the hell, Sara?" Ben demanded. "I was in the middle of a game, and not the Asshole for once in my life."

She shook her head and waved a hand, dismissing his complaints. "Sorry, but not sorry — I really need your help."

Ben sobered a bit. "Okay, what's up?" His breath rose in white steam with each word.

"It's Charlie," she said tears welling in her eyes. "He just left, and he looked like he'd been beaten up."

Ben's mahogany eyes widened. "Beaten up? Here?"

Sara nodded. "I think so. I lost track of him for an hour, maybe a little less. He was completely wasted after chugging like five beers in fifteen minutes. I don't know where he went, but he was fine before, and all bloody when I saw him leaving the house. I couldn't catch him to ask him what happened."

"Jesus," Ben said, and ran a hand through his dark hair.

"I need you to help me find out what happened," she pleaded.

Ben nodded. "Okay. I'll ask around, see if anybody knows something. I can't for the life of me imagine who would do that to Charlie, though." He paused. "Unless…"

"What?"

Ben shook his head. "It's probably nothing, but I was thinking about Scott Schlosser. Remember how he'd tried to pick a fight with Charlie that one day in Bio Lab? Hilliard kicked him out of class after that."

"I do remember," she said. The idea that she might have put a target on Charlie's back by standing up for him that day made her a little sick.

"I don't know anything for sure," Ben cautioned. "But I plan to find out."

"So Schlosser isn't the bomber, but he beat Charlie into a bloody pulp?" Lauren asked, incredulous.

Sara shrugged. "I don't know that for sure. I'm waiting for an update from Ben. I'm hoping Charlie comes to Bio Lab on Tuesday too, so I can see him with my own eyes, maybe ask him what happened."

"I hope he's okay," Lauren said.

Me too.

CHAPTER NINETEEN
Tuesday, October 10, 1989

Sara

Charlie didn't show up to Bio Lab.

When Ben arrived, she asked him what he'd learned. He didn't have any news to share. "Our legacy members just left last night," he said apologetically. "Everyone's been partying nonstop and super hung over. We have a chapter meeting Thursday night – I promise I'll ask around while everyone's there."

She didn't much like his answer, but couldn't do much about it. So she sat, too distracted to listen to Hilliard talk about diffusion and osmosis experiments. She didn't know where Charlie was, or what exactly had happened to him, and she was consumed with worry. *My god, how badly was he hurt that he didn't come to Bio Lab to see me?*

Finally she couldn't take it any longer; she stuffed her textbook into her backpack and stood up. Hilliard didn't notice; he was facing the chalkboard, drawing a crude diagram of a cell. The chalk gave an ungodly screech as he made the curved line of the circle.

"Where are you going?" Ben and Lauren turned and whispered in unison.

"I have to find Charlie," she whispered back, and slipped out of the room. As she hurried through the halls and down the stairs, she hoped she wasn't putting the other Sara's grade in jeopardy by leaving early.

She left Noland Hall and walked quickly down Mills Street, trying not to imagine the worst. *I'll check his house first. If he's not there, I'll check St. Mary's Hospital.*

Sara power-walked that mile in record time. When she turned the corner at Mound Street, she decided to jog the last two and a half blocks. Finally she reached 1326 Mound and took the front porch stairs two at a time. Breathing hard, she knocked.

No answer.

Trying to keep the panic at bay, Sara pounded on the door. "Charlie!" She tried to look through the windows on either side of the door, and discovered that the miniblinds had been drawn.

She looked through the beveled glass in the door again and thought she saw movement. She pounded again. "Charlie, it's Sara! Please open the door!"

She watched a dark shape slowly approach. The deadbolt disengaged with a *clack*. The door creaked open. Charlie's face, battered almost beyond recognition, appeared in the six-inch opening between the door and the frame. His coarse blond hair stood out from his head in chunks. He was expressionless.

Sara gasped, shocked at the extent of his injuries. His face was covered with brutal new scrapes and bruises – a whole new set on top of the older injuries from his mishap two weeks ago. His eyes were swollen to the point where he had only slits to see through. Her hand flew to her mouth. "Oh my god. Are – are you all right?"

Charlie closed and then cracked open his black and puffy eyes in a slow blink. "What do you want, Sara?"

"I missed you in Bio Lab, so I wanted to come check on you," she said. She thought he might need cosmetic surgery to repair some of the damage to his face; his nose looked like it had doubled in size. "You left so quickly on Saturday night."

"And now you know why," he muttered, and moved to shut the door.

She stuck her hi-top Reebok in the jamb, blocking the door open. "What happened?"

"Nothing that you need to worry about," he said. "Now please move."

Sara stood her ground. "I'm not moving until you tell me who did this to you."

"It doesn't matter." His voice was a careful monotone. "Why do you even care?"

"Charlie. Of course I care," she said, perplexed.

"You can say something, but saying it doesn't make it the truth," Charlie said. "Please move. Now."

"Would I be here if I didn't care, Charlie?" Sara had gone from terrified to frustrated in a lamb's breath. "I spent all weekend worrying myself sick over you! And when you didn't show up to Bio Lab, I left class to come here and make sure you were okay. Why are you acting like this?"

Charlie didn't respond.

Something occurred to Sara. "Is this about our conversation in the backyard at Sig Tau? Do you feel like I rejected you?"

Silence – although she thought she saw a hint of a reaction in his eyes. What she could see of them, anyway.

"I meant what I said, Charlie. I consider you a very good friend – and I thought you felt the same about me. I thought a connection like ours would be enough for two wounded spirits with so much in common. I'm sorry that we can't be together like you want, but I do have reasons. And they are complicated."

"Goodbye, Sara."

Hurt, Sara stepped back. Charlie closed the door. Her heart made the same noise the deadbolt made when Charlie flipped it back into place: to her, it sounded like a jail cell closing.

Charlie

That may have been the hardest two minutes of my life, he thought as he reengaged the deadbolt and limped back to the dinette table. He wasn't mad at Sara; he'd discovered that there's a certain perspective that comes with making big decisions, and her rejection just didn't bother him that much anymore. Not really. It broke his heart to see her upset, though.

He *wanted* to talk to her, tell her what happened to him; he knew she would understand, and maybe even help him.

But she would not understand or approve of his Project. So he did what he had to do to make her leave. She couldn't be allowed to see what he was up to.

He gazed fondly at the large cardboard box on the table, which was full of items he'd picked up at the Quality True Value hardware store, taking a mental inventory to make sure he had all the supplies he needed for his Project. He touched his beloved new Casio digital wristwatch, which lay on top of the jumble in the box. All he needed to do was visit to the quarry tomorrow night to procure the really powerful stuff, then put them all together. Like a puzzle.

Your Project, Ruth croaked.

Yep, my Project, he thought. *You're gonna get a real bang out of it, Gram. Everyone is. Just wait and see.*

CHAPTER TWENTY
Thursday, October 12, 1989

Sara

"For the love of Pete, will you please sit down?" Lauren implored Sara, who was restlessly pacing around the room in a loop that took her from the phone on her desk to the window to her closet and back to the phone again. "You're making it really difficult to study." She sat at her desk with her Statistics book open in front of her. "I have an exam tomorrow."

"Sorry," Sara said and sat at the head of her bed, closest to the phone. "I'm waiting for Ben to call."

As if on cue, the phone rang. Sara answered it. "Ben?"

Lauren gathered up her book and papers and marched out of the room with a huff.

"Hey," Ben said.

"Did you find out anything about what happened to Charlie?" Sara didn't bother with the niceties. Her anxiety was in high gear.

"I was right," he said. "It was Schlosser."

"Oh no," Sara breathed. Her heart had been hollowed out.

"After Charlie left you in the backyard, he apparently ran into Schlosser in the house, who somehow talked him into joining him down in the basement. There's a bar down there, but we didn't use it that night; I'm sure Schlosser thought it was the perfect place for a little privacy."

Sara thought of the horrific injuries to Charlie's face; tears welled in her eyes and fell down her cheeks.

"Jeff Nicholson said he went looking for Schlosser during the party and found them both at the basement bar. Apparently Schlosser was giving Charlie shots of vodka, one after another. He said something to Nicholson about teaching Charlie a lesson for getting him, quote, 'kicked out of Bio 101.' I guess Schlosser can't graduate this year because of that."

"Schlosser got his own stupid ass kicked out of Bio!" Sara burst out, her voice cracking.

"I know that," Ben said. "Charlie didn't get him kicked out of class — but Schlosser's just the kind of asshole who waits until his senior year to take a required 100-level science class. And then, because he thinks he's hot shit, the rules don't apply to him — so he was invited to leave Physics 103, Chemistry 103, and Biology 101 in a single week. Those are the remedial science classes he had to choose from for his major, and he was banned from every one of them. Bio was his last chance, and poor Charlie gets the blame."

"So Schlosser beat him up," Sara said. "He did a hell of a job, too…you should have seen him, Ben. He was a mess." She gave a sigh that sounded more like a sob. "I feel like this is all my fault."

"It's not your fault, Sara," Ben said.

"I stood up to Schlosser in class that day, and made things worse for Charlie. I invited him to the party. I rejected him when he told me how he felt about me." The tears flowed freely now.

"One other thing Jeff told me," Ben said. "I guess Schlosser was behind Charlie's injuries a couple weeks ago too."

"WHAT?!" Sara shouted, and stood up without realizing that's what she was doing. "His concussion? That nasty gash on his forehead?" She covered her own forehead with her hand.

"Yeah. Schlosser, Jeff, and a couple other guys were hanging out in Peace Park after skipping classes and drinking all day. It was the same night we had our first date. Anyway, they were loitering and looking for trouble. Charlie happened to walk by, and they ganged up on him. Pushed him around some and then caused him to trip and hit his head on a retaining wall."

Sara had to sit back down before her legs gave out. "Oh, my god," she moaned, and moved her hand from her forehead to her eyes. "I had no idea he was going through any of this."

"Don't take it personally. Wasn't it you who told me that it's just easier to keep people at arm's length? Something like that?"

He's right, Sara realized. *I of all people should recognize victim behavior when I see it. I've lived it, for Chrissake. I can't believe I missed it.*

"Sara? You there?"

She sighed. "Yes, I'm here. I was just thinking about how I should have known what was going on."

"I don't know how you could," Ben said. "Give yourself a little grace."

I don't think I can, she thought. *I don't deserve it.*

Charlie

The M9 bus screeched to a halt at the corner of Tiller and Cosgrove Roads. Charlie stepped off and began the mile walk to Hammersley Quarry under cover of darkness. It had been a long ride to the outskirts of town, requiring two bus transfers; his tailbone was killing him. Charlie was glad to be up and walking around.

He carefully shouldered his backpack, wincing when one of the objects inside poked his cracked ribs, and limped east toward Fitchrona Road. The night air was chilly, but Charlie was oblivious in his black sweatsuit, gloves, and stocking cap. He was ready to blend into the night should he see anyone during his clandestine journey.

It took a long time walking slowly along deserted rural roads – some of them not yet paved – but he finally arrived at a huge painted wooden sign next to a gravel driveway that said HAMMERSLEY QUARRY – FITCHBURG, WI – VISITORS CHECK IN AT TRAILER. The gravel driveway opened onto a small parking lot; a doublewide construction trailer sat on the opposite end of the lot, next to the entrance to the quarry itself.

Charlie's ribs and tailbone throbbed, but he kept moving. If he took too much time, there would be no bus back to Madison and he would be stuck here.

He made his way to the trailer, which stood dark and empty this late on a Thursday night. He walked around the perimeter of the trailer, looking for a cabinet or some other form of storage that might contain the stuff he needed for his Project. There was nothing. *Must be somewhere in the quarry*, he thought. *Not too far in, I hope.*

A steel arm gate blocked vehicle access into the quarry, but Charlie simply walked around it, past the signs that said SAFETY FIRST – HARD HATS REQUIRED and followed the gravel road down a gentle slope. About two hundred yards in, he encountered a twenty-foot square steel storage building on the left side of the road. The building had two doors: an ordinary access door that swung open and closed, and a single-car garage door. During the workday, workers would be able to pull in here on their way into or out of the quarry and pick up or drop off supplies. Charlie knew he'd found what he was looking for.

He limped up to the doors and inspected them. The garage door didn't have any outwardly visible locking mechanism, and when Charlie bent over and tried to raise it – setting his ribs off again in the process and very nearly crying out in pain – it wouldn't budge. *Latched tight from the inside*, Charlie thought.

The access door, however, looked much more promising. Charlie didn't see the deadbolt or latch-and-padlock he'd expected, just a single locking doorknob. *Is it really going to be that easy?* he wondered. *I brought these damn boltcutters for nothing.*

He was glad he brought the crowbar, however. He pulled it out of his backpack and stuck the flat notched end between the door and its frame, easily disengaging the latch and popping the door open without so much as a scratch.

He stepped inside the cold and pitch dark shed and pulled a small flashlight out of his backpack. He turned it on, shooting a bright beam of light on the wall opposite him. The wall was covered floor to ceiling with wooden shelves, which were crammed with cardboard boxes of all sizes. To his left stood various large, heavy-looking tools he couldn't name, and on his right he could see large wooden crates that he guessed held some of the more powerful stuff. Hanging on the wall behind him, next to the door, was a clipboard that held what looked like sign-in and sign-out sheets.

He turned his attention back to the smaller boxes, looking for two in particular. Thanks to the books he'd been reading during his daily visits to the library since last Sunday, he knew exactly what he was looking for. Fortunately the boxes were well-labeled, and it didn't take long for him to find them. He gingerly pulled them off the shelves and tried to stuff them in his backpack. He didn't have enough room in the bag for the boxes and the tools he brought with him, so he pulled the bolt cutters and crowbar out and hid them among the heavier freestanding tools. He finished filling his backpack, zipped it closed, and backed out of the shed – taking care to close and lock the door behind him.

His heart skipped as he limped his way up the hill and down the deserted roads that would take him back to his bus stop – where the M9 bus would pick him up and take him back to Madison. His entire body hurt, but he didn't care. He finally had everything he needed to start assembling his Project.

He couldn't wait.

CHAPTER TWENTY-ONE
Friday, October 13, 1989

Sara

It was a cool and cloudy morning, and once again Sara found herself standing on Charlie's front porch, knocking on his door. She was tired; every time she'd managed to fall asleep last night, vivid images of Charlie taking brutal blows from Scott Schlosser startled her awake again. She still felt terrible for not realizing what was going on, and she felt compelled to tell Charlie that she finally knew – and that she was sorry.

While she waited, she looked longingly at the cute red brick story-and-a-half next door. Her house. *If I somehow manage to succeed in my mission tomorrow, will I see it again in 2019? Will Bat be sitting in the front window waiting for me?*

Charlie didn't come to the door. She knocked again, and tried to look through the glass in the door with her hands cupped around her eyes. The glass was beveled, distorting the shapes inside and casting rainbows everywhere; she couldn't see much of anything.

She stepped to her left, the worn wooden floorboards creaking under her weight, and peered into the window next to the door. The miniblinds had been pulled up to let in the sunlight; she cupped her face with her hands again and blinked until her eyes adjusted to the relative darkness inside. She saw no movement, no shadows, no indication that Charlie was home.

What she did see looked awfully familiar.

A flowered velour couch in brown and gold with wooden arms.

An olive green easy chair in the corner next to the couch.

A heavy brass floor lamp with a macramé shade.

A large television set in an ornate wooden case sitting on the floor.

A portrait photo of a steel-haired old woman with skin that looked like a dried apple hanging on the wall above the TV. The glass in the frame had spiderweb cracks running through it.

Sara gasped and jumped back from the window as if a bee had stung her butt. *Oh my god! It's the same!*

She had assumed that anyone could have abandoned this house between 1989 and 2019. She'd been wrong about that too. The last owner of this house went to the Paws for a Cause event in October of 1989 and never came back. And, because Charlie had inherited the house and a sizable sum of money from his Grandma Ruth, nobody noticed as long as the property taxes were paid – perhaps by automatic withdrawals from a well-stocked bank account.

The house would sit exactly as it was right now for thirty years – a dusty and decrepit shrine to a troubled life cut short.

She peered into the window again, just to make sure her imagination wasn't playing tricks on her. It wasn't; it was still the same room she had crept through in 2019. If she squinted, she could see the jumble of textbooks and school supplies sitting on the dinette table between the living room and kitchen – including the distinctive green Trapper Keeper Charlie had been using in Bio Lab.

Just below her, on the other side of the window, she saw a small wooden table, with a black Bakelite phone sitting on top. Its color was deep and rich; it had been dulled by dust when she first saw it in 2019. Neatly placed on the floor next to the table was a pair of red Converse Chuck Taylor hi-top sneakers.

She'd seen them on his feet once or twice before, noticing how proud he was to wear them. Shoes like that made a guy feel like he fit in.

The sight of them in this house, however, triggered a memory of something she'd read in the Wisconsin State Journal article – a quote from MPD Chief Mike Daniels: *"There wasn't much left of the bomber after the explosion. Pieces, basically, and one red Converse Chuck Taylor shoe."*

Those shoes weren't there when she walked through that living room in 2019.

She stumbled to the porch steps and sank to sitting, her eyes wide, her hands over her mouth and nose. The connection she'd been missing finally fell into place.

It's Charlie. She felt like she'd been punched right in the gut. It had never occurred to her to look outside Kappa or Sig Tau for the bomber.

Charlie, who had been harassed and physically assaulted by a member of Sig Tau — not once, but twice.

Charlie, who had watched the girl he loved fall in love with another member of Sig Tau.

Charlie, who had been bullied his entire life and had finally. had. enough. She imagined him hitting his palm with his fist with each word.

"Oh, god," Sara moaned into her hands. Her eyes were wide, staring at nothing. "I've been so fucking blind."

Charlie is the bomber. That's why she'd been beckoned to Charlie's house by that strange large-crowd-cheering noise; it was the noise that the crowds at Paws for a Cause would probably make tomorrow.

Charlie is the bomber. She now remembered the sparkling mirror in the bathroom too, and how she had felt so compelled to follow that pair of sad blue eyes into it. Eyes that had looked so familiar during her first day of Bio Lab. They were Charlie's eyes.

Charlie is the bomber. That's why she ended up in this Sara Sullivan's body, attending her classes, living her life — because it was the only way to save him.

To save all of them.

Charlie

While Sara sat on his front porch steps in shock, Charlie was in the basement. He was so absorbed in his Project that he hadn't heard Sara pounding on the front door.

The various pieces and parts for his Project were strewn across his grandfather's old workbench. Sitting in the center of the table were two duct-taped bundles of three galvanized steel pipes, each three inches in diameter and twelve inches long with a steel cap tightly screwed onto one end. Charlie had already poured ball bearings into each pipe, and strapped rusty nails and screws he'd found in an old Butter-Nut coffee can to the outside with masking tape. *Shrapnel for maximum damage,* he thought.

Now he was carefully mixing the ammonium nitrate fertilizer he'd picked up at the local Farm & Fleet with the aluminum powder he'd made by pulverizing soda cans in Ruth's old coffee grinder. He filled one pipe with the powdered mixture, leaving about two inches of space. Then, using a glass measuring cup, he poured diesel fuel – siphoned under the cover of darkness from a box delivery truck parked in a neighbor's driveway – on top of the powder and shrapnel, taking care to let it soak in. He stuck an electric blasting cap in the pipe and packed the remaining space with PETN powder – both liberated from Hammersley Quarry. Once he was satisfied that the materials were packed as tightly into the pipe as possible, he threaded the blasting cap's wire through the small hole he had already drilled in the second end cap, then screwed it on as tightly as it would go. He carefully repeated the process for the rest of the pipes, standing each bundle, wire end up, in a stand he'd crudely fashioned from scraps of two-by-fours.

By the time all of the pipes had been filled, he was lightheaded from diesel fumes; he hadn't thought to ventilate the basement. He cracked an egress window, and fresh, cool air rushed in. He took a couple deep breaths and felt a bit better.

Can't quit now, he thought. *I'm almost done. This is the hard part.* He wired the blasting caps, the Casio watch, and two 9-volt battery snap connectors together. If he'd done it correctly, the alarm on his watch would trigger an electrical charge from the batteries, sending it down the wire and into the blasting cap.

And then, KA-BOOM — bye-bye fraternity! Ruth rasped gleefully.

That's right, he thought. *Wouldn't wanna be ya.* He would wait to set the alarm and attach the batteries until just before he set out for the Humane Society benefit Sara had told him about. He wasn't 100% certain he wouldn't blow himself to smithereens before he could get to his intended targets on Library Mall, but that was a risk he was willing to take. His empty backpack stood open and at the ready on the floor next to the workbench.

Because they're gonna pay, he thought, a humorless grin stretching across his face. *That asshole Schlosser wrote himself a check that he and all his little friends are gonna cash tomorrow. With interest.*

Charlie felt remarkably unconcerned that tomorrow would bring certain death. There was a weird sense of peace that came with knowing exactly how, when, and where he was going out — and that he had complete control. *Is this how other people feel just before they kill themselves?* he wondered. He was sure nobody would miss him; the only family he'd had was the grandmother who hated him. He was taking everyone he even remotely cared about — pretty much just Sara — with him tomorrow. There would be collateral damage. It couldn't be avoided.

At least they were going together.

CHAPTER TWENTY-TWO
Saturday, October 14, 1989
Morning

7:00 a.m.

Sara

Sara's original plan had been to go to Charlie's house and stop him well before he could even get to Library Mall. It seemed like a solid plan at first, but with further thought she saw a few holes in it. For one, she didn't know what time he planned to head over to Library Mall; if she missed him, she could very well miss her chance. And, given that he'd literally shut the door in her face when she'd gone to his house to check on him, she thought it unlikely that confronting him on his front porch again would produce different results. Either he wouldn't answer the door, or he would blow them both up – and her goal was to save everyone. Especially him.

So instead she decided on the much riskier Plan B: waiting for him at the event and confronting him there, in the hopes that she could talk him out of it. At least there he wouldn't be able to ignore or avoid her.

After another restless night's sleep, Sara arrived on Library Mall just before dawn and decided to perch on the concrete elevated stage. It was roughly twelve feet tall and had a 360 degree view of the entire mall, making it the perfect vantage point. She would be able to see Charlie coming long before he would see her.

She climbed the concrete steps and looked around; the mall was quiet. There was no movement on Langdon and Park Streets, which were usually quite busy with vehicle traffic. State Street was empty, its storefronts shuttered until later in the morning. She was alone. She sat facing roughly to the south, the direction from which she expected Charlie to come.

While she waited, she tried to keep her mind clear; she was afraid that if she allowed herself to think too much about this crazy situation, she might freak out and flee, or just lose her mind altogether. Instead she focused on the unseasonably pleasant morning air, the haunting wails of two loons that floated to her from Lake Mendota, her hands, anything.

She noticed her shoes. *Well, not really my shoes*, she reminded herself. *The other Sara's shoes.* She'd put them on her feet countless times over the past six weeks, but never looked at them closely. Now, with nothing but time on her hands, she bent over her knees and examined them.

They were white Reebok Freestyle hi-top athletic shoes, the kind with laces over the foot and two hook-and-loop straps over the tongue. Sara remembered her mother having a pair just like this when Sara was a kid. The name Reebok was stitched into the side of each shoe with silver thread.

Sara frowned, then took off the right shoe and laid it next to her. She adjusted the angle a bit…and the photo from the State Journal article she'd read in 2019, which showed the solitary shoe lying among the rubble of the ruined Library Mall, immediately flashed behind her eyes. Her heart raced.

It hadn't really occurred to Sara to think about what might happen to *her* if she failed in her mission; she'd been completely focused on saving the lives of Charlie, Lauren, Ben, and all the other victims. Now she understood the full stakes here: she too would die if she couldn't stop Charlie. *Turns out I'm in the body of a bombing victim*, she thought. *The shoe in the photo is the other Sara's shoe.*

7:30 a.m.
Sara

People from Kappa Delta and Sigma Alpha Tau had started to arrive and bustled about as they set up for the event. She was still thinking about her own fate if she couldn't stop Charlie when Lauren arrived and called up from the base of the tower. "Morning, love. Want some coffee?"

"That would be great," Sara said. She heard her voice shaking.

Lauren brought her a cup and sat next to her at the top of the steps. "How are you doing, love?"

Sara gratefully accepted the warm Styrofoam cup, and breathed the delicious steam. "I'm scared, Lo."

"Me too," Lauren said, and laid her head on Sara's shoulder. Sara leaned her head on Lauren's, and they sat that way for several minutes, not speaking. Just listening to the bustle of event setup below them and thinking about the monumental task that lay ahead.

"You're sure it's Charlie?" Lauren asked.

Sara nodded, her cheek rubbing against Lauren's kinky hair. "Positive."

"Think it's too late to go tell Detective Dipshit?"

This made both of them laugh, which helped dispel the tension a bit. "Are you kidding?" Sara asked. "He's got better things to do than actually investigate a crime before it happens."

Lauren sat up. "I have to go help finish setting up. Are you okay here?"

"Yeah," Sara said.

Lauren stood and started walking back down the steps. At the landing halfway down, she stopped and turned to face Sara. The terror in her dark eyes was clear. "Please stop him, Sara. Please. You're the only one who can."

A block of raw, churning emotion strangled Sara, leaving her unable to speak. So she just nodded. Lauren turned and disappeared.

9:00 a.m.
Sara

The event got underway promptly at nine o'clock. Ben and Lauren stood on the concrete platform that connected to the tower, which served as their stage. They wore their respective Greek letter shirts and held microphones, introducing themselves and their chapters, and getting the crowd excited. Waving banners and speakers on tall stands surrounded the platform, and metal cages covered with black cloth stood in the shade of the trees growing out of the platform.

Sara had moved from her post on the tower and now stood roughly fifty feet west of the platform, in front of the University Club, methodically scanning every face in the crowd and every bag that walked past her on its way to find a spot on the Mall. The size of the crowd was impressive, and she was proud of Lauren. Proud of her for putting together what stood to become a highly successful fundraiser, but also proud of her brave face. Lauren entertained the crowd, holding cats and dogs and laughing as if nothing was wrong – but Sara knew how frightened she actually was.

So many *what if*s tried to bubble up into Sara's consciousness as she watched the crowd. *What if I miss him? What if I can't talk him out of it? What if I can talk him out of it but he can't stop the bomb?* All of the scenarios running through her mind had the same sad, violent ending – and she pushed the scary thoughts out of her mind. Her ability to focus right now was the difference between normal life and massive death and injury for everyone within a hundred-yard radius of the platform.

9:15 a.m.
Charlie

He set the alarm on the digital watch for ten o'clock, double checking that he'd selected AM and not PM, then carefully snapped two fresh 9-volt batteries into the connectors with shaking fingers. He gingerly placed both bundles in his backpack, zipped it closed, and carried it up from the basement. It was damn heavy.

He didn't have a moment to waste, but adrenaline had been coursing through his veins all morning – and he had to pee. He trudged up the stairs and used the toilet; one of the bundles in the backpack stuck painfully in his still-healing ribcage. He zipped his pants and turned to the sink to wash his hands. He chuckled humorlessly at the futile gesture as he wiped his hands on the threadbare towel. *Why am I bothering when I'll be vaporized in less than an hour?*

He glanced up at the mirror. His own eyes, blue, red-rimmed, haggard, stared back at him. He grimaced, shifted the backpack's weight on his shoulders, and turned away. It was time to go.

9:35 a.m.
Sara

She turned her head to the right, scanning the crowd that stretched down toward State Street and the University Bookstore. She slowly brought her face forward, looking for Charlie but not seeing him in the masses that covered Library Mall. She glanced at her watch: nine thirty-five. If she remembered correctly, the bomb was going to go off at ten o'clock sharp. Her heart lurched with a sudden adrenaline surge. *Where is he?*

Bouncing nervously on the balls of her feet, she continued turning her head to the left, looking over the throngs of people between the Wisconsin Historical Society building and the Memorial Library, until finally she was looking up the sidewalk toward Bascom Hill. That's when she saw a familiar lanky figure emerge from the shadows of the Humanities building and lope down the sidewalk in her direction, red backpack on his back. The same red backpack she had carried when she accompanied a badly concussed Charlie back to his house.

There he is, she breathed. His face had healed some, although the green shadow of old bruises and black crust of old scabs still remained. She could see that his face was set with determination: jaw squared, eyes cold. Her heart broke all over again for him. *I can't believe he thinks this is the only way to solve his problems,* she thought. And then she started running.

"Charlie!" she cried, quickly closing the distance between them.

His blue eyes flared like a horse's at the sight of Sara. He reset his face and hunched over, determined to ignore her and keep walking.

She got to him and placed her hands on his skinny upper arms, trying to make him stop walking. "Charlie," she pleaded. He pushed hard enough against her to make her walk backwards. "Please stop."

"What do you want, Sara?" he mumbled, still pushing her backward and looking at the ground; Sara almost couldn't hear him over the cheering and clapping crowd. They had drawn even with the platform where Lauren and Ben were hamming it up.

"I WANT YOU TO STOP!" she shouted. She didn't know she had that loud, authoritative, Hilliard-like voice, but she welcomed it. Startled, Charlie did stop. He lifted his eyes and met hers. The pain and confusion and anger swirling behind them was almost more than Sara could bear.

"You don't have to do this," she said.

His eyes widened again. "How do you —"

"I know everything, Charlie." She turned and gestured to Lauren, who had heard Sara's deafening shout and stopped the show. Lauren, eyes huge and full of naked terror, timidly walked over and handed her microphone to Sara, then quickly retreated to stand with a group of Kappas who were grouped next to the pet cages.

Sara took Charlie's hand and pulled him up the concrete steps and onto the platform with her. The entire crowd had gone silent, watching and waiting to see what would happen next. She took a few seconds to look around her. Ben stood at the top of the tower, where Sara had been sitting not an hour earlier, an adorable black puppy in his hands and a look of surprise on his face. Scott Schlosser stood with his small cadre of college losers under one of the speaker stands toward the back of the platform. She knew right away which one was Jeff Nicholson; the look of shame on his face at the sight of Charlie's injuries was impossible to miss. She made eye contact with Lauren and winked, making her smile a little. Then she looked at Charlie, who was clearly confused and scared; his eyes darted to and fro, trying to find an escape. She had no idea what she was going to say until the words started falling out of her mouth.

"I know everything," she said into her microphone. Her amplified voice bounced off the buildings around them, creating a weird urban echo effect. She looked at Charlie, holding his gaze while she spoke. "And I'm sorry. I'm so sorry, Charlie. I'm sorry that I wasn't a very good friend." She paused, taking a shaky breath. "I took it upon myself to stand up to that asshole Scott Schlosser –" she pointed at Schlosser, who immediately looked guilty and angry at the same time, "—when he was picking on you in Bio Lab. I tried to help, but all I really did was put a big target on your back. I know how that feels."

Schlosser, in his gravelly voice: "You fucking bitch, you better shut your mouth." She turned to see him start toward her, his meaty face red and murderous rage in his eyes.

She turned to face him fully, feeling no fear. "What are you going to do, Scott? Beat the shit out of me like you did to Charlie?"

Schlosser stopped dead in his tracks in the middle of the platform, in front of the crowd and God, the red quickly draining out of his face.

"That's right, I know all about it. Actually, I know all about both of the times you damn near sent my friend to the hospital." Sara's ears felt like they were on fire, she was so angry.

"Would one of those times have been in Peace Park, about three weeks ago?" Sara didn't recognize the voice, which belonged to a police officer who had appeared at the edge of the platform. The name M DANIELS was embroidered on his navy blue uniform shirt.

"Actually, Officer, it would," Sara said. "This guy –" she pointed at Schlosser, who now looked just plain scared, "—beat my friend up and gave him a serious concussion. You can still see the scabs and scar tissue." She pointed at Charlie's forehead.

"Yes, I remember," Officer Daniels said. He stepped up onto the platform and looked at Charlie. "Is what she says true? Did this fellow cause the injuries I saw on you that night?"

Charlie, eyes wide and too overwhelmed to speak, just nodded.

"He assaulted Charlie at least one other time, Officer," Sara said. "That's why he has all these newer scrapes and bruises." She pointed at the scrapes and bruises in question. She also noticed, gratefully, that Ben and other Sig Taus had slowly moved in to surround Schlosser, in case he got the idea to try and run.

Daniels looked at Charlie, his eyebrows cocked. Charlie nodded again. Tears flowed freely down his face now.

"Well," Daniels said, unsnapping the belt case that held his handcuffs. Sara thought she saw the name *Louise* engraved in the leather of his gun holster. "That sounds like probable cause to me." He stepped over to Schlosser and said, "You, sir, are under arrest for felony assault. Give me your wrists."

Schlosser exploded. "No! Fuck you!" He turned to run, only to find a wall of his Sig Tau brothers standing there. Ben, who had been a star fullback on the Menasha High School football team, tackled him at the knees, bringing him down on his belly with a meaty *oof*. The crowd erupted in applause. Daniels put a knee into Schlosser's back and handcuffed him while shouting the Miranda warning. Once Schlosser was safely handcuffed, Daniels used the CB radio on his shoulder to call for backup. "Can't be too careful," he said to Sara and Charlie. "This guy's a brute."

"He doesn't look so scary now, does he?" Sara asked Charlie, and pointed at Schlosser, who was lying on his belly, his hands cuffed behind him, sobbing and blubbering.

Charlie stood dumbfounded, still holding Sara's hand, staring at Schlosser. Sara thought he was probably shocked to see the guy who had once been huge and intimidating now look smaller, deflated…and terrified.

Another officer made his way through the crowd and helped Daniels pull Schlosser up to standing. "Best of luck to you," Daniels said to Charlie and nodded his head once. "I'd been worrying about you since that night I found you in Peace Park." And he was off to load Schlosser into the other officer's car for the trip to the Dane County Jail.

Satisfied, Sara gave the microphone back to Lauren, who got the event started again with a cheery "Hey folks, isn't it satisfying to see a mean ol' bully get his comeuppance?" The crowd cheered, and they all got back to the business of finding homes for deserving cats and dogs.

9:55 a.m.
Sara

Sara held on to Charlie's hand and guided him to the edge of the crowd, near the fountain outside Memorial Library. "I'm sorry that you were hurting and I didn't see the real reasons why. I should have."

Charlie closed his eyes and dropped his head.

"I honestly didn't mean to hurt you, Charlie." Sara said, tears finally rising to the surface in her own eyes. "I love you. You've been a good friend to a girl who has really needed one of those these last few weeks."

Charlie shook his head and finally spoke. His voice was a little croaky with emotion. "It's okay, Sara. I know you didn't mean to."

She couldn't help herself; she let go of Charlie's hand and hugged him around the neck. *It's so weird that just a couple of weeks ago I couldn't bear anyone touching me. Now it seems like I'm hugging everyone.* His arms circled her waist and squeezed. They both cried. The event carried on behind them.

Then something occurred to Sara: the bomb. She gasped and let go of Charlie, nearly pushed him away from her. "Shit! What time is it?"

Charlie glanced at his watch. "We have less than three minutes," he shouted. "Run! To the lake!"

9:57 a.m.
Charlie

He sprinted north across Library Mall as if his life depended on it, with Sara right behind him. They crossed Langdon Street at full speed – causing the drivers of several cars to slam on the brakes and lean on the horn – then ran through the parking lot that separated the Memorial Union from the Red Gym. They followed the asphalt to the lake's edge. Charlie jogged left, shoving through crowds that had gathered on the Union Terrace to enjoy this warm October day, and out onto the dock that extended into the lake. Nobody was fishing today. *Thank god for small favors.*

He stopped, breathing hard, and tried to unshoulder his backpack. His bony elbows kept getting stuck, thwarting his desperate efforts. He had no idea how much time was left on the timer; this wasn't like the movies, where all the timers beep as they get closer to the end. "Goddammit," Charlie gasped. "It's stuck."

"What do you mean, it's stuck?" Sara gasped back. "Here, let me help."

Panic bubbled in his chest. *I'm going to be turned into hamburger meat if I can't get this thing off,* he thought wildly.

Together he and Sara finally wrestled the red backpack off of Charlie. He grasped it by one shoulder strap, wound up like an Olympic hammer thrower, and hurled the bag out into the lake as hard as he could. The muscles in his right arm and shoulder strained with the effort; he would be sore for days afterward.

9:59:56 a.m.
Sara

She watched the red backpack fly through the air silently, almost unremarkably, for about seventy-five feet, and hit the water with a splash. It sank almost immediately. *I wonder how big that bomb was,* Sara thought. *Looks like it was pretty hea—*

The air around them contracted suddenly, as if Lake Mendota was trying to suck it all in at once. Sara's ears popped painfully. Then the lake exploded, sending a giant column of water into the air. Sara watched confused fish and more than a little lakeweed, as well as a sailboat or two, fly up and then splash back down as gravity took over and the water broke apart. She reached for Charlie and hugged him tightly, pressing her face into his narrow chest.

People on Union Terrace, who had a moment ago been minding their own business and enjoying what would become a rare 78-degree day in October, screamed and ducked for cover under the small metal sunburst tables.

Then, complete silence.

Sara lifted her face, stood back, and cautiously turned in a circle to survey the damage. *However bad it is, it can't be worse than how this was supposed to go,* she thought.

Surprisingly, damage was minimal; Lake Mendota had dispersed most of the bomb's energy across its massive surface area, minimizing the effects of the shock wave. The fish kill would have the university, the city, and lakeshore property owners cleaning their shorelines of rotting fish carcasses for a couple weeks; the state Department of Natural Resources would end up restocking the lake with walleye, northern pike, bass, panfish, carp, and suckers the following spring. Several sailboats were destroyed. The waves might have taken out a dock or two. But that was it. No injuries, no major damage. It was sort of a miracle.

Sara looked out on the lake, where the waves were diminishing to ripples. She breathed a huge sigh of relief. *I did it. I really did it.*

"Sara?"

She glanced at Charlie, who suddenly looked bone tired. People from the terrace were running toward them, followed closely by people from the Paws for a Cause event.

"I'm really sorry —" he started.

"Shut up, Charlie," Sara interrupted with a small, wry smile. "It all turned out okay. You are going to be okay. And that's all that matters to me."

10:01 a.m.
Charlie

"Sara!" Lauren ran up to Sara and yanked her into a tight hug. "Oh my god - thank god you're okay," she sobbed.

216

Ben appeared next to Charlie. "Lauren and I saw you two running toward the lake and were starting to follow you. When we heard the explosion and saw the water shoot up into the air, we thought you guys were done for." He turned to glare at Charlie. "What the hell were you thinking, man?" Anger flashed in his eyes.

Charlie dropped his head, hot shame spreading outward from his chest. "I – I wasn't."

"Do you realize how many people could have died?"

Charlie nodded, mute.

"Ben. If you're going to be mad, be mad at Schlosser," Sara said soberly. "When people are pushed to their absolute limit, they don't always make the most rational decisions."

"I take full responsibility," Charlie said softly. Regret pulsed through his chest with every heartbeat. *I almost killed us all.*

Ben looked at Sara's earnest face, and then at Charlie. He ducked his head and held out his hand. "Listen. If I ever said or did anything..."

Charlie took hold of Ben's hand and shook it, a relieved smile spreading across his face. His chest opened up, and he could breathe freely again. "No worries, Ben. We're good."

Ben grinned. "Excellent."

10:03 a.m.
Sara

Ben stepped over to her, his grin giving way to intense concern. "Are you okay?"

Sara nodded. "I'm fine."

"Did you...did you know he was carrying a bomb?"

Sara shook her head. *He doesn't need to know.* "No, I didn't. I had seen Schlosser standing by the platform, and when I saw Charlie coming from Bascom Hill, I just wanted to take the opportunity to actually, truly help him this time." She sighed. "I had no idea what he had in his backpack."

Ben's eyes said that he didn't really believe her, but was willing to let it go because he was so relieved she was all right.

"I'm sorry I ruined the fundraiser," Sara said.

Ben wrapped his arms around Sara. "You didn't ruin it, Sara – turns out you saved it. Imagine if that bomb had gone off with all those people there. We can always do another one in the spring."

She hugged him back, tears pulsing behind her eyes. She had achieved her mission, and now she knew how to get back to her own time. *I don't want to leave him.*

Sirens wailed; several police cars shot out from behind the Red Gym and came to a screeching halt on the boat ramp. Officers in helmets and bulletproof vests, brandishing assault rifles, spilled out of the cars and ran toward them and the crowds that had gathered around them.

"This ought to be interesting," Charlie muttered.

"Don't worry, Charlie," Sara said, watching Officer Daniels step out of one of the cruisers and start toward them. "I think it's going to be okay."

CHAPTER TWENTY-ONE
Saturday, October 14, 1989
Evening

Charlie

It was dinnertime before Charlie was led out of his holding cell in the lower level of the Madison Police Department. He'd spent hours in a dingy interrogation room turning down offers of coffee (it looked suspiciously like liquid tar to him) and telling his story to MPD detectives and then to agents from the FBI and ATF. He tried to remember how many times he'd gone through it; had to be fifty times at least. He knew they asked the same questions again and again hoping to trip him up and expose holes in his story, but he had nothing to hide. He felt terrible that he'd come within a cat's whisker of killing dozens of innocent people, and he figured the best way to make amends was to tell the truth to law enforcement – consequences be damned.

After interrogation, Charlie was booked into the Dane County Jail. His holding cell sat across a wide hallway from the one Scott Schlosser occupied. Schlosser sat on the floor in the far back corner of his cell, his knees drawn up to his chest and his arms wrapped around them, rocking on his well-cushioned tailbone and staring into space. Charlie regarded him with pity, unable to believe he had once been intimidated by this sad sack.

Because Charlie had no criminal record and Officer Daniels was willing to testify to Charlie's character and his experiences with Schlosser, Stuart Kitchen, the criminal attorney recommended by Jerry Harper, was able to pull some strings and get a judge to sign off on a $25,000 cash bond that same day. Jerry helped Charlie immediately post bond from his grandmother's bank account, and Charlie was released. As the officer led him down the hallway toward freedom, Charlie could not pass up the opportunity to make sure Scott saw him walk out.

"See ya later, loser," Charlie said, grinning. His voice echoed in the large, bare room.

Schlosser scrambled up from the floor and covered the distance to the bars of his cell in less than two steps. "Fuck you, twerp!" he roared. "Fuck you! It's your fault I'm in here, I will fucking GET YOU!"

He just didn't scare Charlie anymore.

"Stay in town, Charlie," Stuart Kitchen told him after the officer had led him back into an interrogation room, where the attorney was waiting for him. His magnified green eyes blinked behind Coke-bottle glasses; Charlie could not stop staring. He could see every brown eyelash in high definition. *Too bad he doesn't have that much hair on his head,* Charlie thought.

"I lost count of all the felonies you committed today," Stuart continued. "However. You don't have a rap sheet, there were no casualties or injuries, damage was minimal, and you're taking full responsibility, so I'm going to try and make a case for probation and restitution – to property owners for any damage, and to the state for the fish kill. I might be able to make it stick too, as long as you follow every single direction to. the. letter. Got it?"

Charlie nodded. "I don't have anywhere to go, anyway."

"Good man," Kitchen said, and slapped Charlie on the back. "I think this will be a pretty open-and-shut case. You look terrible. Go home and get some sleep. I'll have the desk officer call you a cab."

Charlie walked down the hall and was surprised to find Sara, Lauren, and Ben sitting on wooden benches in the front foyer, waiting for him. "You guys are still here?"

Sara stood up. "We couldn't leave you here all alone," she said. "Did it go okay?"

"It went as well as can be expected," Charlie said. "I'll have to face some punishment, but my attorney thinks he can make a case for probation since nobody was hurt. We'll see, I guess."

"I'm starving," Ben remarked.

"You are always hungry," Sara said, grinning.

"Your cab will be here in five," the desk officer called from behind his plexiglass shield.

"Let's all get in the cab and grab some dinner at Regent Street Retreat," Charlie said, feeling uncharacteristically bold. "We can walk to my house from there, and…hang out?" This came out sounding terribly awkward to him. He couldn't believe these three people still wanted to be around him, after what he'd almost done to them. "I'm sure you have…questions."

"That sounds excellent," Lauren said. "I hear good things about their chicken strips."

Sara

The chicken strips at Regent Street Retreat were indeed delicious. Sara thought she detected a hint of Cajun seasoning in the batter. They were all so famished, they basically ate without talking, then set out to walk the three blocks to Charlie's house.

As she climbed Charlie's front porch steps, Sara glanced at the house next door. Her house. She looked forward to getting home – but also dreaded it. She sighed and followed the rest of them into Charlie's house.

They sat around for an hour – Sara and Ben holding hands on the brown and gold velour couch, Lauren on the green armchair, Charlie on the floor leaning against the old console TV – and talked about the day. They did indeed have questions for Charlie.

"A bomb, Charlie? Really?" Lauren said, half laughing. "Kind of a drastic solution, isn't it?"

"I guess I felt like I needed to make a big statement," he replied.

"Was Schlosser your real target?" Ben asked.

"Yes," Charlie said.

"And you would have been okay taking out a bunch of innocent people?"

"Well…no," Charlie admitted. "I didn't like that part so much. But in my head, it was unavoidable."

"How did you even know how to make a bomb?" Sara demanded.

"There's a branch of the Madison Public Library right over on Monroe Street. For a week or so, after the party at Sig Tau, if I wasn't here at home, I was there researching. It was actually pretty easy, and most of the stuff to make it was at the hardware store."

"Does one buy explosives at the hardware store, Charlie?" Lauren asked.

"Well…that was a little trickier. I may have liberated one or two key components from the quarry in Fitchburg."

"So you can add theft to your list of charges," Ben observed.

Charlie shrugged. "Maybe. I'm going to let Stuart worry about that. Whatever the judge sees fit to give me, I'll take. I deserve it."

"Such a change of heart," Lauren said. "Just think, you started out the day so…so angry. Now look at you; you're calm, resigned, and ready to face the consequences."

Charlie blushed. "I have you guys to thank for that. Especially Sara." He looked at Sara shyly. "You showed me that people who bully are only as scary as you let them be. Schlosser looked so pathetic when the cops dragged him away, and even more so trapped in his holding cell like a circus bear. I couldn't – still can't – believe I ever gave him the power to intimidate me." He shook his head.

Sara thought there might be a lesson for her here too, somewhere. She remembered Ben telling her that *Hurt people hurt people* and thought it possible that Mandy Huber had taken on a mythical size in her own mind in much the same way. Maybe Sara could finally let her go.

Suddenly she heard it: that sound of a large crowd cheering. It was soft at first, as if far away, and grew louder. Then soft again. Swirling around her head. She could tell that nobody else could hear these strange noises; they were only for her. Her heart quickened. *Oh my god! It's time!*

Without thinking, she sat up and announced, "I have to pee."

"Upstairs, take a right at the top of the stairs." Charlie pointed to the stairway behind the kitchen. "You can't miss it."

She turned to Ben and smiled, then reached out and pulled him into a hug. "Oh!" he squeaked, surprised, before wrapping his own arms around her. She closed her eyes and savored his warm embrace. She pulled back, kissed him gently, and said, "Thank you. For everything."

His forehead creased with confusion. "Um. You're welcome?"

She stood and went to Charlie, sat beside him and slung her arm around his shoulders. The cheering crowd followed her, continuing to swirl around her head. She leaned her head against his, squeezed his shoulders, and whispered, "Thank you for changing your mind."

He nodded, but didn't say anything. The emotion was all over his face.

She stood and went to Lauren. She bent over as if she was going to give her a hug and urgently whispered, "It's time. I need you to come upstairs with me."

Lauren, bless her, didn't ask questions, just stood up with Sara. "I have to go too. You know how it is with girls."

Both Ben and Charlie rolled their eyes. Sara's heart swelled with affection for them both; she would miss them terribly. Tears effervesced behind her eyes. She took Lauren's hand and led her through the kitchen before Sara could do anything stupid, like change her mind about going home. The cheering crowd sounds stopped.

Upstairs, Lauren closed the bathroom door and looked at Sara with wide eyes. "It's time? Are you sure?"

"Yep," Sara said, and gestured at the mirror. "Look."

"Whoa," Lauren breathed. The mirror had transformed back to the sparkling clean glass etched with glowing Greek letters that Sara had seen the first time she entered Charlie's house.

They both leaned over the sink to get a better look. The surface of the mirror rippled with their movement. A shadow gradually appeared and slowly took shape; it was a head. Then, as if a dim spotlight had been turned on, a face appeared. 2019 Sara's face. With basically the same hair as 1989 Sara. *Dear god. I need to do something about that.*

"Oh my god," Lauren whispered. "Oh my god Sara, it's you! You…you look different, but still kind of the same."

Conflicting emotions churned in Sara's gut. *That's me, all right. Older. But how much wiser, really?*

"And you look so…so much older!" Lauren whispered, mesmerized. "Is that you in 2019?"

"Yep, that's me," Sara said, resigned. *I have to go back.*

"So when you go back to 2019, what will happen to the you standing here with me?" Lauren wanted to know.

"I don't know, Lo," Sara said. "Hopefully the real 1989 Sara Sullivan comes back, and it'll be like nothing happened."

"It won't be the same," Lauren said, tears welling in her eyes. "You and she might look alike, but your personalities are so different. It won't take long for Ben and Charlie to notice."

Sara shrugged. "You'll have to prepare her, then. The guys don't know anything about this."

Lauren nodded. "I know."

Sara threw her arms around Lauren and hugged her hard. "I don't know what I would have done without you, Lo. Thank you for everything."

Lauren squeezed Sara back. "I'm going to miss you so fucking much." A sob escaped her.

Sara started to cry too. Her voice was hoarse with emotion. "I love you, Lo."

Lauren released Sara and wiped her eyes, smearing her mascara down her latte-colored cheeks. "I love you too, Sullivan. Now get the hell out of here. Maybe I'll catch up with you in thirty years."

Sara nodded. She reached out and touched the mirror; once again her fingers went right through the cool surface like water. She leaned into the mirror's glass...

2019

CHAPTER TWENTY-THREE
Tuesday, October 15, 2019

Sara

She had the filmstrip dream again, or a new version of it…for what would turn out to be the last time.

"Mommy? These are the ones you should wear to work." Her little arms holding up her mother's heavy steel-toed work boots.

"I'll be fine just for today. Come on, we're going to be late."

"No, Mommy. Not until you put on your real boots." Her own little voice was stubborn…and more than a little authoritative. "I don't want you to get hurt, Mommy."

A pause, then her mother's disembodied voice. "All right, baby. Give them here, I'll put them on."

Clackity-clack. Scene change.

"I'm so glad I asked him to be my lab partner." Still Lauren's face, with a mischievous little glint in her eye, and the other Sara's voice. "I think he likes me, Lauren – he asked me out for an ice cream cone! And I said yes! Maybe next time you and Ben should come with us, and we'll have a double date!"

Clackity-clack. Scene change.

"No matter what, I always have you." Bat's furry black face. She heard a faint meow, as if he were saying, *I know, now would you please come home?*

No more clackity clacks.

Beep. Beep. Beep. The alarm's steady rhythm roused Sara from a deep sleep. Groggy, she sat up in bed, eyes closed, feeling around her for the source of the noise. "Damn it, Lo, you forgot to turn your alarm off again," she muttered.

She heard that familiar meow, like she just had in her dream. *Bat?* Her eyes snapped open. Astonished, she sat up and looked around her; she was in her own bedroom. Her iPhone was on the table next to her, alarm still blaring. And there was Bat on

227

the floor, looking up at her expectantly with green eyes that took up most of his small, furry black face. The cat meowed again and jumped up on the bed. Bat sniffed at Sara, and, recognizing her scent, rubbed his head against Sara's hand. Sara made an involuntary noise that sounded like a combination sob and gasp, picked Bat up, and buried her face in the cat's fur. She didn't try to stop the tears, and they came in a flood. Bat seemed content to sit in Sara's arms; he even started to purr.

After what felt like an eternity, Sara's tears dried and she wobbled out of bed. She turned off her alarm, wrapped herself in her robe and went to the kitchen, Bat on her heels. Everything looked exactly as it should. She rushed into the living room. The boxes marked PILLOWS and KITCHEN SHIT were right where she'd left them.

She spied yesterday's paper lying on the floor next to her tattered easy chair; she slowly sat and picked it up. She shook it out and turned it over; the front page headline read: BADGERS BASK IN BIG HOMECOMING WIN.

She clutched the paper to her chest and leaned back into the chair; the tears came back with a vengeance, running freely down the sides of her face toward her ears. Harsh sobs, even wails, escaped her with the confirmation that it hadn't been a dream. There was nothing for Madison to remember because she really had spent six weeks in 1989 and succeeded in changing the course of history. All of the nearly one hundred people she'd saved had a chance to go on and live a full life. Except Scott Schlosser; with any luck, that bastard was still in jail. She made a mental note to Google him when she had a moment.

The tears gradually subsided, trailing off into sobs and hiccups. Bat sat at her feet, watching her. Sara picked him up again and kissed his furry forehead. "Hungry, huh? Okay, let's get you some breakfast." She stood and headed toward the kitchen, still holding Bat. As she passed the fireplace, an unfamiliar object on the mantel caught her eye. She stopped, set Bat down, and bent over to get a better look.

It was a recent photo of herself standing next to an older, white-haired woman on a path next to Lake Monona, the downtown Madison skyline in the background. Both women wore sleeveless shirts and sunglasses, and flashed identical grins. She frowned and opened the frame. "Me & Mom out for a stroll, 7/6/19" was written on the back in her own precise, spider-like handwriting.

Mom? What the hell? Baffled, Sara put the frame back together and set it in its original spot on the mantel. She started to walk away and then came back and stared at the photo for another minute, wondering how it could possibly be in existence. Her reverie was finally broken by Bat's insistent meow. "All right, all right, I'm coming," she said, tearing herself away from the photo and heading back to the kitchen.

She glanced down at Bat's bowl on the floor next to the stove to find it already full of kibble. *That's odd,* Sara thought. *Bat's bowl is usually completely bare by morning.* Frowning, she looked around the kitchen to see what else might be not quite right. She walked over to the sink and saw an empty bowl and spoon sitting in it. There was a tiny bit of pink milk left sitting in the bottom of the bowl.

Now I know I didn't have a bowl of Froot Loops yesterday, Sara thought. *Who else was here?* Then a realization struck: *Shit, what time is it? I should probably call in sick today.* She headed to her bedroom to grab her cellphone.

She had silenced the alarm without really looking at her phone. Now she saw that she had two text messages:

Mom: Morning sweetie! Want to hit the Capitol Square farmer's market on Saturday? It's the last weekend. Going to make leek soup for dinner on Sunday. LMK!

Luke Marshall: Hey Sullivan. Was going to ask at lunch but chickened out. Can I take you out for dinner this weekend? I know a great little Italian place right by campus. Let's chat in the morning.

Sara wandered back into the kitchen, staring at her phone in complete confusion. *What is going on? I changed my number so my mom can't find me and ask me for money anymore. How am I getting texts? Leek soup? Is this a fucking joke?*

Movement outside the window caught Sara's eye; she leaned over the sink to peer out at the house next door. *Charlie's house.* What she saw took her breath away. She ran to the front door and stepped out onto the stoop, mouth open in awe. Her purse, briefcase, and mail still sat there.

Yesterday the house had been crumbling, the victim of decades of abandonment and neglect. Today it was neat, tidy, and gleaming. The siding was bright white. The trim around the windows, the wood pillars, and the porch stair railings were a freshly-painted red. The tiny lawn was neatly tended, without a weed in sight. A pair of wicker lounge chairs sat on the porch.

A large curly-haired dog appeared from the opposite side of the house; it stopped on the front lawn and looked at her, long tongue hanging out. A lanky man with acne scars and teapot handle ears, carrying a garden hose, emerged – and Sara's heart soared. *Charlie!*

His coarse hair was almost completely white now, but it still stuck up in stubborn clumps. He noticed her and waved. "Hey neighbor!"

Sara waved back tentatively. Before she knew it, the dog was sitting right next to her, begging to be scratched behind the ears. She obliged.

Charlie clearly didn't recognize her. He clomped up onto the porch and shouted through an open window next to the door. "Sara! Come on out here a sec!"

Sara?

A pretty if slightly overweight woman, with white streaks of her own in her long strawberry blonde hair, stepped out and also waved at Sara. Together she and Charlie walked over to retrieve their dog.

"Hilliard!" Charlie growled affectionately. "Get over here."

The dog ignored him, instead licking Sara's hand enthusiastically. Astonished, Sara stared at him, and then at his owners. *Hilliard?*

"I'm so sorry," the other Sara said. "One of these days we'll train him to stay in his own yard." She smiled; her hazel eyes crinkled at the corners. "You just moved in, right?"

"Uh. Yes. Just last week," Sara said. "My name is Sara."

"Me too! I'm Sara, this is my husband Charlie, and this mutt is Hilliard IV." She gestured affectionately at the dog, who was again trying to pet himself on Sara's hand.

Charlie nodded. "We name all of our dogs after the professor of the Biology class where we met as freshmen at the UW back in the late eighties."

Sara's heart lurched, and she very nearly blurted out that she was in that class and also knew Hillard – but noticed an odd, meaningful gleam in the other Sara's eyes, and suddenly she made the connection. *Wait a second. Charlie. Sara. Hilliard? Oh, no way.* Her eyes widened to roughly the size of Cadillac hubcaps, and the other Sara gave an almost imperceptible nod.

Sara looked at Charlie, who had lines across his forehead and crow's feet around his blue eyes in addition to his white hair – but somehow looked exactly the same. He stood there, hands in his jeans pockets, gazing affectionately at his wife. *Holy shit! Charlie got the girl!* She thought her heart might explode with glee. *She does look a lot like me, doesn't she? I wonder if he ever noticed the difference after I left.*

"C'mon Hilliard, it's time to go," Charlie said. The dog obediently stopped licking Sara and descended her front steps to follow Charlie, who had turned back toward his neat little house. "Nice meeting you Sara," he called over his shoulder.

"You too," Sara said and waved; she could not get over that Charlie was here, alive, and living next door to her with his wife and dog.

The other Sara started after Charlie, then stopped on the sidewalk between their houses and turned back to Sara. "Say," she said. "How's your mom, hon?" Her eyes twinkled.

Such a basic question, but its effect on Sara was thunderous. She couldn't breathe. She suddenly realized that she wasn't the only one who had altered history. *I was right!* she thought. *When I woke up in 1989, the other Sara had to go somewhere – so she ended up in my seven-year-old body in Minneapolis for six weeks. Seven-year-old me must have spent last night here and helped herself to a bowl of Froot Loops.*

Sara's head spun, and she stared wide-eyed at the other Sara. A phrase from this morning's dream flashed across her mind: *No, Mommy. Not until you put on your real boots.* She was absolutely gobsmacked; it must have showed on her face, because the other Sara's smile grew wider.

"How…how did you…" Sara trailed off.

"She thought she could go to work without her steel-toed boots one day," the other Sara said. "I stopped her before she left the house and made her change her shoes. She ended up dropping one of those heavy steel molds right on her foot that day. Can you imagine how badly she would have been hurt if she'd had those other shoes on?" The other Sara paused as if considering her next words, then continued. "My own dad was injured at work when I was a kid and became an alcoholic because it was the only way he knew to deal with the pain. I didn't want that to happen to Melinda." She winked and disappeared into her house.

Sara stood there for several minutes, staring at Charlie's house and trying to process everything she'd seen and heard over the last ten minutes. She only jumped about three feet when her phone, which she'd been holding in the hand that hadn't been slobbered on by the dog, rang at top volume. She looked at it; **MOM** flashed on the screen. Her heart skipped a beat, then started racing. Her hand shook slightly as she brought the phone to her ear.

"Hello?"

CHAPTER TWENTY-FOUR
Wednesday, October 16, 2019

Sara

Back at work, Sara spent the morning digging through an inbox full of emails looking for status updates on communications projects. As she responded to each request with the same generic response (*Dear _____, thanks for checking in, I was out of the office yesterday. I will find out the status and get back to you by the end of the day today.*), she thought about the two conversations she'd had with her mother yesterday. It was just like she imagined other people must talk with their moms: easy, familiar, basically nonstop about everything.

"Are you feeling okay, baby?" Melinda had asked at one point during the first conversation. "You sound tired." Her voice sounded so different: clear, confident, full of humor. Sara's heart swelled.

"I am," Sara said, telling the absolute truth. "It's been a long last few weeks."

"Are things still crazy at work?" Melinda asked, throwing Sara a bit off-kilter; she'd never really cared about anything in Sara's life before.

They made plans to hit the Capitol Square farmer's market on Saturday. Sara learned that Melinda did not, in fact, live in a north Minneapolis crack house when she asked Sara, "Want me to pick you up on my way downtown?" Melinda actually had a townhome on Madison's west side – just a few miles from her daughter.

Sara had cried after both conversations. *I still can't believe it. Sara's amazing foresight gave me my mom back. I'll have to do something really nice for her,* she thought. *I don't know what I could possibly –*

"Hey Sullivan." Luke's deep friendly voice shattered her thoughts and made her jump.

Sara tried to give him a stern look, but she couldn't keep a smile from tugging at the corners of her mouth. "Dude. You shouldn't sneak up on people like that."

Luke grinned and leaned against Sara's desk, crossing his arms over his crisp white shirt and red necktie. "Are you feeling better? Did you get my text?"

"I did," Sara said.

"And?" Luke's face was hopeful.

"Well…" Sara said, pretending to hedge as she normally would. "I don't know…"

Luke's face fell. "Oh. Okay."

Grinning, Sara stood and put her hand on his arm. He stared at it in awe. "Luke. I'm kidding. I would love to have dinner with you."

"Really?" Luke's face looked like a little boy's on Christmas. "I mean…really?"

Sara nodded, laughing. His excitement was catching. "Really."

"That's so awesome," he said. "You like Italian? There's a romantic little place on campus. Porta Bella? Ever heard of it?"

Sara smiled. "I hear the Garibaldi sandwich is to die for."

THE END

Acknowledgments

Charlie's Mirror is a dream long in the making. And even though it's my name on the cover, it took a village to make this dream become a reality. Without the skills and encouragement of the following people, Charlie would probably still be sitting in a box in my closet:

My parents, Joel and Penny DeVries, who gave me the gift of words, shared with me their love of reading, and believed in me when I didn't always believe in myself.

My brother, Benjamin DeVries, my first best friend and my biggest fan.

My dear friends Shawn and Jill Whale, who refused to accept any of my lame excuses for not writing.

My friend and colleague Lori Mueller, who made me realize that maybe I should follow my own career advice.

All of my family, friends and colleagues who have offered kind and supportive words throughout my journey, and asked "When can I get a copy of your book?" I'm thrilled to finally deliver!

And finally, my son Price and my daughter Kendall…everything I do, I do for them. Always.

About the author

Brenda Lyne lives just outside Minneapolis, Minnesota with her two busy kids, two cats, two fish, and probably a partridge in a pear tree. She is living, breathing proof that it is never too late to follow your dreams.